CLOSE TO PERFECT

Copyright © 2018 by Barbara Longley
978-0-692-08389-5

All rights reserved. Except for use in any review, the reproduction or utilization of this work in whole or in part in any form by any electronic, mechanical or other means, now known or hereinafter invented, including xerography, photocopying and recording, or in any information storage or retrieval system, is forbidden without the written permission of the publisher.

This is a work of fiction. Names, characters, places and incidents are either the product of the author's imagination or are used fictitiously, and any resemblance to actual persons, living or dead, business establishments, events or locales is entirely coincidental.

Printed in the USA.

Cover Design and Interior Format

CLOSE
to
PERFECT

A LOVE FROM THE HEARTLAND NOVEL

Kitty, Happy reading!

Barbara Longley

Barbara Longley

ALSO BY BARBARA LONGLEY

Heart of the Druid Laird

LOVE FROM THE HEARTLAND SERIES, SET IN PERFECT, INDIANA

Far from Perfect
The Difference a Day Makes
A Change of Heart
The Twisted Road to You

THE NOVELS OF LOCH MOIGH

True to the Highlander
The Highlander's Bargain
The Highlander's Folly
The Highlander's Vow

THE HANEYS SERIES

What You Do to Me
Whatever You Need

THE MACCARTHY SISTERS SERIES

Tangled in Time

To the many readers who asked for Tobias and Mary Lovejoy's story, from the bottom of my heart, thank you for your continued support!

Part One
War's End

Chapter One

Spring of 1865, Atlanta, Georgia

RAGE DUG ITS SPURS INTO Tobias, propelling him forward and lending him strength he did not own. He shoved the barrel of his carbine behind one of the slats nailed across the frame of the charred remains of the door. Putting all his weight into the task, he pried until the plank loosened. He'd known Sherman had burned Atlanta, but knowing had not prepared him for the devastation confronting him. All that remained of his family's mercantile, his home, was a burned-out shell of brick.

Starved, thirsty, and sweating beneath the hot Georgia sun, he leaned against the crumbling brick wall to recover from his efforts and pulled in a long, deep breath. Damn, he reeked—and itched. He'd been host to every kind of vermin imaginable for so long, he'd accepted the discomfort as normal. Hell, he couldn't even remember a time when he wasn't covered in bites, scabs, and crawling things.

What was today's date? He had no idea, but judging by the sun and the heat, he'd guess late May, and it had been mid-April when he'd been turned loose from Fort Sumter. God almighty, it had been one hell of a long walk from South Carolina to Atlanta, Georgia.

Tobias pushed himself off the wall and once again levered the rifle barrel behind the plank and pulled. The *screeeech* of nails loosening from their moorings set him on edge, but he couldn't let up. He needed to get to one of the caches of coin he'd buried in the cellar. Then he'd see about food, a bath, clean clothes, and a place to rest. By tomorrow he'd have a bit of strength back, and then he'd set out in search of his mother and sisters. He swallowed against the tightness in his throat. He'd had no word from his family nor they from him in over a year. Were they safe? Had they survived the war?

He went back to pushing and pulling. Finally the board dropped to the ground, and a flare of triumph lent him another burst of energy. Positioning the barrel under the next slat, Tobias set to work. The effort took what little strength he had left, and the world around him began to spin. He stopped to regain his breath, only to be tortured by the scent of bread baking somewhere down the road. His gut roiled. Sweat burned his eyes and stung the bites on his face.

Swiping his sleeve across his brow, Tobias spat into the dirt between his worn-to-almost-nothing two left boots. He blinked against the sting in his eyes, marshaled his last reserves, and wrapped his hands around the carbine again.

"Here now," a familiar voice said gruffly behind him. "That's private property. You'd best drop that rifle and turn around real slow. Both hands in the air if you please."

His old neighbor didn't recognize him, and why would he? Tobias hardly recognized himself. What if Offermeyer shot first and asked questions later? Terror gripped him, and bile rose to scald the back of his throat.

"Don't shoot. The rifle's not loaded." Tobias turned slowly, hands and rifle held aloft. The muscles in his arms quivered with the effort. He peered through his matted hair at the older man aiming a revolver at his chest. "Don't you recognize me, Ambrose?"

Hunger and fatigue conspired against him then, and spots danced before his eyes. Dizziness took hold. Tobias tried to fight the weakness, tried to remain upright, but then he got the shakes. His knees buckled, and he folded, ending up facedown in the dirt.

"By God, is that you, Lovejoy?"

Tobias nodded, not even attempting to raise himself. Ambrose's shout for help filled the air, and Tobias flinched. Echoes of the battles he'd endured flooded his mind—one brutal skirmish after another, cannons firing, rifles and muskets discharging, smoke

. . . and the constant, sickening stench of blood, unwashed bodies, dysentery, and death.

The horrors of war lived like a glowing ember deep inside him, set to burst into flame at the slightest provocation. Too many men—Confederate and Union alike—had survived the bloody battles only to perish in the deplorable prisons, where disease, filth, and starvation ran rampant. His empty stomach turned as the stink of putrefying wounds and human waste inundated his senses.

He'd nearly died more than once, but somehow, by some miracle, he'd made it home. He heard someone approach, and the next thing Tobias knew, he was being hefted by more than one pair of hands.

"Lord almighty, you smell worse'n a privy," Ambrose Offermeyer remarked. "Let's get some food into your belly. There's nothing to you but skin and bones, son. While you're eating, I'll have the missus fix a nice warm salt bath to get rid of the vermin crawling all over you."

"I can see things moving around in his hair, Pa." The younger Offermeyer grunted. "A salt bath will do for the chiggers and biters, but shaving's the only way to rid him of the nits."

"That too," Ambrose agreed. "Food, a bath, shaving, clean clothes, and you might just feel close to human again. And after a good rest, you can tell us where the hell you been since last we heard. We'd all but given you up for lost."

"Where are my mother and sisters?" he croaked between his cracked lips. "Are . . . are they safe?"

"I'm sorry to have to tell you this, but your uncle passed a month ago. Your mama and sisters are still holed up on his farm and doing about as well as can be expected during these trying times. We'll take you to them tomorrow."

Another blow to the gut. He couldn't even thank his uncle for sheltering his family. "I'm much obliged."

"You were smart to send your kin off when you did, Tobias. Atlanta weren't no place for womenfolk under Sherman's siege."

All he could manage was another nod as Ambrose and Gus supported Tobias as he shuffled across the street.

"After the city burnt, your ma and uncle came back to town to see what was left of the mercantile," Ambrose continued. "We helped salvage what we could and boarded up the doors and windows. My boy and I have been watching over your property ever since. Figured you might want to rebuild. That is, if you made it home at all."

"I owe you, Ambrose."

"Hell, you don't owe me a thing. Your mama shared what she could with us—food, blankets, and such. We're good." He huffed out a wry laugh. "Not so much *good* as *surviving*."

Ambrose and his son set Tobias down on the makeshift boardwalk in front of the butcher shop the Offermeyers had owned and operated since before Tobias was born. Squinting against the brightness of the afternoon sun, he surveyed the building. It appeared his neighbors had already rebuilt, which didn't surprise him.

"You wait right here," Ambrose commanded. "I'll tell the missus to get that bath ready, and we'll come back for you with the wagon."

"I've nowhere else to go," Tobias muttered. Leaning his head against the building, he closed his eyes. The Offermeyers had always been a resourceful, industrious family. Ambrose's and Tobias's fathers had been close friends. Tobias had also been close to Ambrose's older son, Andrew. Because of the history between their two families, he trusted the older man. He'd ask Ambrose for help digging up one of the jars Tobias and his pa had buried in the cellar over the years. *Only silver and gold, son. No paper promises. No banks. Only silver and gold.* That's what Papa used to say, and thank God he'd listened. Confederate paper wasn't worth a damn. May as well keep it on hand in the privies as far as he was concerned. At least then the paper would be useful.

The Offermeyers left him. Tobias sagged against the storefront wall and sighed. He could sleep for a week, and it still wouldn't be enough. His stomach was so empty, he swore his navel pressed against his backbone. *Food.* Ambrose had promised food. His mouth watered at the mere thought. He'd gone far beyond hunger and into starvation long ago. He cringed at the thought of what he'd eaten along the way home just to keep body and soul together.

What would it be like to feel safe again, to sleep in a bed between clean sheets, eat regular meals, and bathe whenever he had a mind to? He'd been deprived for so long, he couldn't recall what it was like to live with the comforts he once took for granted. That had been a lifetime ago, and he wasn't that man any longer.

July 1865, Marilee Hills Plantation, Georgia

MARY KNELT IN THE DIRT and pulled weeds from the vegetable garden behind what had once been a proud plantation mansion. The home where she'd been born and raised now stood a forlorn mockery of its former glory. They'd suffered through raids and lootings by Union and Confederate troops alike before the war had finally ended. At least Marilee Hills hadn't been burned to the ground.

She glanced toward the stables, and her stomach lurched. Anger and grief cut through her as sharp as if her loss had happened today and not six months past. Thrust back to that day, the image of her father hanging from the rafters engulfed her, and a chill crept down her spine despite the midday heat. Her hands curled into tight fists.

Staring at the garden before her, by sheer will alone, she forced her mind away from the internal wound festering like a rotten tooth. "Cabbage, carrots, and peas. Potatoes, okra, string beans . . ." She recited a litany of the vegetables growing in neat rows around her over and over until her breathing returned to normal.

It wasn't as if she couldn't understand her father's despair. She too had despaired. Unable to bear the loss of his sons, his fortune, and his privileged way of life, her father had abandoned her, leaving her to fend for herself. "May God forgive you, Papa," she said, brutally yanking at a particularly stubborn thistle root, "because I cannot."

Guilt nipped at her. She'd been fortunate compared to many of her neighbors. She and her small band of survivors ate regularly. They had a roof over their heads, and only the attic leaked when it rained. Besides, any day now, her fiancé would send for her to join him in Houston, and she would gladly leave everything here behind for the chance to begin anew.

Swiping her brow with her apron, she sat back on her heels as her cousin Beatrice came around the corner of the house. What would become of her widowed cousin and Bea's young son when Mary left to join Eldon in Texas? She worried about the small band of souls in her care, her missing fiancé, and herself. Some days, she feared worry was all that kept her going.

"Was there any mail for us in town, Bea?" she called, tipping her straw hat lower to shield her eyes.

"No, and I don't expect there will be anything for you next week either. I'm sorry to say so again, Mary, but I fear for your dear Mr. Smythe." Bea set her basket on the stoop by the kitchen door before joining her. "What with the war and all, the South is teeming with desperate men willing to kill for anything they might find useful."

Mary bit her lip. It had been nine months since she'd seen Eldon off to Houston. How long should she wait before giving up hope? "One would think his family would have sent word if something had happened to him. They haven't answered a single one of my letters either."

"Perhaps your letters never made it to Savannah. Maybe the Smythes have moved on. Could be they don't know what has befallen their son, and they're waiting same as you." Bea sank down between the rows of peas and pulled out a bit of clover. "I did, however, hear plenty of interesting news while in town."

"Oh?" Mary glanced toward the house. "Before you tell me, where's young Jon?"

"I left him in the kitchen with Mabel and Ezra. He's working on his sums. Just because we've been reduced to poverty doesn't mean I can neglect his education. I want my son to make something of himself."

"Of course he will, Bea. He's bright, and he's already proven he's willing and able to work hard at whatever task we set before him. Tell me what you heard."

"You remember I told you about how Tobias Lovejoy came home nearly starved to death around the end of May?"

"Yes." She remembered the handsome son of one of Atlanta's merchants all right. Every Sunday at church she'd strain to catch a glimpse of him. With his solemn brown eyes, dark wavy hair, and fine physique, he'd been the object of many a young girl's dreams back then. Including hers, but that had been before she'd been packed off to finishing school and long before the war.

Mary tugged at a weed as another pang of guilt hit her. She hadn't attended church services since the day her father had taken his life. She couldn't face the censorious looks or the pity. "What about Mr. Lovejoy?"

"Well, I heard he doesn't intend to stay in Atlanta to run his mercantile after all. But since his mama and sisters refuse to leave with him, he's agreed to rebuild and stock the store before he departs. His older sister Sarah married last month. She and her husband, Mr. Le Duc, will manage the store for the family once Mr. Lovejoy departs."

Young Tobias had always seemed to take in and analyze everything and everyone around him. He'd impressed her as being wise beyond his years. Perhaps it was because he'd been forced by the loss of his father to take over the mercantile at such a tender age. He'd been all of fifteen or sixteen then. "Did you learn what he intends to do instead?"

"I did. Mr. Lovejoy is gathering a like-minded group of folks who want to start fresh somewhere new. He's going to lead a wagon train to Texas next spring." Beatrice made a disapproving sound deep in her throat and shook her head. "He wants to become a rancher. Why he'd want to go from selling dry goods to chasing beeves all over tarnation is beyond me." She tossed a weed out of the garden. "What does a shopkeeper know about ranching anyway?"

Mary hadn't known a thing about gardening, cooking, or surviving on her own either, but look at her now. "I suppose it's like anything else, Bea. He can learn." *Texas.* Tobias was leading a group exactly where she wished to be. Mary's mind opened to a sudden wealth of possibilities. "Why, this is the answer to my prayers."

"How are Mr. Lovejoy's plans to chase beeves through the Texas wilderness going to make a difference to you?"

Mary arched an eyebrow. "To *us.*"

"Us?" Bea blinked. "Whatever do you mean?"

Mary shot up and paced between the rows of cabbages and string beans. "Don't you see? Instead of waiting to hear from Eldon, you, Jon, and I will travel to Texas with Mr. Lovejoy's wagon train. I need to find my fiancé or discover what became of him. I cannot live in limbo like this any longer, not knowing whether he's alive or dead. Bea, I feel as if I've been holding my breath since Eldon's last letter reached me. My entire existence is more about waiting than it is about living."

Still pacing, she took off her gloves, tucked them into her apron pocket, and twisted the sapphire engagement ring on her left hand. "I'll sell this plantation. Of course, I won't get but a fraction of what it's worth, but it'll give us enough to start over." Her throat closed, and she had to swallow a few times before she could continue. "If Eldon is dead—which I fear he may be—why then you and I will open a finishing school for young ladies."

"Oh, Mary, I—"

"Hear me out." Pausing between the rows of vegetables, she gestured to the surrounding fields. "What can we do here? I cannot afford to hire the hands it would take to get this plantation back on its feet, and I have no desire to do so anyway. We can't stay here; there is no future for either of us in Georgia."

She spared her cousin a glance. "If I do find and marry Eldon after all, I'll help you set up some kind of enterprise, so you'll be able to support yourself and your son. A boardinghouse for respectable young ladies perhaps or . . . or a café. What do you say?"

"Well . . . I'd have to think about it." Beatrice sat back and bit her lip. She averted her gaze. "I have nothing left to hold me here," she murmured, her voice hoarse. "But I've never lived anywhere else. I'm not sure what I want to do, but I agree. We cannot go on indefinitely as we are." Bea swallowed a few times and swiped a single tear from her cheek before turning back to her. "I do need to find a way to support myself. *If* I decide to go with you, I still have a few pieces of jewelry and five acres of land left to sell. I could contribute to our journey west."

Bea and Jonathan were all the family Mary had left, and she couldn't leave them behind. She simply couldn't. "All right. Think about it, and let me know the moment you decide. I'll make the next trip into town. While I'm there, I'll speak with Mr. Lovejoy." Excitement hummed through her veins. Finally she had a plan of action, something that would move her forward.

"Bea, we're young yet. We need to get on with our lives, start over while we still can. We cannot live much longer on the pittance we earn selling eggs and a few vegetables to the grocer. Soon enough there will be nothing left to sell but the land. I may as well make the best use of whatever I can get for Marilee Hills."

Her gaze strayed to the stable again, and her heart thumped painfully against her newly found hope. Perhaps being around her had caused Papa even more sorrow. She closely resembled her mother, and surely she reminded him of his earlier loss, a loss from which he'd never recovered. That, the death of both of his sons in the war, and the end of his way of life had been too much for him to bear. She had not meant enough to her father for him to continue living.

No one in Texas need know of her father's mortal sin. More to the point, in new surroundings, a place without constant reminders of everything she'd lost, perhaps she'd be able to forgive Papa for abandoning her when she'd needed him the most.

Lord, how she yearned for a new beginning somewhere far from the misery and loss she'd suffered here. Her eyes burned, and she twisted her ring again, fearing the worst where Eldon was concerned. What other reason could there be for his silence all these months? He'd been an ardent, devoted suitor. The two of them had made such happy plans to start their new life in the growing city of Houston. Back then, she'd thought of little else but becoming Mrs. Eldon Richard Smythe. And now? Now she could hardly recall his features.

She whirled around to face her cousin. "Perhaps Ezra and Mabel might join us. They're free now. I could help them file for a land grant under the Homestead Act. They could farm or find jobs in Houston if . . . if I don't find Eldon and hire them myself. What do you think?"

"You have a big heart. That's what I think." Beatrice shook her head. "You're under no obligation to help me, Jonathan, or freed slaves, but you took us all under your wing anyway. I'll never be able to repay your kindness."

"Nonsense." Mary waved away her cousin's words. "There is nothing to repay. You and Jonathan are family, and Mabel had more to do with raising me and my brothers than my own mama did." Besides, her mama had died when she was very young, and Mary hardly remembered her mother. "Mabel and Ezra are dear to me. I don't know what I would have done without them these past few years."

"We've been through so much together." Bea sighed.

"We have." The five of them had survived the war, often hiding in their secret cellar together when soldiers came to raid whatever they could from their meager stores.

"We'll discuss Texas with Mabel and Ezra this evening," Mary said, brushing dirt from her apron. "Mabel must have supper nearly ready. Let's wash up and see how young Jonathan is doing with his lessons."

Could she leave Georgia without the certainty of knowing Eldon awaited her arrival in Houston? What if he'd sent for her, and his letter never made it to Atlanta? He might wonder what became of her as well. The backs of her eyes stung. So much loss—her dear brothers, both parents, her very way of life. She knew nothing of Texas other than the stories she'd heard. Those tales had been frightening indeed, but surely not any more frightening than facing the rest of her life here on Marilee Hills.

Here her prospects were few, and the reminders of everything and everyone she'd lost were many. Too many. She was far too young to waste away on a plantation she couldn't hope to resurrect. She had a responsibility to the four souls in her care. She needed to look to the future for them as well as for herself. Joining Mr. Lovejoy's party was their best hope, and it had been far too long since she'd hoped for anything beyond day-to-day survival.

Chapter Two

Tobias reached into his apron pocket for a nail and hammered another cedar shingle onto the roof of Lovejoy's Mercantile & Dry Goods. He took off his hat and wiped the sweat from his brow with his sleeve, taking note of the prominence of the bones in his wrist. No matter how much he ate, he couldn't seem to gain any bulk, but at least his hair had grown back some. Even better, he was clean and free of vermin. He moved to the next section and set another shingle in place. Gus Offermeyer worked across from him, and the masons he'd hired to brick the newly framed building worked from the second-story scaffolding below.

The first floor had been completed a week ago, and the carpenters now put their efforts toward the living quarters on the second and third floors. The sound of hammering reverberated through the air. Not just from his family's building but throughout the entire business district of Atlanta.

Lovejoy's Mercantile would reopen by the end of September, ten weeks from now, and orders had already been placed to stock the shelves. Catalogs and pattern books had arrived two days ago. Bolts of cloth, sewing supplies, ready-made clothing, boots, and shoes would soon follow, much to the relief of the female population in the city. Dishes, pots and pans, tools, even children's toys would soon fill the shelves and display cases. His entire family worked together to ready their business, including his sister Sarah's new husband, Terrence.

"Mr. Lovejoy," a woman called up to him from the street.

Tobias moved to the ladder and peered down. A petite woman

stood on the boardwalk. He couldn't see her face beneath the rim of the bonnet she wore.

"Yes?"

"If I might have a word with you, sir," she called. "I'll take only a few moments of your time."

What could she possibly want with him? His curiosity piqued, he climbed down the ladder. Perhaps she wished to place a special order. In which case, he'd direct her inside to speak with his mother.

Tobias studied her as he approached. Reddish-gold curls peeked out from beneath her bonnet to frame large blue eyes—eyes the color of larkspurs. A sprinkle of freckles dotted her nose and cheeks. Ridiculously wide hoops under her crinolines and a gown of blue enhanced the floral impression springing to his mind. "What might I do for you, ma'am?"

"Perhaps you don't remember me." She glanced at him before turning to gaze down the street. "I am Miss Mary Stewart of Marilee Hills."

Now that he took a second look, she did seem familiar, but the Miss Stewart he recalled had been very young, a girl really, and much fuller in the face and figure when he'd known her. Their families had attended the same church, and he'd certainly noticed her at Sunday services. All the young men had, but then she'd been sent off to boarding school, and it had been years since he'd seen her. Still, he hadn't forgotten how her vivacious, congenial disposition had always been as bright and shiny as her strawberry-blonde hair, and he'd always been a little bit infatuated with her.

Ah, but back then, he'd been younger, with more meat on his bones himself, hadn't he? The war had sculpted them all, whittling away at the excess until only what was absolutely necessary to keep body and soul together remained. No doubt her family had also suffered privation. Of course they had. She'd be lucky if her home still stood.

If he wished, Tobias could remain in Atlanta, take up the comfortable life he'd always known, and run his family's store. The Stewarts' way of life had been stripped from them forever, as it had been for many families like hers. Some would adapt; others would not. "Yes, of course. I remember now." He tipped his hat. "How are you, and how is your family, Miss Stewart?"

"I am all that remains of my family, sir, which is why I've come to speak with you."

He frowned. "I'm sorry to hear such grievous news." As he recalled, she had two older brothers and her father, having lost her mother when she was just a child. All gone? Was she here seeking employment with the mercantile? "How might I help?"

"I have recently heard you intend to lead a wagon train to Texas. Is this true?"

"It is."

"I wish to add to the number of your party." She fidgeted with a ring on her left hand as she spoke.

"Are you married, ma'am?" She'd introduced herself as *Miss*, but perhaps she'd said that so he'd recall who she was.

"I am not." Miss Stewart's eyes filled with a determined glint, and her cheeks turned a dusky pink. "I plan to travel with my widowed cousin and her young son."

"In that case, my answer must be no." He wanted no single women in his group. He'd have his hands full as it was, and being responsible for women who had no protection, no adult male relative traveling with them, would stretch him far beyond his breaking point.

"But—"

"The rigors of such a journey are difficult enough for women traveling with their menfolk. For unmarried ladies . . ." He shook his head. "I am sorry, Miss Stewart. It simply will not do." He arched a brow. "Can you even handle a team of oxen or shoot a gun?"

"Which is your greatest concern, Mr. Lovejoy? My unmarried status or your misperceptions regarding my skills? I drove here today. Handling oxen cannot be any more difficult than handling horses."

Her boldness stunned him. Irritation flared, and he clenched his jaw in an effort to control his temper. She did not deserve his wrath. Miss Stewart was more deserving of his sympathy, but he had to think of the welfare of all the people joining him on his journey west. Miss Stewart was exceedingly slender, petite. A tedious journey by covered wagon would tax what few reserves she had. Damnation, she was not likely to withstand the difficulties, and he'd hate to see her succumb after having survived the war.

Besides, having unmarried ladies among the group would stir trouble. As pretty as she was, Miss Stewart would be an unwelcome distraction, and the other women would likely resent her and her widowed cousin's presence.

"You must understand, Miss Stewart. For a lady such as yourself, the journey will be far too arduous, more difficult than you can imagine. Traveling without proper protection, without a man's strength to aid you, is what I find most objectionable."

"Then let me put your mind at ease, sir. I am well acquainted with hardship." Miss Stewart lifted her chin a lofty notch, setting her curls in motion. "I am more than able to protect and care for myself, no matter how dire the circumstances."

Even though he had no intention of agreeing to her request, he couldn't help but admire her determination. The ringlets beneath her bonnet caught the sunlight just then, turning them into strands of spun gold threaded with polished copper. And her eyes, wide-set and lovely, were the bluest he'd ever seen. The bewitching sprinkle of freckles drew his gaze to her pert nose and high cheekbones.

Color once again filled her cheeks, and she studied the bricks behind his shoulder. "It is my understanding you do not intend to depart until next spring. I have until then to prove my abilities. Is that not true?"

"This is not a good idea, Miss Stewart." He rubbed the back of his neck. "I regret having to tell you no, but I fear I must stick to my original plan. No unmarried women. I don't wish to—"

"Mr. Lovejoy," she snapped, stomping a dainty foot, "whether you allow it or not, I *will* be part of your party traveling westward. Even if it means we follow on our own a short distance away."

"I cannot stop you from following, but I will not be responsible for—"

"I do not recall asking you to be responsible for us in any way, sir. All I am asking is that you allow us to travel with you."

She straightened to her full height, which he guessed might be all of five feet two inches at most, to his five feet ten. She was a determined little thing, he'd grant her that. He bit the inside of his cheek to keep his sudden burst of amusement in check. "Now, ma'am, be reasonable."

"I am being *reasonable*, sir. Far more reasonable than you, it would appear." Her eyes narrowed, and she gave him a curt nod, her curls bouncing again. "Good day to you, Mr. Lovejoy. This discussion is not over. I shall be in touch."

With that she turned on her heels and strode away. A tall, middle-aged woman with ebony skin materialized out of the shadows, following in her mistress's wake. Miss Stewart's gown, with its wide hoops beneath, swayed back and forth with each stride. She resembled a handbell one might pick up by the handle and shake. No doubt she'd bring forth a commanding peal.

Tobias grinned as he watched her bell-shaped form proceed down the boardwalk. My, but it had been some time since he'd found humor in anything, and all it took was five minutes in her company to bring forth both irritation and amusement. Mary Stewart was quite the spitfire.

"Goodness, Tobias, was that Miss Stewart I heard you arguing with?" His mother came to stand beside him.

"It was." He folded his arms across his chest. "She and her widowed cousin wish to join my wagon train west."

"You told her no?"

"Of course I told her no. Two single females without protection would cause nothing but trouble."

"Hmm. I recall hearing Miss Stewart became engaged to a young man, must be going on close to a year past. He traveled on ahead to Houston two months before her father died. Her young man was to send for her once he became established. I wonder what became of him?" she mused. "Perhaps he's finally sent word for her to join him, and traveling with you is how she plans to get to Texas."

"A fiancé, you say?" He recalled the way she'd played with the ring on her left hand. Now it made sense.

"What kind of fool would leave a woman like Miss Stewart alone for so long?" If she were his, he wouldn't. He'd be far too concerned some other man might steal her away in his absence. "If the man were any kind of gentleman, he'd return, marry her, and take her to Houston himself."

"Be that as it may, do have some compassion, dearest. Miss Stewart's father took his own life after hearing he'd lost both his sons to the war. Poor thing. Mary has been left all alone in this world."

"Even more reason why her fiancé should have returned for her. She must have sent him word of her plight." A spark of anger ignited. Whoever her fiancé might be, he didn't deserve her. "Do you know his name?"

"If I did, I do not recall it now. I'm sure she did send word, but you know how unreliable the mail service is these days. You'll get no argument from me in her young man's defense. He should have come for her months ago. Compassion, my boy. What would you do if one of your sisters found themselves in similar straits?" She patted his arm.

He grunted in response. If it were one of his sisters who wished to join him on his westward journey, they'd have his protection. Miss Stewart had no one.

"Well, I'd best get back to work. Terrence and Sarah are busy painting the shelving, and Jane is helping me inventory the catalogs and pattern books." She sighed happily. "The first floor is finally beginning to look like a store again." Hesitating, his mother tightened the ties of her apron. "Are you still certain you must leave?" she asked for the hundredth time. "Your father and I had hoped you'd run the business, marry, and raise a family in the town where you were born and raised."

He surveyed the street where their store took up an entire busy corner. So many of their neighbors were gone, moving on after Atlanta had burned. Too many families had lost sons, brothers, fathers, or husbands. Too many wives, daughters, and sisters had perished. So much loss.

A flood of memories swept him into a powerful current, and he could not break free. A shudder racked through him, and he was suddenly transported back to Fort Sumter, back to unending starvation, the sweltering heat of summer, followed by the bone-chilling cold of winter, with no blankets, little food, and only the occasional fire, and finally . . . no hope.

Agony twisted his gut, as he was once again surrounded by death and despair, far from home and separated from those he held most dear. He'd had nothing, no way to send word to his mother and sisters. Endless days of hunger, starvation, and the cruel taunts of the prison guards.

How was it possible the putrid stench of that hell still assaulted his senses? Why was it that, no matter how hard he tried to shake them loose, the cries and moans of the suffering still echoed inside his head? And the nightmares—would he ever be free of this madness? Panting, in a cold sweat, he leaned against the wall, trying like hell to anchor himself in the present.

"Tobias, are you ill? You've gone pale." His mother gripped his arm.

"I'll be fine in a moment. I'm still not . . . not fully recovered from . . . I'm not yet as healthy or as strong as I need to be, and I have moments of . . ." What could he say? That he had moments when the past rose up to swallow him whole? "I suffer from bouts of weakness, and I feel light-headed."

She wrapped an arm around his waist, supporting him. "A strong cup of coffee is what you need, and I'll go make it for you right now."

"Perhaps you're right, but give me a moment to recover." He drew in a breath and slung his arm around her shoulders. Heartache weighed upon his chest like an anvil. As much as he needed to unburden his soul, he couldn't tell her about his visions or the smells that overcame him. He couldn't tell anyone, lest they think him mad and lock him away in some hellish place, never to be free again. After everything else he'd suffered through, that he would not survive.

Life would never be the same for him in Atlanta. It wasn't that he didn't want to stay; he simply couldn't. The war had changed him, as it had changed forever the town he'd known in his youth. Starting over somewhere far away might be his only chance at leaving the nightmares and the terrors behind. He longed to be in a place that held no memories for him. Only then could he begin to hope for peace. Only then could he finally move forward with his life.

He sighed. "As far as wanting to leave, I *am* certain, Mother. Are you sure you don't wish to come with me? Sarah and her husband can run the mercantile well enough on their own. If you join me, Jane will come along as well." They'd tossed this argument back and forth since the day he'd announced his intent to leave. "Think of the adventures we'd have."

"War was adventure enough." She huffed out breath. "I'm far too old for more adventure, Tobias. Besides, all my best memories are here. Soon enough Terrence and Sarah will give me grandchildren." His mother's eyes misted. "They'll need my help, and Jane wishes to stay as well. This is where her friends are, and mine as well. And what about that fine young man who wishes to court Jane?"

"Then let us put this argument behind us once and for all, and say no more on the subject." Tobias squeezed her shoulders. "I'd best get back to work, so you'll have a roof over your heads before I leave."

"It's time for lunch, Tobias. You may as well come in and have that coffee with your meal. I don't like to think of you on that roof after having suffered one of your weak spells. It's not safe. Food and coffee will help; I'm sure of it."

Food and coffee weren't going to fix what was wrong with him, but he nodded and followed his mother into the store anyway. They'd set up a makeshift kitchen of sorts at the very back, and his sisters were there, already putting together a meal for all of them.

Tobias sat at the table as flashing blue eyes and reddish-gold curls replaced the gruesome images in his mind. His mother had urged compassion, and hearing Miss Stewart's story roused his curiosity—that and indignation on her behalf for the way her fiancé had dealt with her. He'd give careful consideration to Miss Stewart's request all right, but he couldn't make any promises. She was a distraction and a responsibility he did not need or want.

"OH, THAT MAN! STUBBORN AS one of the oxen he assumes I cannot manage," Mary muttered as she strode down the street, a mixture of resolve, anger, and attraction chasing around inside her. She'd forgotten how compelling Mr. Lovejoy's soulful brown eyes could be. It broke her heart to see him so gaunt, knowing he'd once been so robust and virile. "Mabel, I must improve my shooting skills."

"You planning on shooting *that man*, child?"

Mary laughed. "As tempting as that is, no. I want to prove my competence to Mr. Lovejoy.

"My Ezra can help, Miss Mary. His aim has improved considerably since it's been up to him to do the hunting and standing guard over us."

"Then we shall begin right away. If I'm to convince Mr. Lovejoy to allow us to join his wagon train, Bea and Jonathan must learn as well." Mary sighed. Lord help her, but she'd already had to learn so very much. If only she'd insisted she and Eldon marry and set out for Houston together. How very different her life would be right now.

No matter. She dealt with her circumstances as they were, not how she wished them to be. Five years ago, no one could have predicted a wealthy plantation owner's daughter such as herself would be reduced to eking out a living as best she could. Mary straightened her shoulders and lifted her chin, taking pride in the fact that she had survived. *And I shall continue to do so.*

"A boy should know how to handle a gun," Mabel agreed.

Her mind went back to Mr. Lovejoy. "Didn't Bea tell us Mr. Lovejoy spent the last year of the war as a prisoner in Fort Sumter?"

"She did, and that's a fact."

"His mercantile burned under Sherman's siege, did it not?" Mary frowned.

"It did. Why?"

"Confederate money is worthless." Mary stopped on the corner. "Where do you suppose he came by the funds to rebuild?"

"Couldn't say," Mabel replied.

Along with gossip, curiosity could also be a distraction and a form of entertainment, and Tobias Lovejoy had certainly presented a challenge. Given the opportunity, she had no doubt she'd be able to chip away at his adamant refusal to allow her and Bea to join his wagon train. Mary needed to assail him every chance she got. She'd prove her skills and wear him down until he agreed to let her join him, just to end her pestering.

Her hopes renewed, a broad smile broke free. The poor man had no idea how persistently annoying she could be when she set her mind to it. "Mabel, I believe it's time I attended Sunday services again."

"Amen to that." Mabel chuckled. "Haven't I been saying as much for months now?"

"You have. There," she said, pointing to the Terminal City Arms Co. "If I am to improve my skill with guns, I'll need to purchase more ammunition." Unfortunately, she had no idea what to buy. "We will begin practicing this very afternoon."

"Miss Mary, we need to be careful. If any of your neighbors find you all with my Ezra . . . a rifle in his hands . . . coming so close upon the heels of the South's defeat and our emancipation, I fear what might follow. Folks around these parts are angry."

"No one will know. We'll practice in the privacy of our own woods, and we'll do so only at dawn and dusk. If anyone should come upon us, I'll say Ezra is simply *attending* us, and no one will dispute my claim." Mary frowned. "Speaking of our neighbors and anger, I wish you and Ezra would reconsider and come with us to Texas."

"No, ma'am." She shook her head. "Texas is still the South. We have kinfolk in Chicago, and that's where we mean to go once we've seen you all safely on your way."

"I'll miss you terribly."

"We'll miss you too. Ezra and I are more than grateful to you, and I'd hug you right now if we weren't in the middle of town."

Her eyes stinging, Mary bit her lip until she regained control over her roiling emotions. "Once my property has sold, you and Ezra will have a portion of the proceeds to see you have a proper start. I owe you wages, after all. And you may take the buggy if you wish. You'll have enough money to buy a decent horse or a mule." So much change, and she'd seen more than her share. Mary forced her thoughts on to more practical matters.

They reached the gun store, and she turned to Mabel. "Wait for me here. I shouldn't be long." Mary knew nothing about purchasing ammunition. Her father had been the one to take care of such matters, but they'd gone through almost all of what her father had stockpiled before his death. She opened the door, her step more determined than ever.

Can you even handle a team of oxen, ma'am, or shoot a gun?

Mr. Lovejoy had issued a challenge, unaware of the multitude of challenges she'd met and mastered these past few years. He had no idea what trials she'd faced or how much stronger she'd grown in the process. Handling a team of oxen or mules could not be any more difficult than handling a team of spirited horses. Hadn't she learned to manage the latter at her father's knee? Even more so with her brothers, who were far less cautious with her. She'd show Tobias Lovejoy, all right.

A bell over the door chimed as she walked into the shop. A narrow-shouldered, balding clerk hurried out from behind the counter and approached, his manner almost furtive. He reminded her of the mice she constantly battled to keep out of their pantry.

"Madam, ah . . . perhaps your husband is joining you shortly?" he asked, glancing around her at the door.

"Is Mr. Thompson here?"

"Ah . . . y-yes, but . . ."

"If you would be so kind, please tell him Miss Mary Stewart is here to see him."

Before she'd made her request to Mr. Lovejoy, Mary had spent the better part of the morning with her father's lawyer, now hers. Her lawyer hadn't wanted to deal with a mere female either. He'd suggested she bring a trusted male relative or friend with her to an appointment he'd be happy to make for a future date.

She'd held her ground. Finally he'd had no choice but to deal with her, and the two of them had gone over her father's last will and testament to be sure all was in order, and she was indeed free to sell her property.

By the time she'd finished batting her eyelashes, cajoling and flattering poor Mr. Henley, he'd also agreed to undertake the sale and transfer of the deed himself. In exchange, he required a commission, and that was fine with her. He threw out an outrageous percentage, and then she'd been forced to haggle him down to a reasonable, single-digit figure. Did he think her a gullible fool simply by virtue of her sex? Would this day of dealing with muleheaded, condescending males never end? She massaged her temples, trying to waylay the beginnings of a throbbing headache.

Hopefully the plantation would sell before spring. She pushed aside the wrenching sensation in her chest. The land had belonged to her family for three generations, but what choice did she have?

"Why, Miss Stewart," Mr. Thompson's voice boomed, "what a lovely surprise."

"Mr. Thompson." Judging by the expression of disapproval he wore, her presence in his store was not a *lovely* surprise at all. Mary pursed her lips.

"We don't ordinarily see young ladies such as yourself in our establishment."

After the morning she'd had, his tone grated. "*Do* forgive me for any impropriety, sir." She pasted on a smile, a smile as sickly sweet as sorghum molasses. "If either of my brothers or my dear papa were still alive, I would not find myself in such a position. However, since I must now take matters into my own capable hands"—she held out said hands, palms up—"here I am."

For an instant, he looked stricken, as if just now recalling she'd lost her entire family. "Ah . . . forgive me." He cleared his throat. "Yes, of course, of course. What can I do for you, ma'am?"

"I find I do not know what to order in the way of ammunition for the guns left to me by my papa and brothers. Do you perchance keep records of prior purchases? I would also like your expert advice about which of the rifles and pistols to keep and which to sell." She studied the glass cabinet filled with different makes and models of guns. Rifles took up most of the wall space, and stacks of small boxes lined the wall behind the counter.

"We do, yes." He snapped his fingers at his nervous clerk. "Bring the ledger to me, Mr. Weber."

The next hour was spent with Mr. Thompson explaining to her all about the most modern rifle purchased by her father, the best of the revolvers, the different calibers and bullets, and how to care for her small arsenal.

"I would advise you to keep the 1861 Whitney rifle and the Witten Bros. five-shooter revolvers, Miss Stewart. The Whitney is fairly light, and the barrel length is thirty-four inches. I'm sure it would be the easiest for you to handle. Of course, it's always good to keep a revolver or two close to hand, and I can find a belt and holsters that might do nicely for you. Whatever firearms you don't wish to keep, bring here. I'd be happy to sell them for you on consignment." He folded the paper he'd written instructions on and handed it to her.

"All right. I'll do that," she said, almost giddy at the prospect of more money coming in. She'd purchase two gun belts, one for her and one for Beatrice. They could each carry one of the revolvers when needed.

"I'll include a pamphlet on gun care, and I recommend you purchase oil, the tools you'll need, and cloths to take care of your guns, since I have no way of knowing what is left to you."

"Thank you. I do appreciate your help, sir. Now, if you'll gather what I need for the rifle and the two revolvers, I'll make the purchase and be on my way." She reached for the small purse she kept in the deep pocket of her skirt. She dreaded spending the coin, but if she sold a number of her guns on consignment, surely she'd come out ahead.

"Right away, ma'am." Mr. Thompson signaled to his clerk, who moved behind the counter and began putting together her order.

While she waited, she created a mental list of things to be accomplished before their journey. Once she secured Tobias Lovejoy's permission to join him, she'd see about a wagon and oxen or mules. She, Bea, and Mabel would have to start sewing practical clothing, and she'd need to order sturdy boots for all of them. Perhaps two pairs for Jonathan, since he grew so quickly these days.

Did she own any dresses worth remaking? Silks were useless to her now. She had no qualms about abandoning the hoops in favor of simpler skirts. She never wore the bulky things or the restrictive corsets while at home. Now and then, she even donned a pair of altered trousers or breeches left behind from when her brothers were young. How would Tobias react if she showed up dressed like a boy on the day of their departure? She grinned. He'd be scandalized, of course, but oh how she loved the ease of movement and lightness breeches afforded her.

Come to think of it, she might just buy a pair or two for herself while she purchased new clothing for Jonathan. That settled the matter. She'd pack trousers, and once there was no turning back, she'd wear them.

"Here you are, Miss Stewart." Mr. Thompson handed her the two parcels wrapped in brown paper.

"Thank you, Mr. Thompson." He told her what she owed, and she counted out the coins. A moment later, she joined Mabel outside and handed her one of the two packages. "I believe we're ready to return home." She held up her wrapped box. "Let the shooting practice begin."

"Lord help us, child." Mabel's eyes widened. "Who would ever have thought a fine lady such as yourself would have need of such a skill?"

Mary grinned. "I'll show Tobias Lovejoy. Beatrice, Jonathan, and I *will* be part of his wagon train, and no matter what, things *will* get better. I cannot tolerate this lack of momentum any longer. Come, we've plans to make, and we have much to tell Ezra and Bea."

Thoughts of proving herself to Tobias buoyed her spirits. She had a task to accomplish and the means to do so. Her goal in sight, she marched down the street to retrieve their only remaining buggy, an ancient affair, hitched to their only remaining horse, a swaybacked old mare. No matter. She'd sell her land, her home, and start over—with or without her errant fiancé.

HIS MOTHER ON ONE ARM and his younger sister on the other, Tobias surveyed the makeshift church. After the original church had burned, the men had gotten together to build a temporary, rectangular hall of pine to use for services and social functions until a new church could be built.

"Oh my," his mother said, her gaze fixed upon an approaching buggy.

"What is it?" his sister Jane asked.

His mother gave his arm a slight squeeze. "Isn't that Miss Stewart with Mr. and Mrs. Greaves?"

Tobias glanced toward the buggy, which had stopped. Mr. Greaves was helping his wife to climb out. Two other women and a young boy still sat. He recognized Miss Stewart right away. "Yes, what of it?"

"She hasn't attended services since her father's unfortunate death," Jane whispered.

"Hmm." Curious, he led his mother and his younger sister toward the Greaves. Sarah and her husband were already climbing the steps to the door into the hall. "Mr. and Mrs. Greaves, Miss Stewart, good morning."

His mother and sister exchanged greetings just as the other woman joined them, the little boy's hand held in hers. Miss Stewart peered at him from beneath the rim of her bonnet. "Mr. Lovejoy, do you remember my cousin, Mrs. Williams?"

"Of course. She and my sister Sarah are good friends. It's good to see you, ma'am." He nodded toward her.

"This is her son, Jonathan. Jon, this is Mr. Lovejoy." Mary's indulgent smile landed on the youngster, and she smoothed down the boy's hair.

"A pleasure to meet you, sir."

"And you," Tobias said. Once Mr. Greaves secured the pair of horses hitched to their buggy, they all headed for the church in a companionable group.

"I wonder, sir, have you given my request any more thought since last we spoke?" Miss Stewart asked him.

She'd taken up the place beside him, and he couldn't help but compare his memories of the girl she'd been not so long ago to the woman she now was. "Can't say that I have."

She pursed her lips for an instant, as if his answer displeased her. "I, on the other hand, have given your objections a great deal of thought."

"Have you?" He studied her.

"Yes, and I insist you allow me to prove that I am capable of taking care of myself and my cousins well enough that you'll allow us to join your party west."

"Oh?" Again she'd managed to amuse and irritate him simultaneously. On top of those conflicting reactions, his curiosity had been piqued. "How do you plan to go about proving your skills, Miss Stewart?"

"I thought we might begin with marksmanship. I propose a demonstration at the end of October. Right here, in fact." She waved a hand toward the land surrounding the makeshift church. "I plan to sell Marilee Hills, and when I do, I shall purchase a wagon and a team of oxen. To prove that I can handle the team, I shall drive the wagon to town for your inspection."

What drove this diminutive spitfire to undertake such an extreme endeavor? "My mother told me of your recent losses, your brothers and your father. I am very sorry to hear of it."

"Thank you." She bit her lip for a second and stopped walking.

She'd been pretty and vivacious as a girl. She was still lovely, perhaps more so now. Though it seemed a lifetime ago, he couldn't help but recall how infatuated with her he'd been. He'd tried so hard to gain her attention, talking a little too loudly with his friends when she was near, all the time trying to stand near her or maneuver his family so he shared the same pew.

Today she radiated inner strength and determination, reminding him of the prow of a ship cutting through ocean waves. "Do you have family in Texas, ma'am? Is that why you are so determined to endure the hardships of a journey west by wagon?"

"Why does anyone make such a journey?" she shot back. "Why are you? Your family and business are here, Mr. Lovejoy. What remains of mine plan to travel with me."

His mother's words urging him to be compassionate came back to him, and he squelched the flare of irritation her tone ignited. She was right. He still had his family, and they'd rebuilt their business, while Miss Stewart had lost her family. One woman alone could not hope to bring a vast plantation back to profitability.

"Miss Stewart, I look forward to your marksmanship exhibition on the last Sunday of October." The warm and genuine smile she rewarded him with nearly punched the air out of his lungs. He gestured toward the door. "Shall we? I'm certain the service is about to begin."

Miss Stewart presented him with a complex puzzle he longed to solve, and before he allowed her to travel with him to Texas, he meant to discover what motivated her to leave all that she knew behind. Perhaps it had something to do with her missing fiancé, perhaps not. That the man had left her to her own devices was yet another puzzle worth solving.

Miss Stewart was not the only one who possessed a great deal of determination. After all, it was determination that had kept him alive during the hellish year he'd been a prisoner of war, and it had been determination that got him home.

He followed Miss Stewart up the stairs and into the church. She joined her family, and he joined his. Perhaps he and Miss Stewart might talk more after the service. Smiling, he settled onto the hard seat, his mind set upon puzzles and a particularly intriguing spitfire with blue eyes and a breath-stealing smile.

Chapter Three

Autumn of 1865

"Come, ladies, or we'll be late for church," Tobias called up the stairs. Lovejoy's Mercantile had reopened nearly two months ago, and business had been brisk. With all the new construction and other establishments reopening, Atlanta was coming around. The railroads were providing jobs for those willing to put their backs into laying rail and building bridges.

"Trying to hurry three females is a wasted effort, Tobias. You may as well save your breath." Terrence came down the stairs and shook his head. "It's like trying to herd chickens with a stick."

Impatient, Tobias buttoned his overcoat and strode toward the front door. "I'll go on ahead then if you don't mind."

"I don't mind in the slightest. Go save us seats, and I'll escort the ladies. We're likely to be late again."

Nodding his farewell, Tobias stepped outside into the freshness of the late October morning, his thoughts drifting to one petite spitfire. His mother had remarked that Mary had stopped coming to church after her father's unfortunate death. Odd that she began attending again the Sunday after she'd demanded a place in his wagon train. Also odd that he'd begun to look forward to their exchanges before and after services. He chuckled. Perhaps not so odd after all. He found verbally sparring with Miss Stewart stimulating, and he always came away somehow enlivened.

He shook his head. She was another man's fiancé, and she should not be filling his thoughts as often as she did. He had no business prying into her personal life, yet he couldn't help himself. No doubt she pined for her long-absent beau. What a shame that her heart was lost forever to a man so callous he'd left her behind without a word. As far as Tobias was concerned, Mary owed the fool nothing, and once she realized that fact, she'd be free.

He grunted. Free to be courted by a man who suffered visions from the past, nightmares and cold sweats? His chest tightened. He couldn't subject her to the terrors he fought. Mary deserved so much more than a man whose future was uncertain—a man attempting to outrun his demons.

"Morning, Tobias," Ambrose called from across the street. He too was dressed in his Sunday best.

He waved. "On your way to church without your wife and son this morning?"

Ambrose crossed the road to walk beside Tobias. "They're already there. Hilda volunteered to organize the refreshments, and Gus went along with her in the wagon. He'll help her carry and move things about." Ambrose glanced askance at him. "I've been meaning to talk to you. I have a favor to ask. Do you mind if we discuss it along the way?"

"Course not."

"I've heard from Andrew. Before joining up, our son took his wife home to her family's farm near Newburgh, Indiana. He figured she'd be safer in a Yankee state known to be sympathetic to the South, and he was right." Ambrose's Adam's apple bobbed. "My boy was badly wounded at Bentonville. It's taking him a long time to recover. Far too long." His expression grave, he took a moment before he continued. "He took ill while being doctored for his wounds, you see. We're grateful he's alive, but he hasn't yet fully regained his strength. He's with Bonnie and her family on their farm."

Tobias recalled Andrew's pretty young wife, Bonnie Schmitt, who'd come to Atlanta as a young teacher a few years before the war. "Hmm." Tobias nodded sympathetically. "What can I do to help?"

"Well, here's the thing." The older man's face reddened. "I hate to ask it of you."

"Our families go way back, Ambrose, and Andrew and I were close as boys. You were my father's closest friend, and I'll never forget how you were there to guide and support me when he passed." Tobias stopped walking.

"For God's sake, you looked after my store when a lesser man would've looted what was left and turned his back. The day I returned, you picked me up from the dirt, bathed, clothed, and fed me. Whatever it is you need, you have only to ask."

"All right." Ambrose cleared his throat. "I've had a letter from my son. Andrew, his wife, and two other families in Newburgh have asked to join your wagon train to Texas."

Tobias rested his hand on Ambrose's shoulder for a moment. "They are more than welcome, and I'll help Andrew in any way I can."

"That's not the favor," Ambrose said, sending him an arch look. "They have no one to lead them here or wherever else you might designate as a meeting spot. Andrew is too weak, and the other two families . . . well . . . one is a widower with a son and a young daughter. The boy is fourteen, and the daughter is ten. The other family is a young, newlywed couple." Ambrose huffed out a long breath. "I'll get to the point. Andrew has asked if you'd be willing to travel to Newburgh first, so that they can join you there and head out under your auspices. He knows how inconvenient it will be, and the three families have pooled their resources to compensate you for your trouble on their behalf."

It would add an extra two weeks at least to get to Newburgh, and another couple of weeks to reach the Santa Fe trail out of Missouri. Inconvenient indeed. His jaw clenched. He'd never been an impatient man before the war, but now irritability and impatience flared to life over the most trivial matters. But his family owed the Offermeyers, and if he must leave earlier than what he'd originally planned, so be it. He still had plenty of time to plan. Shoving his emotions aside, he turned to Ambrose.

"Done. Write to Andrew, and tell him he and the other two families should use their pooled resources to gather adequate supplies for the journey, because it won't be easy. He can expect us by the end of March or early April at the latest." He only hoped the weather would cooperate, and they'd have a drier than average spring.

"God bless you, Tobias," Ambrose said, his voice hoarse. "Your pa would be so very proud of the man you've become."

"It's the least I can do." Would Papa be proud? After all, he was abandoning the business his father and grandfather had built from the ground up, the legacy his father had hoped Tobias would continue. He was abandoning his mother and sisters. He lost his temper and his ability to concentrate far too often, and then there were the nightmares and the moments when he was thrust into the past, reliving the horrors of war.

Though it had been a decade since his father had passed, Tobias still missed him desperately, missed his guidance and his papa's even temperament. If only he were more like his pa. He inhaled deeply, trying to ease the tightness in his chest.

"What does Andrew intend to do in Texas? Will he and his wife file for a land grant?"

"They will." Ambrose nodded, pride shining in his eyes. "But it will have to be close to a growing town. Andrew and his wife plan to open a butcher shop. Bonnie also wants to keep chickens, a milk cow or two, and grow vegetables. They'll sell the eggs, roasters, and whatever surplus vegetables and dairy products they can, along with meat from the ranchers and farmers in the area. Texas is growing fast, and there's a need for butchers and grocers."

"I've no doubt they'll prosper." They'd reached the edge of town, and the church bell began to peal. Surveying the yard, Tobias caught sight of Mary right away. She stood with her neighbors, Mr. and Mrs. Greaves, who brought Mary, her cousin Mrs. Williams, and young Jonathan to church with them every Sunday. How could he not notice Mary? She stood out like a bright, flickering flame on a moonless night. He couldn't help but smile at the sight of her.

Tobias's pace quickened. If he could manage to maneuver things just right, he'd sit beside her during the service again this Sunday. As if she sensed his attention upon her, Mary turned and smiled. Her bright countenance, framed in reddish-gold curls, stole his breath.

"What's your rush, Tobias?" Ambrose huffed and puffed to keep up with Tobias's longer strides.

"Um . . . I've been charged with the task of saving places for my family."

Ambrose's gaze followed his to where Miss Stewart stood. He chuckled. "Go on, then. We'll talk more later."

"Of course." Tobias left him and caught up with Miss Stewart just as she and Mr. and Mrs. Greaves reached the steps leading to the hall's double doors. He removed his hat. "Good morning, Miss Stewart, Mr. and Mrs. Greaves. I hope you're all well this fine Sunday morning."

"We are indeed, Mr. Lovejoy." George shook his hand. "You seem to be missing your womenfolk and brother-in-law this morning. I trust they are well?"

"They are, thank you. My family should be here momentarily."

"Good morning, Mr. Lovejoy," Mary said, her lovely blue eyes sparkling. "I *do* hope you still intend to stay after service today, so I might prove my marksmanship once and for all." She stared out over the grounds. "It is a perfect day for target practice, clear and practically windless."

"Mary," Mrs. Graves chided. "You could not wait until after service to start in on the poor man?"

"Apparently not." Mary smiled sweetly. "I fear pestering poor Mr. Lovejoy has become a habit, and it's a habit I will not quit until my place in his wagon train is assured."

"Miss Stewart, I would not describe our Sunday debates as pestering. I see them more like indefatigable attempts at persuasion."

"What a pretty way to say the same thing as *pestering*, Mr. Lovejoy." She graced him a sweet smile.

She reminded him of a redheaded woodpecker, pecking away at his reasons for denying her until nothing was left of his argument but empty holes. Why did her nagging fail to raise his ire when the slightest provocation from anyone else set him off so easily?

"I wouldn't miss the demonstration for anything, ma'am." Tobias offered her his arm. She accepted his escort, and they climbed the stairs side by side. Her cheeks turned a most becoming shade of pink even as her chin lifted a determined notch. Her blushes reminded him of the wild roses growing in profuse abundance along the railroad tracks, and her pretty blue eyes put the early flowering bluebells to shame.

They filed into the hall, and Tobias handed her into a pew after Mr. and Mrs. Greaves. Her cousin and young Jonathan were already seated behind them. Tobias took his place beside Mary, then took off his overcoat and laid it out on the bench, saving spots for his family. Sitting so close to Mary, his awareness of her took up his entire attention. Mere inches separated them, and the scent she wore, lilies of the valley, enveloped him in a cloud of sweetness.

Lilies of the valley suited her, for she was the very essence of spring's beauty. From the corner of his eye, he stared, fascinated by the fairness of her complexion and each delightful freckle. She removed her cloak, and her feminine curves captured his errant imagination. He shifted, forcing himself to look elsewhere.

"I've had an offer on my property," she whispered, leaning toward him. "And I plan to accept."

Tobias's blood heated, and his pulse raced at her nearness. "Why, that's excellent news. I hope you were offered a fair price."

She sighed, and his attention riveted to her slightly parted lips. Miss Stewart possessed the most kissable mouth he'd ever beheld. Did she taste of sweet, ripe peaches?

"Not nearly as much as I would have liked, but more than I expected," she continued, her voice hushed. "It will be enough, and I shall accept."

"Enough for what, ma'am?" He leaned nearer. "Do tell. What are your future plans?"

"Other than traveling to Texas with you, do you mean? Oh, look." Mary twisted around to peer over her shoulder, flashing him a smug look. "Your family has arrived, sir." She held up her hand to catch their attention.

Tobias stifled his grin. Mary had managed to evade his question yet again. His brother-in-law lifted Tobias's overcoat and draped it over the back of the pew before sending his mother and sisters in to take their places. Greetings were exchanged just as the good Reverend Burns walked to the front of the hall, and the service began.

Tobias's attention strayed again and again to the woman beside him. He barely remembered to stand with everyone else for the hymns. Mary held the hymnal between them to share. He placed his hand under his half, and his fingers brushed hers for the merest instant. His poor heart nearly pounded out of his chest. Had someone fed the fire in the stove? The hall had grown uncomfortably warm.

It would be better for all concerned if Miss Stewart didn't join his wagon train. Better for his soul, at least. He was beginning to covet another man's betrothed. If he had a woman like Mary, someone he loved with all his heart, only death or imprisonment could've kept him from her.

Perhaps Miss Stewart had heard from her missing fiancé, and that was why she wished to travel west. Perhaps like Andrew Offermeyer, Mary's beau had been too gravely wounded in the war to come for her himself. Or could it be she'd been jilted, and she sought the churl so she might give him a piece of her mind? She still wore the sapphire ring, though. Did that mean she intended to reignite the man's passion for her once she found him?

His mind spinning with various scenarios, he missed the cue to sit until his mother tugged at his sleeve. Chagrined, he dropped to the pew to the sound of a few snickers.

Things would be much simpler if he knew the name of Miss Stewart's fiancé. Tobias had friends in Houston, men he'd served with who'd moved on to Texas before him. He'd recently received a letter from Charles Bradford, who was now a Texas Ranger. He was certain Charles would be willing to help him locate Miss Stewart's missing fiancé. Once Tobias had the man's name, he'd send a query to his friend regarding the man's whereabouts.

Surely Miss Stewart would appreciate his efforts on her behalf. Then what? He'd learn she was still engaged, and he'd offer his aid in reuniting the happy couple, or he'd learn she was free to direct her affections elsewhere. The thought of reuniting the couple sent a surge of jealousy coursing through him, while the thought of her being free caused despair. A woman like Mary deserved the best, and he was not the man for her. War had stolen away pieces of him, and he was no longer whole.

MARY WALKED OUT OF THE hall, Tobias close upon her heels. She'd scarcely been able to breathe at all during this morning's service, and it was entirely his fault. He'd sat too close, so close she'd been enveloped in the scent of the bayberry shaving soap he used. The heat radiating between them had kept her warm in the otherwise chilly hall.

She should be focusing on finding her missing fiancé, but more and more she found Tobias Lovejoy filling her thoughts and setting her heart aflutter. Did that make her wicked? Sinful? Frowning, she strode to the Greaves' wagon and lifted the basket holding the cracked crockery she'd gathered.

"You look worried, Miss Stewart." Tobias took the basket from her.

"I assure you, I am not." Not about shooting, anyway. Her worry had far more to do with her growing attraction to him. She reached for her holstered revolver from under the driver's seat and strapped the belt around her waist. "I thought we might set the targets on that old oak stump." She jutted her chin toward the spot. "We'll be in plain view, so there won't be any cause for gossip."

"All right." One side of his wide, generous mouth turned up. "After you, ma'am."

Bea and Mrs. Greaves watched from where the food had been set out for everyone on plank tables in the yard, and young Jonathan chased around the yard with the other children. By the time she and Tobias returned to the hall, only crumbs would remain. Mary's stomach rumbled in protest, but she would eat once she was home. Right now, the need to prove herself once and for all to her far-too-attractive, muleheaded adversary outranked hunger. "If you'd be so kind, please set three of the jars up on the stump for me."

"It would be my pleasure, ma'am." Tobias strode off, her basket in hand.

She couldn't help but admire the manly way he moved. The masculine timbre of his voice never failed to elicit a tingle of awareness, and his compelling eyes . . . Oh, how she longed to banish whatever caused the haunted look she glimpsed in their depths.

Despite whatever haunted him, he planned to lead a group of pioneers to Texas. Since the first Sunday she'd attended services, she'd noticed others gravitated to Tobias, seeking his counsel, looking to him for leadership. He'd make a fine mayor or perhaps even a senator someday, yet he'd decided to become a rancher. Eldon certainly had ambition. Her fiancé hoped to be governor of Texas someday.

"All set, Miss Stewart." His expression held a hint of smugness. "I eagerly await your demonstration."

She clucked her tongue, turning to pace away from her targets. "Do I detect the hint of facetiousness in your tone, sir?"

"Why, not at all, ma'am."

"Humph." She fixed her sights on the crockery. "Prepare to be impressed."

He laughed.

She fired. "One." The first jar flew off the stump. "Two." The second shattered where it stood. "Three." The third joined the first, flying off the stump. Triumphant, she met his gaze. He no longer laughed, and his eyes held a glimmer of respect. "Well?" She batted her eyelashes at him.

"I am impressed. Do you shoot as well with a rifle?"

"Better. My cousin and her son are equally as skilled." A small exaggeration, but at least they knew how to shoot and how to disassemble, clean, oil, and reassemble all the guns in her possession. Bea wasn't interested in shooting anything, but that would change if they faced hunger along the journey and were forced to hunt. Jonathan was still too young and fidgety to hone his skill, but he'd shown promise and an eagerness to learn.

She, on the other hand, had a driving need to be the best. Was it pride or desperation that drove her? "*Now* will you agree to let us join you on your journey west?"

"Hmm." His stance relaxed, and he rubbed his chin, his expression pensive. "I will—"

"Finally!" Triumph flared.

"—agree on one condition."

Mary's heart dropped. Hadn't she done enough? "What impossible condition do you intend to impose now?" she managed to grit out through her clenched teeth. "It seems to me I'm being singled out for trials no one else is being subjected to." She glowered at him. "Do you see it as *my* fault *all* my male relations are dead? Is that it? Or, somehow, by virtue of my sex, I have no right to . . . to determine the course of my own life?" she sputtered. "Do you think me somehow less capable of—"

"I have a few questions to ask. That is all." He clasped his hands behind his back, a single eyebrow arched.

"Oh?" Her revolver dangling from her right hand, she canted her head to peer at him from beneath the rim of her bonnet. "What do you wish to know, Mr. Lovejoy?"

"Why do you want to leave everything and everyone behind? Why move to Texas?"

"Same as you, I'm sure. I wish to start over. I have lost my entire family, sir, and my way of life. Surely even *you* can understand why I'd wish for change. I cannot run a plantation, and even if I could, I have no wish to."

"Fair enough. What do you plan to do once we reach Texas?"

"I thought I'd open a finishing school for young ladies." She walked over to the basket for more targets and set two more jars on the stump. "As much schooling as I've had, I'm certainly qualified."

This time she paced farther away from her targets. What had he heard? Did he know she'd lost a fiancé somewhere between Savannah, where Eldon was born and raised, and Houston? She lifted the revolver, aimed, and fired the last two bullets in the chamber. Both targets shattered to bits. "Perhaps I'll teach young ladies in my finishing school how to shoot. I hear Texas is a dangerous place."

He chuckled and walked to her side. "My mother tells me you're engaged. She says your betrothed left for Texas about a year ago, promising to send for you once he'd settled. Is that true?"

So he did know. Mortification burned a path from her head to her toes. She couldn't bear the weight of his pity. "My personal life is none of your concern, and I fail to see how this has any bearing upon whether or not I travel with you. Have you asked everyone else joining you such impertinent questions?"

Consternation clouded his features. "No, I haven't."

Her face still flaming, she studied the shards of crockery littering the ground. "If you can impose conditions upon me, it's only fair that I'm allowed to do the same to you. Why do you wish to know about my affairs? If you have a good reason for asking, perhaps I'll answer."

"I don't know why exactly." He removed his hat and plowed his fingers through his hair, leaving furrows in their wake. "Perhaps it's because you present such a puzzle. Wanting to solve the puzzle gives me respite . . ." he grunted, "from thinking about the ugliness of the past few years, I suppose. I am curious, Miss Stewart, and curiosity has recently become a most welcome diversion."

Once again she glimpsed the haunted look behind his gaze, but she had her own ghosts to fight. "Gossip."

"I beg your pardon?" His eyes lost the haunted look, and his focus on her sharpened.

"I used to attend dances, afternoon teas, dinner parties, plays, musicales, and other social functions. We all did. The war put an end to entertainments of that sort, at least for me. I will confess I have found gossip provides me with an alternative, a reprieve from worry and hardship. Gossip has become a form of entertainment. Don't you see?"

Her chest ached. He wanted to satisfy his *curiosity*, and she was nothing more than the object of his speculation. "I must thank you, Mr. Lovejoy, for you have brought my hens home to roost." She sighed. "Now that I know what it feels like to be the object of such curiosity, I can assure you, gossip will no longer be a pastime of mine."

"Ah, I do see, and it's clear I've fallen into a bad habit. I apologize, Miss Stewart. You are . . . You don't deserve to be viewed as entertainment or as a distraction from my own dark thoughts. I have been unforgivably rude. Your personal life is none of my business." His expression pained, he bowed slightly. "If you will excuse me, I must rejoin my family."

"Mr. Lovejoy," she called out to his retreating back.

"Yes?" Though he stopped, he didn't turn to face her.

"You have not granted me a place in your train west." Tears threatened as she faced yet another loss, yet another abandonment. *Tobias?* That made no sense. Until she knew otherwise, she was still engaged to Eldon.

His shoulders slumped. "You have it, Miss Stewart. You, your cousin, and her son are most welcome."

Mary nodded to herself. Victory was hers, so why did this crushing sadness and disappointment sit so heavily upon her heart?

Chapter Four

Tobias stood behind the counter at the back of the mercantile, fountain pen in hand, gazing absently at the ledger before him. It had been two long, miserable weeks since the disastrous target practice with Miss Stewart. Two weeks of Sunday services where she'd been cool, polite, and distant, avoiding him when she could. He missed their conversations, even their verbal sparring. He missed *her*, and he had only himself to blame. He blew out a resignation-tinged breath and tried to concentrate on the ledger, only to find his thumb and fingers covered in black ink. He dropped the pen and reached for a rag. "Damnation."

"Tobias, what is wrong?" Sarah appeared from between the shelves to stand across the counter from him, concern clouding her features.

"Besides a leaking pen?" He wiped at the ink he knew would not come off. "It's guilt at my own foolishness that rankles." Thank heavens he hadn't been holding the pen over the ledger, or he would've had to start all over on a fresh page with the day's tallies.

"If you don't mind my asking, what have you done now, Toby?" Sarah pulled the ledger away, put the ribbon over his most recent entries, and closed the leather-bound book.

The two of them were only twenty months apart in age. Her chiding tone brought him back to when they were children. He'd frequently gotten himself into mischief, while she'd been the perfect daughter. "Do you remember how you always used to ask me that very same question when we were children? What have you done now, Toby?" he mimicked.

"I do, and often it was when I found you standing in a corner where Papa had put you after you'd broken something, or you'd failed to pay heed to his warnings to cease with your shenanigans." A wistful smile played across her face. "I miss Papa so."

"As do I." Perhaps he missed his father's steadying influence and unwavering love now more than ever.

"So . . . what did you do this time, Toby?" She gestured over her shoulder, her eyes sparkling with amusement. "Would you like to stand in a corner while you confess? It'll be like old times."

"I think not." He and Sarah had always been close, sharing secrets with each other they hadn't dared share with anyone else. She'd never once betrayed his trust, nor had he ever betrayed hers. He tossed the rag onto the counter.

"Through my own selfish curiosity, I fear I caused another considerable insult and hurt. I demanded answers to questions I had no right to ask."

"Miss Mary Stewart?"

"Yes." Remorse bit at his conscience. "Was I that obvious?"

"You were, but if it's any consolation, you aren't the only one to speculate where she's concerned. Most of us believe her poor Mr. Smythe met with an untimely end on his way to Houston. Anyone who ever saw the two together could have no doubt regarding his devotion to her."

"Smythe . . . that's her fiancé's name?" For weeks he'd been trying to discover the man's name, and his sister casually dropped the missing piece of the puzzle into his hands. His pulse leaped, and all his nerves tingled. "You knew him? You know his full name?"

"Yes, of course. Eldon Richard Smythe attended Sunday services with Miss Stewart and her father whenever he was in town, but you had already gone off to war by then." Sarah sighed and shook her head. "Poor Miss Stewart. I suppose she must feel as if she cannot move forward until she knows for certain what became of him."

He reeled from the sudden revelation. "All this time you've known who he was, and you said nothing?"

"You never asked." Her brow creased. "Why did you wish to know?"

Tobias raked ink-stained fingers through his hair. "Because I

. . . I—"

"Oh, Tobias, do you want Miss Stewart for yourself?"

His heart stumbled and tripped. His sister had always been far too perceptive where he was concerned. "I can help her discover what has become of her fiancé. I have friends in Houston who could make inquiries for her. She doesn't need to uproot her entire life and deal with the hardship of traveling to Texas by covered wagon." He frowned. If Sarah had figured him out so easily, others could as well. Unless he wished to add scandal to his list of offenses, he needed to be a great deal more circumspect.

"My dear brother, do not forget I know you better than anyone else."

"She's engaged to another man," he blurted.

"I doubt that's still the case. If he is alive, she has most certainly been jilted. Miss Stewart has not heard from him since he left Savannah for Houston. You wouldn't scandalize anyone by courting her."

"From Savannah, you say?"

She nodded. "His family lives there. They are . . . er . . . were her father's business associates, distributors for his cotton and sorghum, I believe."

"I have grievously insulted Miss Stewart, and she's avoiding me." The ember of hope ignited by his sister's revelations snuffed out. "Even if courting her would cause no scandal, I doubt she'd welcome my attentions now. Not after the way I've insulted her."

"Oh, Toby." Sarah rolled her eyes. "Go apologize to the woman, and bring her a gift while you're at it."

"She's sold Marilee Hills. I don't know where she's living at present."

"She's still at home, and there she will remain until your party leaves at the end of March. That was part of the negotiations when she accepted the offer for her land."

"How do you *know* all this, Sarah?"

She shrugged. "Her cousin and I are good friends. Bea and I often meet at the post office during her visits to town. Afterward, we take tea together at the hotel and chat."

"Tea. I'll bring Miss Stewart tea as a peace offering." He untied his apron and moved out from behind the counter. "It's suitably impersonal."

"Hmm." Sarah tapped her chin. "She prefers coffee, and why don't you include a cone or two of sugar? I'm sure she'd appreciate the gesture."

"Brilliant." He strode off to gather a sack of roasted coffee beans and a few cones of sugar.

"Tobias," Sarah called after him.

"Yes?"

"Do wait until tomorrow. It's suppertime, which is why I came to fetch you in the first place. By the time you ride out to Miss Stewart's, it will be dark, and that will cause a scandal, whether she is spoken for or not."

Jane appeared at the end of the aisle. "Hey, you two. The food is getting cold. We're all waiting."

"Right. Sorry." Supper, and then he'd write a letter to Charles Bradford in Houston. His friend would receive the request long before Tobias left for Indiana—if his mail got through at all. Bradford would be able to investigate Mr. Smythe's whereabouts and send a reply long before the end of March.

Perhaps he'd best send a telegram as well. Though things were slowly returning to normal, too many robberies still disrupted the mail coaches. Should he mention his efforts to Mary? He'd wait and see how receptive she was to his apology first, and then he'd decide. He needed to tread carefully if he wished to regain her trust, and more than anything he longed for her trust.

MARY ADDED WOOD TO THE fire under the large cauldron. The wind shifted slightly, and smoke blew into her face. Coughing and blinking, she moved to stand by the pile of linens and clothing awaiting a good wash. Mabel and Bea would join her soon, and the three of them would work together to get the odious weekly chore completed.

Out of everything she'd been forced to learn, laundering was her least favorite. Still, odd as it seemed, she didn't miss the pampered life she'd once lived. Idleness had never suited her, and the business of living gave her purpose and a deep satisfaction. After a day's labor, she certainly slept better, and the nightmares happened less frequently.

Beatrice walked out the back door, tying on an apron over her coat. "Mary, you have a visitor." Her eyes danced with glee.

"I do?" She straightened. "Mrs. Greaves?"

"No. Mr. Lovejoy is here, and he's brought a gift."

Her heart flipped, and dismay charged through her. "Oh my. Today of all days." Her hands flew to her hair, which she'd wound into a tight, unattractive bun to keep it out of the way. "I smell like woodsmoke." And her simple workday gown was the most drab color of mud imaginable.

"I did explain to him the inconvenience of his timing. Nonetheless, he awaits your presence in the front parlor. After he's gone to the trouble of riding all the way out here, you should at least see why he's come to call. I'll take over here. Jonathan is keeping your guest entertained at present."

Her ruffled feathers still hadn't settled since learning he viewed her as nothing more than a distraction from his own dark thoughts. Miffed, she kept her apron on. Fine, let him see how he'd inconvenienced her. She squared her shoulders. "Whatever can he want?"

Bea picked up one of the wooden paddles and stirred flakes of soap into the heated water. "You won't know unless you talk to him. Go."

"Humph." Smoothing her hair back, she shot her cousin a disgruntled look. "Truly, I'd rather do the wash."

"You hate doing the wash."

"Precisely my point." Mary strode toward the kitchen door, Bea's laughter echoing behind her.

Mabel stood at the kitchen counter, arranging a tray. "I made coffee, Miss Mary, but all we had left is the half-chicory blend. I hope that's all right."

"I'm sure it's fine, thank you. I'll take it with me to the parlor." She moved to stand beside Mabel. "Where is Ezra?"

"Out rounding up piglets that escaped from their pen, or so he said. I don't know if you've noticed, but that man always disappears on laundry day."

"I have, and I don't mind. He'd only get in the way, and tending to the animals falls mostly to him." Mary lifted the tray. "I'll rejoin you and Bea shortly. I don't plan on this being a long visit."

Mabel sighed. "Mr. Lovejoy is a fine young man, and he could use a bit of your charity about now."

"Charity? It seems to me he's well-off enough," she said with a huff of disdain.

"I don't mean that kind of charity, and well you know it, child. He fought in a war and spent more than a year as a prisoner in Fort Sumter, only to come home to find his home destroyed. The poor man was starved near to death. We both know he's been through things, seen horrors you cannot imagine."

Mary's chest tightened, and the image of her father, his vacant eyes bulging and bloodshot, his face a mottled purple, flashed through her mind. She shuddered, remembering the sheer terror she'd experienced the first time soldiers came to Marilee Hills, and she, her father, Mabel, and Ezra were forced into hiding. She too had been through things, seen things she wished she hadn't.

"Perhaps you're right, Mabel. I'll be civil." Tray in hand, Mary set out for the front parlor. Her breath caught at the sight of him where he sat beside Jonathan. Tobias had taken great care in his appearance for this visit, wearing his Sunday best. For her?

"Mr. Lovejoy. What a surprise." She set the tray on the one remaining end table. "Can I pour you a cup of coffee? It's partially chicory, I'm afraid."

"Miss Stewart." He shot up from the settee. "Yes, thank you."

Next to Mr. Lovejoy's overcoat, hat, and gloves, a parcel wrapped in brown paper and tied with twine rested on the settee. Her curiosity sparked to life.

"Cousin Mary," Jonathan said, bolting up from his spot, "am I supposed to stay here, or should I find Mama?"

"You can go help tend the fire out back, Jonathan. Thank you." She poured two cups of the steaming brew.

"It was a pleasure meeting you, young man," Tobias said, holding out his hand for Jonathan to shake. "I'm certain you'll be a big help to your mother and cousin on their journey to Texas."

Jonathan grinned, shook his hand, and peered up at him. "I will be, sir. I know how to shoot a revolver now, and I'm learning how to harness the team and how to drive the wagon." He stood a little taller as he made his pronouncement, and then he ran off to help Mabel and Bea.

Mary's heart filled with pride for her young cousin. "Jon is a most determined and hardworking boy." She handed a steaming cup to Tobias. "Please sit, Mr. Lovejoy."

She settled herself on a ladder-back chair across from him. "What brings you out to Marilee Hills in this chilly weather?" Not only chilly, but damp. They'd have to hang the wash inside, since the overcast sky promised rain at any moment.

He cleared his throat, tugged at his tight collar, and studied the room. Mary had a difficult time keeping her smile in check. Clearly he was uncomfortable, but he had it coming. She sipped her coffee and waited. She had no intention of making anything easier for *him* after the trials he'd foisted upon her.

"I've come here today to beg your forgiveness," he said in a rush while lifting the parcel. He handed it to her. "I should never have made it so difficult for you to secure your place in my wagon train, and I should not have pried into your personal life. I've brought a peace offering, and I am hoping we can start over. It is my greatest wish that we might become friends."

The earnestness of his gaze softened her resolve to make things uncomfortable for him. "As I recall, you already apologized, sir."

"Not sufficiently, or you would still be . . ." His face grew ruddy.

Her gaze flew to his. "I would still be what?"

He shrugged, his expression chagrined. "I . . . well, I miss our conversations, our verbal sparring, especially on Sundays before and after service."

She laughed. "That is the last thing I would expect you'd miss."

"And yet I do. You have a quick mind and a sharp wit, and I appreciate both." He shifted. "I never meant to insult you, Miss Stewart. I thought perhaps I might be able to help discover the whereabouts of your fiancé, and I guess I was hoping you might trust me enough to share some of the worry you carry." He tugged at his collar again. "Presumptuous, was it not?"

"How would you go about helping me locate my missing fiancé?" She flashed him a questioning look before turning her gaze to her cup. "Of course, I should've known you would've heard my tale of woe."

"I have friends in Houston, one of whom is a Texas Ranger. If you will permit me, I'd like to send him a letter asking him to look into the matter. I had thought doing so might save you the trouble of uprooting your entire life here in Georgia."

Mary's brow rose, and she stared at the peace offering upon her lap. "My life has already been uprooted in every way imaginable, Mr. Lovejoy."

As unreasonable as it was, she floundered in a well of abandonment, barely keeping her head above the surface. In her short life—hadn't she just turned twenty?—she'd lost her mother to illness, her brothers to war, and her father to despair. Most likely she'd also lost her fiancé. She smoothed down the brown paper and fixed her stare on the bare floorboards, where once a luxurious, thick rug had graced the surface.

"If your friend can tell me what became of Eldon, I would be much obliged, but I still intend to leave this place. I meant it when I said I want a new start."

"As do I," he murmured.

"I too would love to be your friend, and I hope you might see me as someone you could . . ." She bit her lip.

"Yes?" His gaze met hers, his expression inscrutable.

"Sometimes I see shadows clouding your eyes, and as one who carries more dark memories than I care to acknowledge, I can only imagine the visions that haunt you."

A look of alarm suffused his features. "Visions?"

She'd been too bold, but he'd said he wanted her trust. Trust grew out of revelation and compassion. "If we are to be friends, let us be honest with one another. I am the one who found my father hanging from the rafters in our stable. It was I who climbed the rafters and cut him down." She blinked against the sudden sting at the back of her eyes, recalling the way his body fell to the ground below, a lifeless thud against the packed dirt. "I have . . . nightmares about that day."

She could scarcely breathe. "And sometimes I'm so overcome with terror, I believe soldiers are once again in my yard, come to raid my home or worse." She cast him a look of sympathy and shrugged. "I can only imagine what it must have been like for you in Fort Sumter or enduring the hardships of war. I just thought perhaps you might have similar . . . experiences."

Tobias grunted. "I believed I was alone in such matters," he muttered, his tone hushed. "It's true. I am haunted by visions from the past. I haven't said a word about them to anyone for fear I'd be perceived as mad, and someone would have me committed." He frowned. "It's the oddest thing. Smells come back to me, sounds trigger memories, and sometimes I find it hard to remain in the present."

Mary nodded. "It's the same for me. So you can understand why I want so badly to leave. This house, the land . . . it's saturated in tragedy and loss. I'm desperate to be free of this place. When you speak of sparing me the turbulence of uprooting my life, such a thing is not possible. Do you see?"

"I am sorry for all you were forced to endure and for all you have lost, Miss Stewart." He laid his hand over hers, his expression filled with warmth and compassion, tinged with his own heavy sadness.

Mary's heart ached for them both, even as tingles at his touch coursed through her. "As I am sorry for what you too have suffered, Mr. Lovejoy."

He removed his hand, and they sat in silence for several minutes, but there was nothing awkward between them now. Theirs was the quiet sharing of two souls offering companionship and comfort. Mary drew in that comfort and offered him a conciliatory smile. "Your apology is accepted, and I would very much like to be friends, sir."

His entire countenance brightened. "In that case, please call me Tobias."

"I will, and you may call me Mary."

"Mary." His smile broadened. "Will you open your gift?"

"Oh." She stared at the parcel in her lap. "I'd forgotten." She untied the twine and peeled back the paper. "Sugar!" She beamed. "Oh, and coffee. How very thoughtful. Thank you, Tobias. Your peace offering is very much appreciated."

"You're most welcome." His eyes caught and held hers. "Mary, if there is anything you need, please do not hesitate to let me know. I'll do whatever I can on your behalf."

Again her heart flipped, and she could not tear her gaze from him. His expression was so sincere and intense, he robbed her of reason. This time, the silence stretching between them was fraught with a different kind of tension . . . an awareness of his maleness, how very attractive he was, the broadness of his shoulders. Her pulse raced, and heat pooled deep in her belly.

"Well," he said, rising from the settee, "I should be going. I have taken up enough of your time, and I must get back to the mercantile."

"I confess, I didn't want to make this visit easy for you." She also rose and set the coffee and sugar on the tray, along with their cups.

Tobias chuckled. "I didn't expect you would." He put on his coat and hat. His gloves he tucked into a pocket. "I'd like to invite you and your cousins to join my family for dinner this coming Sunday." Once again his face reddened. "If you're free, you could return home with us after the service."

"That would be lovely. Thank you." She saw him to the front door. Torn between wanting him to stay longer and needing the distance between them in order to regain control over her rioting reactions to him. "I'm glad you came by, Tobias, and I'm glad we are to be friends." He reached for her hand, setting off a cascade of internal flutters. She savored the warmth of his skin against hers.

He held her hand between both of his as if entreating her. "Do I have your permission to enlist the aid of my friend in Houston on your behalf?"

"You do. Perhaps he will be more successful than I have been."

He let her go. Mary opened the front door and followed him out onto the veranda.

A fine buckskin gelding stood hitched to the post in front, and Tobias strode to his mount's side. "I look forward to Sunday."

"As do I. Tell your mother we'll bring dessert."

"I will, and will you please resume your pestering?" he teased. "So that I might feel that all is truly right between us?"

She laughed. "If you insist."

He tipped his hat, mounted, and rode down the lane toward town. The smell of woodsmoke drifted to her. A reminder there were chores to be done, yet she couldn't tear her eyes from Tobias. She followed his progress until he reached the end of their lane. Only when he was out of sight did she finally shut the door. Smiling, she made her way back to the parlor, taking the tray to the kitchen on her way to the back door.

Coffee and sugar! Such a luxury. After the laundry was done, she'd brew a fresh pot as a treat. Still smiling, she set out for the backyard, her heart considerably lighter.

"Well?" Mabel straightened beside the cauldron of laundry,

eyeing her curiously.

"Well, what?" Mary took up one of the washboards and joined the two women.

"My dear, do not keep us in suspense," Beatrice chided. "What did Mr. Lovejoy want, and what did he bring?"

"He apologized for viewing my situation as a means of entertainment, and he brought coffee and sugar."

"Thanks be," Mabel muttered. "We haven't had sugar here in . . . Why, I think it's been a year if it's been a day."

Bea stretched and rubbed the small of her back. "Did you accept his apology?"

"I did." That he asked to be her friend and held her hand in his more than once she kept close, her secret to take out and savor whenever she pleased. "He's also going to have a friend in Houston look into Eldon's disappearance for me."

Beatrice arched a brow. "Or . . . perhaps he wishes to know for himself."

"Whatever do you mean?" Mary asked.

"I don't mean anything, other than the man has an overabundance of interest where you're concerned." Bea cast a speculative look her way.

"Well, no matter, I appreciate his help, especially if it leads me to answers." She was not free, could not be free until she knew for certain what had become of one Mr. Eldon Richard Smythe.

Images of Tobias filled her mind—his rare smiles, the way his expressive face shifted and changed with every emotion, his broad shoulders, and the delicious way he smelled, like his shaving soap mixed with his own unique masculine scent. She'd found him incredibly attractive as a girl, even more so now that she was a woman. Still, if she allowed him to get too close, she'd put herself at risk for yet another abandonment. Holding on to the fantasy that her betrothed was somewhere in Texas, needing her to find and nurse him back to health, was far safer.

Good heavens, but she needed to steer her thoughts in another direction. Her throat tight, she grabbed a few linen shifts and shoved them into her pail of soapy water. Tobias wanted to be her friend, and she wished to be his, and that was all there was to that. "I thought we'd brew a fresh pot of coffee and treat ourselves once we're finished with the laundry."

"Perhaps we might make a small batch of sugar cookies," Bea said, pressing one of Jon's shirts against the washboard.

"Could we?" Jon's face lit with excitement.

"Of course." Mary smiled and settled into her task. She had a friend in Tobias, and he'd offered his help should she need it. She did. Oh, how she needed a strong shoulder to lean on. "By the way, the three of us are invited to Sunday dinner this week at the Lovejoys.'"

"Oh?" Bea's brow rose. "How lovely. We shall have to bring something to contribute."

Mary nodded. "Dessert." Her mind filled with the day's revelations and the confidences she'd shared with one solemn-eyed gentleman.

Chapter Five

Inviting Mary and her cousins to Sunday supper had been one of his better ideas, and having her sit beside him at the table filled him with indescribable pleasure. Or was it pride? He listened to her chatting happily with his mother and sisters, and the meal passed in a blur . . . for him anyway. His thoughts were on how he might find a few moments alone with her.

Hadn't his sister assured him no scandal would attach itself to either of them if he were to court her? Ever since his visit to Marilee Hills, he'd thought of little else. She too suffered nightmares and visions. Because of their shared confidences, he couldn't help but feel a deepening connection between them. Mary was the only soul he'd told about his visions, and his burden had lightened as a result. Had her burden eased as well? He hoped so.

Besides the bond of friendship they'd formed, he couldn't deny she stirred his passion. Was that enough to build something lasting, something far deeper? Perhaps, but she did provoke him at times, and she did possess an undeniable stubborn streak.

Studying her out of the corner of his eye, he couldn't help but smile again. When animated as she was now, he found her utterly beautiful. Hell, he found her irresistible even when she'd pestered him or when she argued with him over current events. Tobias swallowed a mouthful of dessert. "This peach cobbler is delicious."

"Thank you," Mary said, an expression of pleasure flitting across her face. "I find I enjoy baking."

"We made cookies too," Jon added. "I helped."

"You brought cookies too?" Tobias teased, searching the table.

"No." Jon's face reddened. "We ate them all."

"Perhaps the next time you help your mama and cousin bake, you might consider saving me a sample?" Tobias cocked a brow at the lad.

"Sure, Mr. Lovejoy." Grinning, Jon stuffed his last forkful of cobbler into his mouth.

"Everything was delicious," Terrence announced. "My compliments and gratitude to the cooks."

"Shall we retire to the parlor with our coffee?" Tobias's mother asked, placing her napkin on the table.

Beatrice rose from her place. "Thank you so much for a wonderful meal, but we really should head home before the sun sets."

"I'll escort you." Armed with his carbine, in fact. Tobias stood up and strode to the front parlor to the gun cabinet. Mary and her cousins followed.

"That is most kind, Tobias, but not necessary." Mary glanced at the rifle in his hands, flashing him a puzzled look.

"Indulge me. There have been reports of thieves in the area. I escorted you to my home, and now I shall escort you to yours."

"We've heard the same reports you have." Mary's chin came up. "My Whitney rifle is beneath the seat of the buggy."

"And I've no doubt you're able to fend for yourselves, but I'd feel more at ease if I saw the three of you safely home."

"Your company would be greatly appreciated," Bea said, sending Mary an arch look.

Mary opened her mouth as if to argue, but then she closed it again.

"I'll fetch your wraps." Jane hurried off to get their things.

Bea set the cobbler dish into its basket, and then she placed a hand on her son's shoulder. "Don't you have something to say, young man?"

"Yes, ma'am," Jonathan said. "Thank you for the wonderful dinner, Mrs. Lovejoy."

"You are most welcome." Tobias's mother tousled the boy's hair. "I am impressed with your manners, young man."

Jonathan beamed at her praise, and Bea patted his shoulder. "We hope you will join us at Marilee for dinner in the near future," Bea said.

"Perhaps the first Sunday in December?" Mary added as she fastened her cloak.

"We'll look forward to it." His mother's eyes filled with warmth.

Tobias slipped into his coat, and then he sidled closer to Mary. "Will you walk with me to the horses?"

"If you wish." She peered at him, her curiosity obvious.

While Bea lingered to talk with Sarah and bundled Jonathan into his coat and hat for the ride home, Tobias managed to steal Mary away and down the stairs. Was it his imagination, or was Mary's cousin lingering on purpose? Tobias's heart lodged itself in his throat, and his mouth went dry as he led Mary to the rear of their building and opened the gate to the paddock. Having to take over the running of their business at sixteen. Going off to war soon after, he hadn't had the opportunity to do much in the way of courting.

As Tobias entered the corral to fetch her mare, his buckskin wandered over to give Mary a friendly snuffle. She stroked the horse's forehead. "I had a lovely time today, Tobias. Thank you for inviting us."

"As did I." His pulse pounded so hard his ears rang. He had no idea how to broach the subject consuming him. Should he come right out and admit he wanted more than friendship with her? Was he even certain he did?

"This is a fine fellow." She scratched the gelding behind his ears.

"His name is Horace." Tobias led the old mare out and began to harness her to the buggy. Mary's laughter dissipated some of his anxiety.

"Horace the horse?" she chortled. "Whose brilliant idea was that?"

"Mine." He flashed her a wry grin. "I've had him for ten years—since my sixteenth birthday in fact. Horace was the last birthday gift my father ever gave me. Three months later my father was gone." Memories of that day flashed through his mind. His father had complained that he must have injured himself somehow, because he suffered pain in his left arm and jaw. Then, while they all sat down for their noon meal together, Papa had doubled over and fallen to the floor. A moment later, he was gone.

"Losing your father must have been very difficult for you. I was only four when I lost my mama." She sighed. "I hardly remember her."

"It seems a lifetime ago, and yet I still miss Papa terribly." Tobias fastened the last buckle and patted the mare's rump. He went back into the corral and strode to the lean-to for his tack. Placing his rifle into the scabbard, he returned to where his gelding continued to enjoy Mary's gentle ministrations. He was jealous . . . of his horse. Snorting, he shook his head at his own folly.

"Mary, I've been wondering . . ."

"Hmm?" She stroked Horace's neck.

"It's been quite some time since your fiancé set out for Houston, has it not?"

"Yes. It's been a little over a year." She gazed toward the street.

"Would you consider . . . that is, might you be open to . . ."—he sucked in a breath, and heat rose to his face—"another man's attention?" He was not handling this well at all. "An honorable suitor, of course, for you deserve no less." He slipped the bridle over Horace's head and slid the bit into his mouth. "*If* there were someone worthy who—"

"I don't know how to answer your question, Tobias. I don't feel . . . I'm not free to even consider such a prospect." She touched the sapphire ring through her glove with her thumb, as if reassuring herself it was still there. "I take my promise to Mr. Smythe seriously, and until I know for certain—"

"No one has ever doubted your integrity. I didn't mean to suggest otherwise." His heart dropped to the ground, there to wallow in a pool of mortification. "It's just that it has been so long without word. If it turns out you've been ill-used by your Mr. Smythe, I might have to find him myself and give him a piece of my mind." *More like give him a good beating for leaving Mary to fend for herself all this time.*

He swung the saddle over the top rung of the fence, and then he set the saddle blanket over Horace's back. "If it turns out he has no excuse for neglecting you as he has or if it turns out he's reneged on his promise, I will be truly angry on your behalf." He cast her a quick glance. "As any friend would be," he muttered.

"Your sentiments might be entirely misplaced. Eldon could

have taken ill, or he may have been seriously injured and very slow to heal. Perhaps things didn't go as planned with his career, and he's fallen into desperate straits."

"I did send my ranger friend Bradford a letter and a telegram. I expect we'll hear back from him before we set out for Texas." He placed the saddle over the blanket and reached for the girth strap under Horace's belly. "I hope my friend will provide you with answers, Mary." More accurately, the answers *he* needed, answers that would set Mary free at last.

"I hope so." She gazed toward the corner of their building where it met the sidewalk.

Bea and Jonathan appeared, as if Mary's will had summoned them. Tobias's heart thumped painfully at the relief he glimpsed in her expression. Ah, well. He'd taken a chance and been rebuffed. He'd suffered through far worse and survived.

"Will you drive, Bea?" Mary took the basket from her cousin's hand and tucked it under the buggy seat.

Bea's brow rose slightly. "If you wish."

Jonathan clambered into the buggy, while Tobias helped the ladies to their places. He reached for the Whitney rifle under the seat and handed it to Mary. "Hold this where it can be seen." Without another word, he strode to Horace and hoisted himself into the saddle, his carbine within easy reach. Bea started the mare toward the road, and he followed.

Struggling to alter his expectations where Mary was concerned, he rode along beside them in silence. He needed a friend who understood what he was going through, and so did she. Fine. Unless something changed drastically—and she'd have to be the one to let him know—he'd stifle his attraction to her.

A knot of disappointment twisted his gut as Tobias plodded along beside Mary's buggy. This was going to be a very long, uncomfortable ride, but he'd meant what he said. He wouldn't rest easy until he knew Mary and her cousins were safely home.

MARY STARED STRAIGHT AHEAD AND gripped the rifle Tobias had thrust into her hands. Plainly he was upset. Well, so was she. When he'd asked if she might consider accepting the attentions of an honorable suitor, panic had risen to swallow her whole.

It wasn't as if Tobias had asked if *he* could pay her his addresses. No. His had been a general question. Hadn't it? She frowned. Of course his question had been impersonal. He'd been curious, and so he'd asked what everyone in Atlanta wished to know. Good heavens, how she hated being the object of speculation. Even worse, Tobias had pointed out what must be obvious to all and sundry. Clearly her fiancé had either died, or she'd been jilted. Either way, why didn't she move on?

She couldn't. The thought of yet another blow to her heart set her insides to quaking. Better to cling to the illusion she'd fabricated to protect herself. She would find Eldon, and he would welcome her back into his life with open arms.

Glancing at Tobias out of the corner of her eye, she couldn't deny she found him attractive. She genuinely admired and respected him too. Still, if he had asked if he might pursue something deeper than friendship with her, her panic would have been a hundred times worse. She needed to nip her attraction to him in the bud.

"Are you ill?" Bea asked, her tone filled with concern.

She blew out a breath. "No. Just tired."

"Hmm." Bea's gaze shot to Tobias and back to her. "Did you and Mr. Lovejoy have some sort of disagreement? Both of you are like porcupines with all your quills standing on end," she whispered. "I thought you two were getting along so much better since his apology. What happened?"

"Can we speak of something else, Bea? This is not the time or the place." Thankfully, Tobias had ridden ahead, well out of hearing range, and Jonathan had fallen asleep between them.

"Of course. Having dinner with the Lovejoys certainly was pleasant, wasn't it? I shall miss Sarah very much once we set out for Texas."

"Perhaps in the future we'll have opportunities to visit. The railroads are expanding, and things in the South will settle eventually. There's no reason why we shouldn't travel, and I'm sure Tobias's family will want to see his ranch once he's established. They're likely to pass through Houston if they do, and I'm certain they'd be willing to spend a few days with us."

She would carve out a new life in Houston, and Tobias would

homestead somewhere in the vast Texas wilderness. The two of them were bound to part ways. She'd lose his support and friendship. Anxiety welled. Her insides clenched at the thought of losing the one person who understood how she still suffered the effects of war.

The rest of the ride went by in uncomfortable silence. Tobias seemed lost in his own thoughts, dark thoughts if the tightness of his expression was anything to go by. After an eternity, they finally turned into their lane. Mary heaved a sigh, eliciting an arched brow from Bea. "I promise we'll talk as soon as we find a moment of privacy, Bea."

The sun sat low upon the western horizon in a blaze of azure and orange as they drew the buggy to the front of the veranda. Tobias dismounted and approached. His gaze met hers for an instant, and the air between them grew fraught with tension. Was he angry with her? He offered his hand to help her climb down. Jon woke, rubbed his eyes, and yawned.

"I'll take care of the buggy and your horse," Tobias informed her.

"Can I help?" Jon straightened.

"*May* I," Bea corrected. "You are certainly able, Jon."

Jonathan rolled his eyes. "*May* I help, Mr. Lovejoy?"

"Of course you may." Tobias lifted Jon from the buggy, swinging him through the air in a broad arc. Jon giggled as his feet landed upon the ground.

"I have to visit the privy," Jon cried, already running off. "I'll be right back."

"Thank you again, Mr. Lovejoy," Bea said. "Jonathan and I had a lovely afternoon, and we look forward to hosting you and your family for supper here at Marilee Hills." She glanced at Mary. "I'll take the rifle in with me if you wish."

Nodding, Mary handed the rifle to Bea as she passed. Drawing a fortifying breath, she turned back to Tobias. "Thank you again for a most enjoyable afternoon, sir."

"Sir?" His brow furrowed, Tobias tied Horace's reins to the hitching post. "I thought we were past that formality."

"It's habit."

"A habit you resort to when you are displeased with me."

"I am not displeased with you. Your question took me by

surprise is all, and it made me think."

"About?"

"About what everyone in Atlanta must be thinking or saying about me." She hated the way her eyes filled whenever she tried to talk about *anything* having to do with her feelings.

"Everyone in Atlanta loves you, Mary." His expression softened. "How could they not? If anyone has given your situation any thought at all, I can assure you it is out of concern and caring, not out of pettiness."

She nodded and said nothing, lest the unsteadiness of her voice betray her.

Tobias lifted her chin, forcing her to meet his gaze. "Do you believe me?"

She shook her head, and an unladylike snort escaped. A blush heated her cheeks, and she still couldn't speak without her voice quavering.

"Here now," he murmured, drawing her into his arms. He patted her back as if calming a fretful child. "If anyone in my presence says even one word regarding you or your missing beau in a disparaging tone, you have my promise that I will put a quick end to the conversation."

She couldn't help but smile. "You sound quite fierce right now."

"We're friends, and friends look out for each other." He released her, stepped back, and studied her intently. "Wouldn't you do the same for me?"

She swallowed, attempting to dislodge the lump in her throat. "I would."

"Mr. Lovejoy," Jon called from the stable. "Are you coming soon?"

"On my way," he called back. "See you next Sunday, Mary." Tobias took her hands in his and squeezed. "By then I hope you will have forgiven me for the distress I have caused you."

"There's nothing to forgive." Mary squeezed back before freeing her hands from his. She watched as Tobias led her horse and buggy toward the stable. She had no doubt Bea awaited her inside. It wasn't as if her cousin hadn't raised the same issues regarding Eldon with her several times already. Her cousin didn't understand. No one did. She'd lost every single member of her immediate family. Her fiancé was God knows where or more likely also dead and gone. Who in their right mind would set themselves up for the possibility of more loss? One more devastating heartbreak would be the end of her. That much she knew for certain.

Part Two
The Journey

Chapter Six

Spring of 1866

IT HAD BEEN AN UNUSUALLY inhospitable spring, and Tobias had been wet and cold since he and his band of pioneers had set out from Atlanta a week ago. As miserable as perdition, he huddled deeper into his oiled duster. Then he tugged the wide brim of his hat lower over his forehead to keep the worst of the pounding rain out of his eyes. His gloves were soaked through, as were his boots and his trousers below the knee. Thick wet clay sucked at the wheels of his wagon and the hooves of his oxen. Mud covered everything and slowed them to a crawl. At this rate, it would be July before they reached Newburgh, Indiana.

A single gunshot rent the air, signaling the train to stop. "Damnation. What now?" he muttered, steering his oxen slightly off the road and onto firmer ground. They'd all been forced to deal with one crisis after another since setting out. Stuck wagons, broken wheels, and bad tempers wreaked havoc on his peace of mind. Tobias engaged the brake and wrapped the reins around the handle before climbing down. Stiff and aching from the chill, he went around to the back of the wagon and untied his gelding's lead. Would he ever be warm and dry again?

Suddenly he was plunged back to the winter he'd spent in Fort Sumter, and a shudder racked through him. Images of gaunt men appeared before him. Their ribs showing, they paced the small confines of their foul prison, trying to keep warm. Every morning was the same. He would wake in hell, only to find more had died during the night. Dull-eyed, lifeless stares accused the living—condemning him for surviving another night while they had not. Tobias couldn't draw enough air. His mouth had gone dry, and his hands formed tight fists.

Brutally shoving the memories back to the dark recesses of his mind, Tobias bit the inside of his cheek until the pain and the taste of blood brought him back to the present. It took his entire focus to remove the oiled canvas protecting his saddle. He tossed the tarp over the back of his wagon, and then he tightened the girth strap around Horace's belly. Everything he owned was going to rot. Hell, he might rot. Groaning, he mounted and nudged his horse into a canter along the line of wagons, staying off the road in an attempt to prevent splattering even more mud.

Three wagons from the end, he detected movement through the sheet of rain obscuring his vision. Items were being unloaded, the action seemingly being directed by a diminutive figure in a coat and broad-brimmed hat similar to his. He did a mental inventory of the families in his charge, trying to ascertain whose son was around that height and build. There were no boys he could name to match whoever it was directing the flurry of activity.

It was Cyrus Oglethorpe's belongings being unloaded. The widower's wagon was stuck up to the hubs of his front wheels. A line of men had been formed, and items from inside were being handed out of the wagon and passed along to be placed upon the grass. There, a group of women hurriedly covered the furniture and trunks with sheets of canvas. Impressed by the smooth efficiency of the operation, Tobias dismounted. Clearly this crisis was being well handled, and he wasn't needed.

The individual responsible for organizing everyone separated from those who were working and approached. "Mr. Lovejoy."

His breath caught. "Miss Stewart?" He couldn't help but look her over from hat to boots. She wore . . . trousers. Thank God she also had on a coat reaching her knees, because the thought of her legs and curves being so clearly visible to every man in their party sent a wave of possessiveness through him so powerfully that he was robbed of rational thought.

Irritation flared. With a great deal of effort, he tamped it down. Despite the respect and deepening friendship they shared, in this venue, he found Mary unruly, independent, and as stubborn as granite. She'd quickly proven herself to be a thorn in his side from day one of their journey. Too often she countermanded his orders.

He figured he had a choice: He could turn her over his knee, or he could simply hand over command to her for the entire enterprise. Then he'd ride off into the sunset to enjoy blissful silence and a total lack of responsibility. Right now, seeing her in trousers, turning her over his knee held a slight advantage over abandonment. "I see you have things well in hand," he muttered.

Mary leaned over to adjust her boot, stomping and pulling at the leather, and her long braid escaped from beneath her coat. She straightened and faced him. "I thought we might use a couple of planks under the wheels once everything is out of the wagon." She gestured toward two boards that had been set upon slightly drier ground.

Where she had gotten the lumber, he had no idea. Of course she knew best how they should proceed. Mary always knew best. "Might work."

Without thinking, Tobias reached over, lifted her braid, and tucked it down the back of her coat so it wouldn't get drenched. If he weren't so bloody annoyed with her, he might think about how much he longed to unbraid her reddish-gold mass of curls. He'd fantasized plenty about how soft her hair would feel as he ran his fingers through the lustrous tresses, how it might tickle his skin should it fall over his bare chest while she straddled him. A welcome heat suffused him. Perhaps thinking erotic thoughts might be the best way to keep warm in his present situation.

"I've been thinking. . . ."

"You don't say," he said, his tone the only dry spot to be had for miles around.

Mary cast him a look of consternation. "What if we drive the wagons off the road? The thick grass might prevent the wheels from becoming stuck so frequently, and we'd make better time."

He grunted, annoyed that her idea had merit. He peered westward through the rain. Every time he tilted his head, water dripped from the brim of his hat down the back of his neck. "Mary, I can't help but notice you're wearing trousers. I don't like it one little bit. It's not at all proper." It put ideas in a man's head, in *his* head. Pants hugging her legs, leading a man's gaze to the apex of her thighs, clinging to the contours of her hips, shapely derrière, and the slender curve of her waist . . .

"I prefer trousers." She tugged at the leather work gloves on her hands. "The freedom of movement and the lightness make everything easier. You try wearing petticoats and a long woolen skirt in all this rain and mud, Tobias. All that fabric gets tangled between your legs when you walk, and wet wool is heavy."

"I cannot imagine wearing petticoats or skirts, nor do I wish to. However . . ."

Mary walked away from him midsentence, and he was left to struggle alone with his exasperation. The wagon had been emptied, and Mary must feel she needed to personally direct the placement of the two wooden planks beneath the front wheels, because of course she knew how to do so better than anyone else. Oglethorpe's twelve-year-old son climbed to the seat of the wagon and unwound the reins from the brake lever, while several men took up positions alongside and behind to push. "Jonathan," Tobias called to Bea's son, who was helping the women protect Oglethorpe's belongings from the downpour.

"Yes, sir?" He hustled over to stand before Tobias.

"Take Horace's reins." Resigned, dreading the thought of his boots filling with mud, Tobias handed Horace's reins to the boy, and then he stepped into the quagmire to do his part.

Between the oxen, the planks, and the manpower, they managed to free the wagon from the sticky clay and move it off the road. Tobias pulled one foot up, almost losing his boot to the sucking mud in the process. He crouched and held on to the top of his boot, almost toppling forward as he tried to free himself. "Damnation," he muttered, slogging one foot free and then the other.

By the time he made it to the grassy slope, sweat covered his brow. He took his place in the relay, handing things back into the wagon, while Mary directed their placement, completely reorganizing the interior of Oglethorpe's wagon no doubt. The crisis over, he swiped mud from his coat and stomped his feet. Cyrus joined him.

"Ain't she somethin'?" Cyrus's gaze was fixed upon Mary.

"Indeed." Another surge of possessiveness overtook him, that and frustration. He hadn't heard back from Charles Bradford until the week his westward journey was to begin. Charles had apologized, saying Tobias's letter had taken months to arrive, and then he'd been out in the field. His friend promised to look into the whereabouts of Mary's missing fiancé and asked where he might send any information he gathered.

Tobias had written back, telling the ranger to send word in care of Andrew Offermeyer, residing at the Schmitts' farm via the town of Newburgh, Indiana, along with when they expected to arrive. How long would it take for Tobias's answering letter to reach Houston this time? He might reach Texas before his letter did.

"Do you know Miss Stewart's story, Cyrus?"

"Course I do." He grinned. "Don't matter none. She's been on her own and alone for far too long. Might just have to rectify the situation."

Tobias must not be over the shock of seeing Mary dressed like a boy yet, because planting his fist in the man's face appealed to him greatly. Doing so just might divest Cyrus of any notion he had of pursuing Mary, but he had no right. Tobias held no claim over her no matter how much he wished he did.

As irritated as he was with her, he couldn't help but admire her indomitable spirit or her ability to organize everyone into action. He also had a great deal of respect for her intelligence, and he couldn't deny wanting her by his side. Hell, he wanted her in his bed. "You don't find her managing and far too outspoken?"

"Aya." Cyrus chuckled. "She's just the kind of managing female a man needs to make his life easier. Miss Mary Stewart ain't no shirker. She's smart as a whip and easy on the eyes."

What could he say? Cyrus was right. Mary was more than capable. Forging a new life in the wilderness would be difficult. Having a wife who worked just as hard as he did would be a blessing. The problem was, he didn't want Mary to work that hard. He couldn't bear thinking of her toiling away in such a harsh environment as the wilds of Texas.

She'd already gone through enough. With all the losses she'd suffered, she deserved a life of comfort—a life like the one he'd left behind in Atlanta as a well-to-do merchant. His gut tightened, and not for the first time since their journey began, he questioned his decision. He'd given up the mercantile, a comfortable home, all the things he'd had to offer a woman like Mary, in exchange for the uncertainty of homesteading and ranching. It would take years of hard work to see a profit, and a single year of drought could wipe him out.

His gaze caught on her. She and Cyrus's younger son were making their way to where he and Cyrus stood. She rested a gloved hand on the boy's shoulder.

"Winston did a fine job driving your team, Mr. Oglethorpe." Mary beamed and patted the boy's shoulder.

Her smiles were warm rays of sunshine in the endless, gloomy gray. Dammit, her light and warmth should be turned toward him and him alone. Tobias swallowed the growl of frustration rising in his throat.

"Why, thank 'ee, ma'am." Even though it was still raining, Cyrus removed his hat and nodded agreeably. "Both Winston and Junior are good boys. Hard workers, mannerly. If there's anything you and your cousin need, you jus' let me know, and we'll lend a hand."

"That's very kind of you, sir. We will." Oglethorpe received another ray of sunshine before Mary turned to Tobias. "What do you think about my suggestion, Mr. Lovejoy?"

"That I try wearing petticoats and a woolen skirt in all this mud?" He arched a brow. "I think I'll pass."

Oglethorpe let loose a guffaw and put on his hat.

Mary's cheeks flushed. "The suggestion I made that we continue our journey slightly off the road, driving the wagons on the grass."

"I think doing so will work for the wagons in front, but by the time those at the rear follow, the grass will have been churned into the same thing we face in the road. Mud."

"Hmm." Mary glanced toward the wagons and then to the road. "We could divide into two groups. Six wagons on one side, and six on the other, lessening the impact."

"Can't hurt to give it a try," Cyrus added. His stare was fixed upon Mary, his blatant admiration clear as day. "Might even make some progress yet today."

He was going to have to stomp Cyrus into the oozing mud if he kept looking at Mary that way. "All right. I'll direct the first six to the left. Oglethorpe, you lead the back six to the right." He tipped his hat and walked away before he did something foolish.

MARY WOKE TO THE SOUND of birdsong. Stretching, she yawned and peered out the back of the wagon. Framed by the canvas, a few stars still glittered in the sky, and the horizon was just beginning to lighten. Relief coursed through her. Hopefully they would have a clear day at last. The promise of warm spring sunshine to dry their belongings buoyed her sagging spirits immensely.

Pushing the covers aside, she crawled to the box where she stored dry tinder. Her mouth watered at the thought of a cup of fresh, hot coffee as she gathered what she needed. She slipped out of her nightgown and into her damp clothes, and then she crept quietly out of the wagon without waking Jonathan or Bea.

Breathing in the fresh spring air, she gazed toward the east. The sun was not yet visible, but the sky grew lighter by the minute, and rosy streaks stretched across the horizon. She was careful not to jangle the coffeepot and their water barrel dipper as she set about preparing a large pot of coffee to boil. She'd gladly share with anyone who wished to join her. Perhaps doing so might lift the cloud of moodiness that had marked their progress thus far.

They'd camped by an aspen grove, and last night she'd had Jonathan gather firewood, storing it under the wagon and out of the rain. Mary crouched down to light the fire she'd laid. It took a while, but the dry tinder finally coaxed the wet branches to ignite. Moisture hissed and steamed out of the wood as she set up the tripod and hung the coffeepot to boil.

Everyone's tempers had been short by the time they'd decided to stop for the day, especially Tobias's. Didn't he realize he set the tone for the rest of them? Oh, she'd tried her hardest to counteract his surliness, bolstering flagging spirits where she could. But that only seemed to irritate him more, and it was a mystery to her as to why that might be.

She missed Tobias sorely, missed their weekly conversations and planning together for their journey west. Tobias had even helped her purchase the wagon and oxen team, his presence preventing the merchant from taking advantage of her ignorance and her gender. And now they were back to butting heads. How had that happened? *Why* had that happened? She'd been nothing but helpful since the day they'd set out for Indiana. Hadn't she?

Soon the delicious aroma of coffee filled the air. Mary moved the pot slightly so it could percolate without scorching. Then she straightened and surveyed the six wagons on the far side of the river of mud that had once been a road. Satisfaction surged. Her idea to move the wagons onto the grass had been successful, and Mr. Oglethorpe, bless his heart, had insisted she lead their half.

A lone male appeared next to the first wagon on the far side, his silhouette a darker shadow against the coming dawn. *Tobias.* Would he cross the muddy divide to join her? Surely he could smell the coffee, and he'd see the fire she'd coaxed to life. A skillet. She needed a skillet and the ingredients for a hot breakfast. If Tobias did come to their wagon, she wanted to have something to offer besides coffee. Mary hurried to the back of their wagon and gathered what she needed.

"Did you make coffee?" Bea sat up and rubbed her eyes. "Smells good."

"I did, and I'm about to make breakfast." Mary sifted flour into a bowl and added baking soda and a bit of salt. "The rain is gone, Bea. We're finally going to have a clear day."

"If it doesn't cloud up again." Bea groaned. "How can you be so cheerful after this past week of muddy misery?"

"Even the thought of sunshine has lightened my mood, that and the prospect of a hot breakfast. Join me when you're ready." She hurried back to the fire just as Tobias approached. Her heart turned to hummingbird's wings, fluttering rapidly inside her chest. "Good morning, Tobias. Looks like we'll have sunshine today. That should give us all a welcome respite and cheer everyone's spirits."

"Humph."

"I'm making biscuits and bacon. Will you join us for breakfast?" She grabbed a folded square of wool and moved the pot of coffee from the fire, setting it upon the ground. "Coffee's ready." She poured steaming coffee into an enameled cup, inhaling the rich aroma. "Here," she said, handing the cup to him handle first. "You may have the first cup."

"Thank you."

Though his words were polite, his grudging tone chafed. "Tobias, you do realize your demeanor sets the tone for everyone.

As our leader—"

"Am I leading this expedition?" His brow rose. "I rather thought you saw yourself filling that role."

Her jaw dropped, and she bristled. "I am sure I don't know what you mean, sir. If you will excuse me, I have things to do." Blinking back angry tears, she gave Tobias her back and sliced bacon for the skillet.

"Mary, every time I give an order, you change it. Like when I arranged the placement of each wagon in line as we travel. You rearranged the entire order without even consulting me!"

"Yes, I did. For heaven's sake, Tobias, you put us in alphabetical order! We are a group of families, not a needlepoint sampler. Each family has different—"

"Before I can even arrive on the scene of one emergency or another, you're there, ordering everyone around, and I . . .You undermine my authority at every turn."

"I see." She scowled as she placed strips of bacon in the skillet and set it near the flames. "If your foul temper didn't set everyone off, perhaps my interference wouldn't be necessary. I was only trying to help."

"A great deal less help on your part would be much appreciated," he grumbled. "Thank you for the coffee. If you don't mind, I'll take it with me and return the empty cup once we're ready to set out for the day." He began to walk away, only to turn back again. "And while we're clearing the air, I—"

"*We* aren't clearing the air, Tobias. Other than mentioning your surliness, I have not yet begun to voice my grievances with you." Had she gone too far, interfered where her advice was not welcome?

Grunting, he pointed at her legs. "I'd appreciate it if you would refrain from wearing those infernal trousers. It is disturbing to everyone, and we don't need the added distraction."

With that he departed, and she was left reeling. How dare he! Her throat clogged with anger and hurt, Mary sliced viciously at the smoked bacon.

"What was that all about?" Bea asked, tying on her apron.

"Mr. Lovejoy made it abundantly clear my help is not appreciated."

"Ah." Bea poured them both a mug of coffee. "Well, for what

it's worth, I appreciate how very efficient and organized you are, my dear. I would follow your lead anywhere."

Mary gave her cousin a sharp look. Did she detect a hint of facetiousness? "He also ordered me not to wear trousers," she groused. "He has no right to tell me what I can and cannot wear."

Bea crouched by the fire and took up the fork to turn the frying bacon. "A woman wearing boy's clothing is provocative to say the least."

"You're taking his side?"

"Not exactly, but . . ."

" But what?" Frowning, Mary added water to the biscuits and stirred. "Out with it, Bea."

"All right." Bea sighed. "It's obvious Tobias is attracted to you. No, that's putting it mildly. He's smitten, and until you know what has become of Eldon, out of respect for you, there's nothing he can do but offer friendship. Imagine what it must be like for him, seeing you in trousers while every man takes note. You must have noticed Oglethorpe can't keep his eyes off you, and even the married men stare. Poor Tobias must be beside himself."

Tobias smitten? Was he? Her pulse raced, and a pang of guilt soon followed. "Oh. I hadn't thought . . . I didn't consider . . ."

"Don't misconstrue my meaning. There is no blame attached to what I am pointing out. I'm only suggesting you consider things from Mr. Lovejoy's perspective." Bea placed her hand on Mary's shoulder. "Of course he needs your help. He knows how very capable you are, but if you wait until he asks, your contribution might be more appreciated. Do you see?"

Shame burned through her, but also indignation. Had she been more meddlesome than helpful? She didn't think so. She gazed across the road to where Tobias was hitching his team. "I was only trying to help," she huffed. "I was *attempting* to bolster everyone's drooping spirits. I didn't meant to . . . to—"

"Provoke? I know, and for my part, I appreciate everything you do. Perhaps you and I have been on our own for so long, we've become self-reliant to the point where we've forgotten how very fragile a man's pride can be."

Mary laughed. "Bea, I'm well aware you're casting yourself in the same light only to soothe my own fragile pride. I love you for it, but we both know you've always been a paragon of ladylike behavior, while I have rebelled at every turn. From now on, I will keep to myself until Tobias comes asking for my help." She'd wait until the stubborn man was desperate. Then he'd come begging. She nodded.

"And you'll wear a skirt?"

"Sometimes." She groaned. "All right. If I must, with the trousers underneath and no petticoats. You heard every word Tobias and I exchanged, didn't you?"

"I did."

Bea removed the crisp, aromatic bacon from the skillet, setting it on a tin plate, and Mary dropped balls of biscuit dough into the hot grease. "Will you have Jonathan bring a plate to Tobias for me?"

"A peace offering?" Bea grinned.

"I suppose." Would he see it as such? Did she want him to see her offering of a hot breakfast as a peace offering? No, she did not. It wasn't her fault his foolish pride had been wounded. After all, her intentions had been good. Her gesture was the neighborly thing to do, that's all.

"I thought we could string a line inside the wagon to dry our bedding," Mary said. "We can also hang clothing over the canvas covering the wagon. There doesn't seem to be any wind today, so things should stay put."

Sighing, Mary put the lid over the biscuits and moved the skillet to the side of the fire. "Speaking of Jon, best roust him. Breakfast will be ready in a few minutes."

"I'm up," Jon called from inside the wagon.

Wonderful. No doubt he'd been eavesdropping as well. "Good. I have an errand for you." Mary squelched the desire to take Tobias's breakfast to him herself. Smitten with her? Could it be true? She'd been wrestling with her attraction to him herself. From the first moment she'd laid eyes on him the day she'd asked to join this wagon train, that attraction had grown. Twisting the engagement ring on her finger, guilt assailed her.

Tobias filled her thoughts and her dreams. Stubborn, prideful man that he was, she wanted him with a fierceness she'd never experienced with Eldon, and that frightened the wits right out of her.

She hadn't wanted to care this much for Tobias. Especially

knowing they'd have to say goodbye at the end of their journey. If nothing came of her search for Eldon, Mary intended to start a school for young girls, and Tobias planned to become a rancher in the Texas wilderness. One way or the other, she and Tobias were bound to part. Her gut wrenched at the thought of losing his presence in her life. Straightening her spine, she bolstered her resolve to stay strong. After all, she'd survived far worse than the parting sure to come.

Chapter Seven

Tobias surveyed his weary group of travelers and their surroundings. As the men unhitched their teams, the women lit fires to prepare the evening meal, and the youngsters flitted about, gathering firewood. He set himself to the task of unhitching his oxen, and his gaze drifted toward the tributary they'd camped beside. Crystal clear water frothed and tumbled over submerged boulders; the cheerful sound was music to his ears and a balm to his tattered nerves.

Once his livestock had been tended, Tobias strode down to the riverbank and stood quietly for a spell, content to soak in the peaceful surroundings under the budding canopy of walnut trees. Branches on both banks stretched across the gurgling water, as if trying to reach their brethren on the other side. Some of the limbs touched midway, forming a sort of natural cathedral, dappling the stream with patches of late afternoon sunlight and shadow. A rare, bone-deep calm settled inside him.

Tobias toed the damp earth with his boot, uncovering a few walnuts the squirrels had missed. He picked them up and slid them into a pocket. He'd try to find land in Texas with a stream running through it, and he'd plant walnut trees along the banks. The promise of walnut saplings brought on a smile, and with his entire being, he latched on to the contentment now filling him. Perhaps the good feelings would take root and drive out the demons haunting his dreams.

"Mr. Lovejoy?" a feminine voice said from behind him.

He glanced over his shoulder to find Caroline Cummings standing a few yards away. "Good evening, ma'am. What can I do for you?"

"The ladies and I have been talking. Is it true we'll cross into Indiana within the next two days?"

"Barring any disasters, yes." Tobias turned to face her and caught movement next to the wagon behind his. Was that Mary peering around the end? Their eyes met for a brief instant before she pulled back out of sight. What was she up to now?

"Well . . ." Mrs. Cummings twisted her fingers into the fabric of her skirt. "Even though tomorrow is not the Sabbath, the women have asked me to inform you that we want to remain here for a day. The water in this river is so wonderfully clear, and all of us need to do laundry, bathe, and air our bedding and such. After being on the trail for ten days . . ." She glanced toward the wagon where Tobias had caught a glimpse of Mary. "What with those days being so wet and muddy . . ."

Tobias's gaze followed hers, just in time to see Mary nod encouragement and wave a "go on" gesture with both hands. He bit down on the urge to laugh, his heart gladdened simply by the sight of her. Mrs. Cummings cleared her throat, bringing his attention back to her.

"We *insist* upon a day off. We wish to enter Indiana with our families wearing clean clothing, and—"

"Your wish is granted. We could all do with a day off to reorganize and inventory our supplies before we reach Newburgh."

"Oh." Mrs. Cummings blinked as if she hadn't expected things to go her way quite so easily. "All right. I'll tell the others if you wish."

"I'd be grateful."

"Join me and George for supper this evening, Mr. Lovejoy. We'd love to have you."

"Thank you. I will." He grinned and bobbed his head. It had become the habit among the families to take turns feeding him supper, and he shared what supplies he could in return. From conversations he'd had with his hosts, he'd learned Mary had been behind the arrangement.

It warmed him to know she cared enough to see that he ate well, but her actions also pricked at his pride. He was a grown man, more than capable of taking care of himself. Had she not considered what he'd already managed to survive in the past three years? And without her help, mind.

Still, that Mary hadn't been the one to come to him with this latest request laid him low. She'd stopped interfering—in an overt manner, at any rate. He should be delirious with relief, not bereaved. Since the morning he'd scolded her, she'd avoided him. Regret had been a pebble in his boot ever since.

He returned to his chores, his mind on the spirited Miss Stewart, with her beguiling smiles and sharp wit. By the time everyone had finished setting up camp, twilight had descended, and a few stars had made their appearance. Cool night air blanketed the area, and the smell of wood-smoke, bacon, and beans permeated the entire camp.

His stomach rumbling, Tobias walked along the stream toward George and Caroline's wagon. He paused to study the western horizon streaked with deep orange, pink, and grey against the dome of deepening indigo. They'd had a string of dry, warm days, and everyone's mood had lightened considerably, including his.

"Good evening, sir."

His pulse surged. "Mary."

She held a bucket of water in each hand. "Lovely evening, is it not?"

Words he longed to say crowded together, causing a logjam before they could leave his mouth. "It is," he managed, trying to corral his thoughts. "You could have come to me with the request to camp for a day. You didn't need to prod someone else into—"

"*I* did not *prod* anyone; I encouraged. There's a difference." Rather than look at him, she inspected the string of wagons, as if assuring herself all was well. "I did not wish to interfere or to *undermine* your authority."

Her words were laced with hurt, and the pebble in his boot turned to a jagged shard of broken crockery. "Mary, I didn't mean to—"

"I must get back to our wagon." She lifted her buckets. "Bea and Jonathan are waiting for me."

"Let me carry those for you." Tobias reached for the pails in her hands.

She stepped out of his reach. "I can manage just fine, but I thank you kindly for the offer."

With that, she strode away, taking his good mood with her. *Confound it*, he missed her interference as much or more than he'd missed her pestering when she'd been so determined to win her place in his wagon train. Why could the two of them never meet on level ground? He'd have no peace until he made things right between them, but how to go about that eluded him.

STAYING PUT TODAY HAD BEEN a good idea. Not a single cloud marred the early morning sky. Everyone, including him, had risen with the dawn, filled with determination to put their lives in order before continuing on their way. Tobias added water to the cauldron heating over his fire, and then he glanced toward Mary's wagon. She and her cousin were already doing their wash. Even in her drab work dress and apron, with her hair in a tight knot at the back of her head, the sight of her stole his breath. He was on the verge of walking over to apologize to her when Cyrus and two other men approached.

"We're off to do some huntin' in the woods yonder." Cyrus pointed to the forest. "We could all do with a bit of fresh meat, even if we get nothin' but rabbits and a turkey or two. You want to join us, Tobias?"

Tobias scratched his bearded chin and considered. "You all go on ahead. I'll stay here and keep an eye on things. Anything you manage to bring back will be much appreciated by all." Besides washing his clothes, he had all his tack to clean and oil, and a multitude of items needed seeing to. Unlike the men standing before him, he had no one to help with his chores.

"My brother Daniel's wife and mine have offered to organize a supper for everyone with whatever we manage to bring back," David Morris added. David had just turned twenty-one and Daniel was nineteen, yet both were already married and carrying a lot of responsibility. "Miss Stewart and her cousin are making biscuits and providing two jars of blackberry jam. Every family has offered to contribute something, and old man MacGregor has agreed to bring out his fiddle afterward."

Anticipation thrummed through Tobias at the prospect of a social, especially one including dancing. He'd ask Mary to be his partner straight off, and if she agreed, he'd have the opportunity to smooth things over between them. Warmth surged at the thought of holding her in his arms. "We could all do with an evening to relax. Good hunting." He waved the three men on their way before returning to his wash.

AS FAR AS HIS CHORES went, the morning had been productive, and by early afternoon Tobias caught sight of the hunters returning. He set out to meet them. "I see you were successful," he said, nodding toward the feral pig they carried strung to a pole. Daniel held two turkeys as well. Tobias's mouth watered at the thought of the feast to come.

Oglethorpe grinned. "Me and my boys will roast this here pig, and we'll have a fine meal come suppertime."

Daniel lifted the birds. "My wife and I will see to the birds. Can't hardly keep from drooling at the thought of tonight's spread." He laughed. "I've had my fill of bacon and beans."

"You're not alone," Tobias agreed. He walked back to camp with the triumphant hunters, anticipating a fine feast and dancing the night away with Mary in his arms.

Before long, the delicious scents of roasting pork and the turkeys spread through the camp. Laughter and conversation filled the air. Children played tag or threw pebbles into the stream, supervised by a few fathers and older children bearing fishing poles.

"Tobias."

"Yes, Mary?" He shot up from the log he'd been sitting on while working on his saddle.

"I'm not interfering, but I thought you should know . . ." She nodded ever so slightly toward the road behind him and held her rifle at her waist. "We have company coming, and I don't like their looks at all."

Tobias tamped down his disappointment. It had been far too long since the two of them had shared a bit of friendly conversation, and he had no one to blame but himself. He peered in the direction she'd indicated. Sure enough, three men on horseback were headed their way. Even from where he stood, he could see they were lean, hardened men. All three were armed with six-shooters strapped to their waists and rifles hanging in scabbards from their saddles. "Perhaps they'll ride on by," he murmured.

"Not likely."

"I know. Just wishful thinking." He nodded. "As unobtrusively as you are able, make your way through camp." Tobias glanced sideways at her. "Warn everyone to arm themselves, and send Cyrus to join me, please."

"I will. Where's your carbine?" she asked, her expression tight with concern.

"Just inside the back of my wagon."

"Is it loaded?"

"It is."

"Take mine. I'll grab yours on my way to warn the others." She sidled nearer and pressed the stock into his hands.

"Thank you." Cradling her gun in his arms, Tobias studied Mary's profile, the way she stood, her shoulders squared and her chin lifted. That was Mary for you, always ready to meet whatever challenge came her way. The years of turmoil had tempered her strength, sharpened her already agile mind, and deepened her character. She shone with an inner beauty, and her bravery humbled him. He caught her by the wrist before she could walk away.

"Have I ever told you how much I appreciate your perspicacity?" The need to protect her nearly overwhelmed him.

"You haven't, but you have mentioned a time or two how much you resent my—"

"I was wrong, and I promise to beg for your forgiveness later. Go. Warn the others." He spared her a pointed look. Their gazes locked for an intense instant. Mary was nothing if not a lioness when it came to looking after those she cared about, and he hoped like hell she still counted him in that circle. She nodded before disappearing between the wagons.

Tobias set out to meet the men, forcing himself to appear calm.

"Howdy." One of the three riders brought his horse to a stop slightly ahead of the other two. "Couldn't help but follow the delicious smell of whatever you folks got cooking. Can you spare us a meal? We been on the road for a good while with nothing but hardtack and beans."

"We have families to feed, but there's good hunting nearby. I'm sure you three are capable of providing for yourselves." Tobias lifted the rifle resting in the crook of his elbow and used the barrel to indicate the direction of the woods. He kept his finger on the trigger.

"Now that ain't at all hospitable," one of the men behind the one who spoke grumbled. He spat a wad of chewing tobacco, and it landed a mere inch from the toe of Tobias's left boot.

"Quiet, Roy," the man in front snarled. He tugged at the brim of his hat. "Are you in charge of this here outfit?"

"I am." Tobias widened his stance.

The third man leaned forward in his saddle. "Is that where you all come by whatever smells so good? In them woods yonder?"

"Aya." Cyrus appeared at Tobias's side, six-shooters now strapped to his hips. "There's a good-size sounder of swine in them woods, gone feral durin' the war, I suspect. You'd best be movin' along if you want light to hunt by yet today."

"Guess we'll be heading toward them woods then. Much obliged for the information." The man in front surveyed their camp as if weighing the risks against the gains. He glanced over his shoulder at the other two, cocked his head in the direction of the road, and spurred his horse into a trot.

Those three men didn't need to be told where to hunt any more than he did. They'd stopped for one reason only. "I reckon they'll be back once they believe we're all bedded down for the night." Tobias set the barrel of Mary's rifle over his shoulder.

"Sure enough." Cyrus followed their progress as the men rode away.

"We'd best triple the night watch—work in pairs, keep the campfires burning."

"What do you think about posting a few men on the rise by the road?" Cyrus asked.

Tobias shook his head. "There's no cover there. We'd be better off hiding in the bushes near camp and drawing them to us. That way we can capture them before they do any harm. I've a feeling they've made a habit of robbing folks traveling this road. We'd be doing everyone a favor by turning them over to the law once we reach a town."

"I see your point."

Mary walked over to stand beside him, a holstered revolver now strapped to her waist. "Everyone has been warned, and supper is ready," she said, trading his rifle for hers.

"Best skip the music for tonight," Tobias muttered. "Was I wrong to turn them away?" He glanced at Mary, inviting her opinion. Of course he wasn't wrong, but he wanted her to know he welcomed her input. From this day forward, he'd seek her counsel and never again scold her for the very qualities he so admired—the same qualities that vexed him sorely.

"Of course not. Bringing those men into our midst would only have made robbing us easier for them."

She started out for the center of camp, and Tobias took up his place beside her. Cyrus walked alongside him, turning again and again to peer at the trio riding away.

The ladies had managed to set up makeshift tables bearing the feast, adding a festive touch with a few mason jars holding early-blooming wildflowers. Families set down their offerings for the meal and milled about. All the men were armed, and many of their wives were as well. The youngsters kept close, their energy subdued.

Cyrus removed his hat and scratched his head. "Least with yon stream bordering our camp and the wagons forming a semicircle, they won't be able to approach without our seeing them."

"It's going to be a clear night, and the moon is nearly full," Mary added. "The advantage is ours."

"Shame we won't be dancin' tonight," Cyrus said, his glance sliding toward her.

Possessiveness once again rose within Tobias. He moved closer to Mary's side and placed his hand at the small of her back. Though she cast him a look of puzzlement, she didn't move away.

"We'll have other opportunities," Tobias said. "I propose we celebrate our arrival in Newburgh with a social. We can include the three families there who will be joining us for the rest of our journey. It will be a nice way to welcome them."

"An excellent idea." Mary graced him with a smile.

He needed to tell Mary what he had in mind, and to hell with her missing fiancé. Surely after all this time, she'd gotten over the man who'd left her high and dry. What might he say to her when the time was right? He'd start off pointing out how good it would be to have each other to rely upon as they forged a new life in the wilderness. She'd have his strength to aid her, and he'd have . . . He frowned.

Clearly he'd be the one to benefit the most. He was still a broken man, prone to irritability and nightmares. He had no home or livelihood to offer. Would she even consider the uncertainty of a life ranching?

"Mary, I know you're going to want to join the watch tonight, but I'd prefer it if you remained near your wagon," he said, casting her a sideways look.

"I'm a good shot." Her eyes narrowed. "You know I am."

"There's no denying your competence or your bravery, but I don't want you in harm's way. Just this once will you *please* listen? Stay with your wagon. Protect your cousins. It would ease my mind considerably."

She huffed and bristled—no doubt working herself up to an argument—and it was all he could do to keep from hauling her into his arms and kissing her silent. "For my sake, please do what I ask."

"Oh, all right," she grumbled. "But if you get hurt because I'm not there to watch your back, I'll never forgive you, sir."

"Wouldn't expect you to." He chuckled, even as relief weakened his knees. Once again he placed his hand at the small of her back, guiding her toward the feast spread out before them. Soon, very soon, he'd ask her how she felt about him, and he'd make it clear he had the best, most honorable intentions where she was concerned. She was worth risking his pride once again. If they were to prosper, they needed each other.

*"*T*HE SOLDIERS ARE BACK." MARY'S father hissed the warning into her ear and shook her roughly. "Quick, now." He tossed her robe on the bed. "We need to head for the hidey-hole. Now."*

Terror brought her fully awake in an instant. She threw the covers back, slipped her feet into the boots she always kept beside her bed, and put on her robe even as she headed for the door. "Have you woken—"

"Yes, yes. I have Mabel gathering food, and Ezra is setting the pigs free to hide in the woods."

Mary grabbed her small box of jewelry, tucked it into a pocket, and followed her father, his favorite rifle in hand, down the broad stairway. They ran toward the kitchen. Mabel was tying a bundle of food into a tablecloth. The older woman glanced at Mary, fear showing plain on her face.

Oh God. This could be the time the raiding soldiers burned the house. Worse, what if they discovered their hiding place? Panic surged, and her heart beat hard enough to break a rib.

It didn't matter if the soldiers were Confederate or Union. As the war went on and on, both sides became more desperate. Both committed atrocities.

"Let's go," her father hissed again.

Mary's insides in a knot, she followed her father out the back door and ran for the woods, Mabel trailing behind her. The unmistakable sound of soldiers approaching, the jingle of spurs, the muffled exchanges, and the occasional hoofbeat prodded her onward.

Mary woke with a start, breathing hard. A cold sweat beaded her brow, and it took a moment to recall where she was. Ah, yes, in her bedroll on the cold ground beneath her wagon, where she had meant to keep guard over Bea and Jon. She'd become a light sleeper since the war, waking at the slightest sound.

Sighing, she rubbed her eyes as a familiar niggling certainty lodged itself deep in her gut. If the appearance of the hardened men earlier hadn't been enough, she knew better than to ignore her nightmarish warning. Dammit, she needed to help guard the families she'd come to know.

Without a doubt, the three hardened men from earlier today meant to rob them, and they'd come back tonight. After suffering through so many similar scenarios during the war, Mary's instincts never failed her. Soldiers would come, their greedy eyes surveying her property even as she turned them away. They'd return in the dark of night to steal what they could. They *always* returned to rob them, and she'd quickly learned to take steps to protect herself and the people she sheltered under her roof.

Mary glanced at the moon, judging the time to be near midnight. She threw off her blankets and crawled out from beneath her wagon. She grabbed the gun belt she'd kept beside her and strapped the belt around her waist. Then she donned her coat and hat. Moving as quietly as possible so as not to wake Bea or Jonathan, she crept to the front to retrieve the rifle she'd stashed beneath the seat. She wore her trousers of course—all the better to sneak around without the whoosh of a skirt and petticoats.

Tobias would be furious with her, but when it came to the safety of the people she cared about, disobeying his request to stay put was her only option. Campfires lit both ends of their encampment, and she knew their men were dispersed throughout camp, hiding in the shadows and behind the surrounding brush. She intended to do the same, only from a different vantage point. The more eyes watching out, the better.

When the outlaws appeared, she'd fire a warning shot into the air, alerting Tobias and the rest of their men. If she drew the outlaws' gunshots, she could return their fire easily enough from behind the boulders, even in the moonlight. Still, she hoped a warning shot would be enough to chase them off.

Crouching low, she crept toward the rise overlooking their campsite. The clothing and hat she wore would blend into the landscape. She'd be invisible against the cluster of exposed granite she'd chosen for her hideout.

Mary reached the boulders and hunkered down in their midst, with her rifle across her lap. Tugging down the rim of her hat, she faced the road. From this vantage point she could see anyone's approach from all directions. Settled into the center of her rocky nest, she drew her woolen coat tighter around her to ward off the chill.

Weariness tugged at her eyelids, and she yawned. The day had been long, and she'd risen early and worked hard all day. The moon continued to make its nightly journey toward the southwest horizon while she waited and watched. Sighing, she closed her eyes to ease the grittiness for a second, only for a moment.

Mary woke with a start. Hushed voices drew her attention, and her heart nearly leaped from her chest. She twisted around and peered over the boulders. *Hellfire and damnation!*

She'd fallen asleep. She'd failed to keep watch, and now two of the thieves, armed with six-shooters, were between her and the wagons. Where was the third? Was he behind her or already in the camp? She couldn't fire a warning shot now, not without knowing the location of the third outlaw.

Cursing herself for her own stupid weakness, she waited and watched as the thieves headed straight for everyone in the world she held dear. Her best bet was to sneak into camp and find one of their men. Perhaps between the two of them, they could stop the thieves.

Once the intruders were out of hearing range, she drifted over the grass like morning mist, following after the two she kept in her sights. Her ears rang with the pounding of her pulse, and fear gripped her as the outlaws split up, melted into the shadows, and disappeared. She crouched on the ground, frozen with indecision. Too late she realized how vulnerable her position left her. Without cover, she was a sitting duck.

"Hands up, mister." Tobias's voice rang out through the early-morning stillness. "Come on out now, nice and slow."

Mary gasped as Tobias appeared from behind a cluster of bushes. He approached the gap between the second and third wagon cautiously, hugging the side of the second, with his rifle up and aimed. Movement caught her eye, and dread chilled her to the marrow. The third outlaw, the leader, stepped out of the darkness behind him, his revolver aimed at Tobias's back.

"Tobias, watch out!" She shot up, aimed, and fired a fraction of a second before the outlaw's gun went off. Mary cried out as Tobias fell forward. His head slammed into the corner of the wagon as he collapsed in a heap on the ground. Shouts, gunfire, and the sound of pounding feet filled the air.

"Tobias!" Heedless of her own safety, she ran to him. Mary dropped to her knees and rolled him onto his back. "Oh, Tobias."

Tears streamed down her cheeks as she reached for his hand. *Dear God, let him be alive. Please, let him be alive.* Tobias groaned, and she nearly fainted with relief. Blood trickled from his temple, and a dark stain spread at an alarming rate from beneath his coat. She dropped his hand and opened his duster and then his shirt. He'd been hit in the upper right side of his chest, just beneath his shoulder. She pressed her palm against the wound, frantic to staunch the flow of blood. "Help!"

Cyrus and David ran to her side. "I need something to stop the bleeding," she sobbed. "Tobias has been hit. He . . . he's been shot."

Chapter Eight

MARY ADJUSTED THE WICK OF the oil lamp hanging overhead, while her cousin propped Tobias on his side. "Thank God, the bullet passed clean through. Can you keep him on his side for another minute, Bea?"

"I can." Bea wedged her knees against Tobias's lower back.

"He's still losing blood, although it has slowed considerably." Mary reached for the soapy cloth and washed the exit wound on his back. "Should I stitch this, do you think?"

"I don't know." Bea frowned. "My knowledge is extremely limited when it comes to gunshot wounds, though I expect I'll have to learn." She sighed. "From all I've heard, Texas is a lawless state since the war ended, and the men there are prone to violence at the slightest provocation."

The canvas curtain at the end of the wagon lifted, and Cyrus appeared in the dim light of the lantern. "I brought a healing salve." Cyrus leaned in. "Here," he said, handing Mary a small mason jar. "Old family recipe. Put this on the bullet holes, and it'll prevent festering. Lay a folded square of clean cloth over the entrance and the exit wounds, then bandage him up good and tight. Change the dressing each day, and he should come right as rain."

"I shouldn't stitch the lesions closed?" She accepted the jar.

"No, ma'am. Bullet holes don't need stitching, not like gashes and cuts. They'll close up on their own; you'll see. He'll heal just fine."

"Thank you, Cyrus."

He nodded and left. Now that she knew what to do, another

surge of relief left her exhausted and weak. Mary took off the lid and gave the contents a sniff. She detected the faint hint of honey, along with something earthy and herbal. Were those bits of moss mixed in?

Her vision blurred as she smeared the concoction over the bullet holes, and worry clogged her throat. Once Tobias was out of the woods, she was going to give him a piece of her mind. He should not have stepped into plain view like that without another man guarding his back.

The sound of cutting and the tearing of fabric filled the confines of the wagon. Bea handed her folded squares of clean flannel and strips of muslin to bandage him as Cyrus had instructed. "He'll need a sling to keep his arm still once he's up and about," Mary remarked, winding the bandages over his shoulder and under his arm.

Tobias moaned and thrashed as they resettled him upon his pallet. "Please be still," Mary murmured. She reached for a cool, damp cloth to press against the swelling at his temple.

David Morris appeared at the end of the wagon. He held up a poster that had been folded so many times, the paper was on the point of tearing at the creases "Found this in the dead man's pocket. He was the leader of the gang, and all three are wanted dead or alive. They've been robbing and killing folks traveling this way since before the war ended."

"Was anyone else hurt?" Bea asked. "Were the other two outlaws caught?"

"Daniel was knocked out by one of them. He has a lump at the back of his head the size of a crab apple, but he's awake and talking. As for the other two outlaws, we got 'em tied to wagon wheels for now. We'll turn them over to the sheriff once we reach town."

David caught Mary's eye. "There's a reward, ma'am. We all talked and decided. Since you killed their leader, you'll get a full third, and the rest of the bounty we'll divide between those of us who were on watch." He folded the poster and set it on the floorboards. "Does that sound fair?"

She shook her head. Money was the last thing on her mind. "We'll split it equally. That will leave more for the rest of you." Bile burned the back of her throat. She'd killed a man, but she'd had no choice. Everything had happened so fast. "That awful man shot Tobias in the back. He tried to kill him in cold blood without a second thought." She was just glad she fired when she had, wrecking the murderer's aim, or Tobias would be dead. Tears filled her eyes again.

"Mary," Tobias called out as he thrashed.

"I'm here." She caught his hand and held it with both of hers, trying to settle him through touch alone. "Be still."

"Don't let me die. Can't die . . . must tell you . . ."

"You're not going to die." She smoothed the hair from his brow, determination igniting into a fierce blaze within her. "I won't let you. I promise."

"Stay with me." He brought her hand up and pressed it against his cheek. "My Mary . . ."

His Mary? A thrill sluiced through her, and mortification cast it off as quickly as it came.

"Don't . . . don't you leave me. I . . . I need you." Tobias drifted off again, his body going slack.

Bea gasped, and Daniel muttered, "Well, I'll be."

"He's speaking out of his head," Mary snapped. "None of that made any sense, and you can't form conjectures based upon the ramblings of a wounded man. I'm sure he meant he needs me to nurse him back to health, that's all."

"If you say so, ma'am." Grinning, David tugged at the front of his hat and walked away, no doubt to tell everyone what he'd just witnessed.

Damnation. This was not the time to worry about gossip. Tobias wasn't out of danger, not by a long shot. His head wound troubled her more than the bullet holes. He'd been drifting in and out of consciousness. More worrisome, he'd cast up the contents of his stomach when the men first tried to move him to his wagon. "Bea, would you fetch me a fresh bucket of cold water? I want to keep a compress on his temple."

"Of course. I'll be right back." She reached for the pail. "Told you so," she whispered as she passed by.

"You cannot be serious. He's taken a blow to the head. He has no idea what he's saying, and—"

"He begged you not to leave him and called you his, while saying he needs you. I believe his sentiments were crystal clear.

The blow to his head has removed the restraints imposed by convention for now. The question is, how do you feel about him?"

"I am not free to speak of any feelings I might harbor for Mr. Lovejoy until I know what has become of my fiancé."

Bea shook her head and sighed. "There ought to be a time limit for such things. You have not heard a single word from Mr. Smythe in—"

"I know how long it's been." It had now been a year and a half. Mary scowled. "You need not remind me. What would you have me do that I have not already done?"

"I would have you let it go. Regardless of whether or not you ever learn what became of Mr. Smythe, let *him* go. Enough is enough." Bea rested her hand on Mary's shoulder. "My dear cousin, you deserve happiness." Bucket in hand, Bea left.

"Happiness?" She frowned and sat back on her heels. Images of her father hanging from the rafters flashed before her. Then the stark terror of having soldiers invade her home took over, and gooseflesh skittered along her arms and at the back of her neck. Survival was all she'd thought about for so long, she knew nothing else.

She'd held tightly to the possibility that Eldon would rescue her from the hellish misery of war and grief. He'd become nothing but a means for her to cope and as insubstantial to her as morning fog. So much so that she never thought of the flesh-and-blood man anymore. Did she cling to him solely to protect her heart? Silly question, because she couldn't deny the truth she'd known all along.

Tobias had told her she was brave, but she knew better. She feared opening herself to the possibility of more loss and from yet another abandonment. A fist-size lump lodged in her throat.

"Mary," Tobias whispered.

She looked at him, only to find his gaze fixed upon her, his expression pained, fraught with anxiety but lucid. "I'm here, Tobias."

"You'll stay?"

"Of course I'll stay."

"Good." He brought her hand to his lips and kissed her knuckles, then he pressed her palm to his breast.

His chest rose and fell as he breathed, and his heart beat steady and strong beneath her hand. "Rest," she said, "because once you're feeling better, I'm going to give you hell for scaring the living daylights out of me."

"Course you are." He sighed and pressed her hand closer. "Head hurts." He grimaced and closed his eyes. "Everything hurts."

"I know, and if I could take away the pain I would." What she felt for Tobias was so very deep and abiding. She respected him, knowing without a doubt he was a man of integrity. He embodied every characteristic worthy of admiration. She couldn't deny that the friendship they'd forged over the past year meant the world to her, even though they butted heads as often as they agreed.

She ached inside, hurting for the little girl who'd lost her mama, for all the hopes and dreams that had fallen along the wayside as war raged. She mourned all over again, thinking about how, one by one, her family had left her behind in a cruel and uncertain world. Sadness pressed heavily upon her. She was tired of being strong, exhausted with the effort to keep moving forward when what she needed most was to stay still.

Reassured by the steady rhythm of Tobias's heartbeat, she stretched out beside him, so weary she could no longer keep her eyes open another second. Resting her cheek against Tobias's good shoulder, she was lulled by the steady, reassuring rhythm of his breathing. Soon she found herself drifting upon a raft of concern, exhaustion, and despair, all bound together to whisk her away into the welcome relief of oblivion.

THE HAMMERING PULSE INSIDE HIS aching head woke Tobias. That, and the feel of a cold, wet cloth being pressed against his temple. A warm body pressed against his good side. Confused, he opened an eye a crack and took a look. Tenderness washed through him. Mary slept soundly beside him on his pallet. She'd flung an arm across his waist, and her cheek rested against his bare shoulder.

Ever so carefully he extricated his good arm from where it was trapped between them and slid it beneath her neck and around her shoulders. This way, he could cradle her beside him. If he could've managed it, he would've kissed her forehead, but his wound protested even the bit of effort he'd already made.

"I didn't have the heart to wake her," Bea whispered. She took the cloth from his head and dropped it into a bucket.

Tobias had been so intent upon Mary, he hadn't been aware of anything else. His gaze flew to Bea and then to the canvas covering the opening at the back of his wagon. Dim light filtered in around the edges, and birdsong filled the air.

"What happened?" he asked, keeping his voice low. "The last thing I remember, I was stalking a thief hiding between two wagons."

She smiled. "Our Mary interfered yet again. Another thief came out from hiding behind you, and Mary saved your life. She fired on him a second before his revolver discharged, ruining his aim. The gunfire alerted everyone that the three outlaws were in camp. After that, they didn't stand a chance." She wrung out the cloth over the bucket and brought it back to his temple.

It took a few moments for him to digest that bit of news, and then warmth surged through him. "Mary spent the night by my side."

"She was seeing to your care and succumbed to exhaustion. You need not be concerned. Everyone knows you were incapacitated, and besides, I was here the entire time as well. No one would dare think poorly of Mary. She saved your life and likely many others."

Tobias settled back, humbled by what Bea had revealed. Vague recollections from the night before came back to him. Had he called out for Mary, commanding her not to let him die? Lord, he was thirsty. "Where is your son?"

"Jonathan spent the night with Mr. Oglethorpe and his boys. How are you feeling this morning?"

"My head aches abominably. My shoulder burns and throbs, and I'm mighty parched."

"The parched part I can help you with." Bea reached for his canteen, took off the top, and handed it to him. Drinking meant letting go of the bundle of warmth and softness he held close. Reluctantly he removed his good arm from under Mary and accepted the canteen. She stirred beside him. Then her breathing steadied, and she slept soundly again. Though it hurt to raise his head, he did so and drank his fill of the cool water.

"I should wake her," he said, handing Bea the nearly empty container.

"Indeed. As much as I'd prefer to let her sleep, I imagine someone will appear soon with breakfast."

Still, he couldn't resist the pleasure of having her close for another moment or two. He spent those moments memorizing the way Mary's lips parted slightly while she slept, the absence of worry so often creasing her brow, and the way her lashes fanned against her cheeks. "Mary," he said into her ear. "Wake up." She groaned and stretched but didn't open her eyes. Tobias nudged her with his shoulder. "Time to rise."

She blinked and glared her displeasure at him. Did she always greet the morning with a scowl? As pained as he was, he had to stifle the urge to laugh. The longing for a lifetime together to find out settled in his chest.

"Oh! You appear to be fully alert, a good sign." She studied him. "I didn't mean to fall asleep. I beg your pardon if I caused you any discomfort, sir." Mary pushed herself up to sitting and yawned.

Sir. A moment ago she'd lain pressed against his bare side, and now he was *sir*. His heart on his sleeve, he smiled at her, hiding none of the tender emotions churning through him. She'd saved his life. "You caused me nothing but the comfort of your presence, ma'am."

One of her delicate eyebrows rose, and she averted her gaze. "Coffee. I smell coffee brewing."

"I asked Mr. Oglethorpe to make us a pot. Do take care of your appearance, Mary," Bea admonished, handing her a comb she pulled from her pocket. "I'll raise the canvas in a moment, and no doubt we'll have visitors soon after."

Mary accepted the comb and sat a little straighter. "Of course."

"I believe a clean shirt is in order, Mr. Lovejoy. Are you able to sit up?" Bea fished through one of his trunks.

"I think so." Tobias rolled slightly to his good side and pushed himself to sitting. The world spun around him. He scooted back to lean against the back of the driver's bench. "Give me a moment."

Closing his eyes, he drew in a long, steadying breath and let it out slowly. The dizziness passed, and Bea handed him a shirt. He tugged a sleeve over his wounded arm. "I'm afraid I need help getting this around my back."

"Of course." Bea crawled over to help him. "We need to get that arm in a sling. Do you want help buttoning the front?" Bea asked.

"I can manage, thank you." Tobias's gaze drifted to Mary. She'd undone her braid. and waves of reddish-gold curls cascaded over her shoulders and down her back. She pulled the comb through her glorious hair. Lord almighty, how he yearned to run his fingers through those silken tresses. What little blood he had left heated, and his groin tightened. Tobias bunched the blanket over his lap to hide his reaction to her. Then he concentrated on fastening the buttons of his shirt, forcing his mind away from lustful thoughts.

Mary braided her hair with efficient dispatch, of course. Everything she did was done with efficiency. She crawled to the back of the wagon. "I shall be back shortly," she muttered. Mary rolled up the canvas curtain and fastened the ties, and then she disappeared.

Sunlight poured into the wagon. Tobias blinked, and a new discomfort insinuated itself into the cluster of physical complaints plaguing him. He needed to relieve himself, but he couldn't bring himself to say so. And in his weakened state, could he even make it outside on his own? For that matter, he'd have to accept help putting on a pair of pants. Wait. Who had removed his pants in the first place? *Damnation.*

"We thought Mary could drive your wagon, and I'll drive ours," Bea said.

"We?"

"Cyrus and I." Color rose to Bea's cheeks.

"Ah." Tobias nodded. "Speaking of Cyrus, I could surely use his aid to . . . uh . . . I need to go outside."

"I'll fetch him for you." Bea handed him a folded, wet cloth. "Keep this on your temple."

"Yes, ma'am." With that he was left alone with his thoughts, and all of them centered upon one petite, curvy nuisance. Smiling, he recalled all the ways she provoked him, relishing each and every memory. Lord, life with Mary would surely be a trial. She'd keep him on his toes, pushing him to be a better man, for she deserved the best. As if his thoughts conjured her, she appeared once again.

"I've brought your breakfast." Mary set a plate and two steaming mugs on the floor of his wagon before climbing in. "Oglethorpe is on his way to help you, and we'll depart shortly after we have you straightened away."

"I do believe you could manage this entire undertaking and get us to Texas safely without any help at all." Tobias grinned like a fool. He kept his hands to himself, though he longed to brush his knuckles along her cheek or tuck that errant ringlet behind her delicate ear.

"Perhaps, but I have no wish to manage anything." She set a plate of biscuits and leftover turkey on his lap and reached back for the coffees.

"Is that so? I don't think you can help yourself, Mary, and I mean that as a compliment." His mouth watered at the smell of food, and he noticed someone—probably Mary—had already cut his meat into bite-size pieces. Tobias picked up a biscuit and took a bite. Mary would make an excellent mother, not that he needed mothering. He'd always planned on having a family of his own, though.

"Hmm." Setting his coffee within reach of his good hand, she scrutinized him, her brow once again creased with worry. "You're still awfully pale, and you did lose quite a lot of blood. Maybe it would be best if you rested in the back of your wagon while we travel today."

"I'll ride up front with you, confident that if I should faint, you will catch me before I fall." Ah, but he'd already fallen, hadn't he?

"Why are you all smiles this morning, Tobias? You nearly died last night, and you could still develop a fever from your wounds." She waved a hand toward his head. "You might even suffer some ill effects from your head injury."

"You would not allow it of me. I will recover my full health, or you will pester me until I do."

She blinked and stared, then canted her head. "I do believe you're showing signs the blow to your head has addled your thinking. Since when have you been happy about my pestering?"

"Oh, I've always appreciated your pestering, my dear, but it's just now that I've finally come to terms and surrendered my resistance." He laughed at her stunned look. Hope for his future—a future with Mary by his side and in his bed—blazed to life.

Nothing like a brush with death to alter a man's outlook. Everything had shifted in his mind, and he could no longer deny the truth. Lord help him: he'd fallen in love with the thorn in his side.

Chapter Nine

From her perch on his wagon, Mary took up the team's traces and eyed Tobias where he sat beside her. Deep creases bracketed his mouth and the corners of his eyes, a testament to the toll it took for him to sit upright. Beads of sweat dotted his brow, and he was still far too pale. After having lost so much blood, he'd likely grow light-headed at any moment. A longing to ease his pain and to nurse him back to health swept through her.

She couldn't cosset Tobias, but she could encourage him to take better care of himself. Sighing, she released the brake. "It's obvious you're in pain. You should be in back resting, not sitting on this hard bench, where every rut and bump in the road will cause you a great deal of discomfort."

"The ruts and bumps won't be any less agonizing because I'm lying down. I am not exerting myself. Is that not the same as resting?"

"Not at all." *Stubborn man.*

"I'll be fine."

"Suit yourself. Get up," she called to the oxen and started the team moving. Mary peered behind her, making sure the rest of the wagons followed suit. Satisfied, she commanded the team to increase their pace. They had a day and a half of travel ahead before they'd reach the ferry landing to cross the Ohio River. "Sleep is what you need to recover your strength, Tobias."

"I can't sleep any more than I already have, and I'd be bored to tears lying on my back in the confines of my wagon. I prefer to be where I can see what's going on around me." He flashed her a lopsided grin. "Besides, time will pass much more pleasantly with you to talk to. Come to think of it"—he faced her, his smile widening—"this is the first day since we began our journey that I've had company while driving. Perhaps I should've suffered an injury sooner."

"Humph. I'm sure if you'd asked for company, any number of individuals would have joined you, regardless of whether or not you were injured." She eyed the carbine resting on his lap. They all kept a weapon near at hand, but now, most wore or carried their guns where they were plainly visible. With the two outlaws still in their midst, reminding them of what could happen, being armed seemed prudent.

Her stomach lurched at the thought of what had happened. They'd buried the man she'd killed in an unmarked grave, and the other two were tied to their mounts with their horses fastened to leads—one behind Cyrus's wagon, the other behind George's. Both outlaws were watched carefully by everyone. "Do you think we'll be set upon by more thieves along the way?"

"I do. The closer we get to more populated areas, the more likely it is we'll encounter desperate men hell-bent on robbery."

He was probably right, and knowing so brought back a host of recollections. The soldiers trespassing upon her family's land had also been desperate to steal . . . or worse. Her rifle rested beneath the bench within easy reach, and she wore her five-shooter strapped to her hip. "Wounded as you are, how will you manage that rifle if trouble comes calling?"

"I'll risk the pain if need be." He patted the rifle on his lap. "Have I told you how I came by this Gallager carbine?"

"No, you haven't." Mary studied him. Talking seemed to ease his discomfort, and some of the pinched look around his mouth and eyes eased.

"When we were set free from Fort Sumter, those of us lucky enough to have survived walked away. None of us owned anything but the rags we wore. I set out for home without provisions—barefoot, starving, and without any means to defend myself or to hunt."

"Oh, Tobias." She'd had help and a home in which to take shelter. She couldn't imagine what it must have been like to be set free from a deplorable prison with nothing but your wits and the will to survive. "How ever did you make it home? How did you keep from starving to death?"

He shrugged his good shoulder. "I traveled along what streams and rivers I could find, so I'd have water at least. Occasionally I managed to catch fish by constructing a trap of twigs woven together into a kind of basket, baiting the contraption with grubs or worms." He grunted. "Hell, if I didn't catch a fish, I ate the grubs and worms."

His Adam's apple bobbed, and he turned away. "Birds eat them, so I reckoned it was safe enough. I *had* to make it home, you see. My mother and sisters . . . I didn't know whether or not they were still safe, and I was near frantic to get to them. I foraged for whatever I could along the way, raiding birds' nests for eggs, catching turtles and frogs, nuts left from the previous year, and even a few dried berries still clinging to their branches." His voice had gone hoarse at the telling.

"I am so very grateful you made it home." Her heart turned over for him and ached for herself. If only Papa had possessed even a smidgeon of the concern for her welfare Tobias showed for his family, she wouldn't be alone and without protection in the world. "Your devotion to your mama and sisters speaks volumes about your good character."

"Does it?" He huffed out a breath, still not meeting her eyes.

Mary frowned. "Surely you're not ashamed by what you were reduced to eat in order to survive."

"I'd be lying if I said I wasn't."

"Don't be." She arched a brow, fixing a pointed look his way. "I'm impressed by your determination and resourcefulness. Truly, I am beyond impressed and more than a little in awe. I could not have managed half so well."

"Is that really how you see my ghastly tale?"

He shifted, and his gaze bored into hers as if searching for something he needed that only she could offer. If only she knew what he sought—Absolution? Acceptance?—she would give it and gladly so.

"Is that how you see *me*?" he rasped out.

"It is." Her breath hitched, and her heart raced. How was it he could turn her insides to mush with nothing but a look? "You're a good man, Tobias Lovejoy, the very best, and I'm proud to have you as my friend." Though she spoke the truth, her feelings for him ran far deeper than friendship. Some days, the yearning for something more between them nearly drove her mad. To think, she'd almost lost him last night. Her heart thudded painfully. More than likely she'd lose him still. Once their journey came to an end, their paths would part.

"When that awful man pointed his revolver at your back." Her voice broke, and a shaky breath escaped. "I . . . I had no choice but to shoot, and when his gun went off, I feared he'd killed you. For as long as I live, I shall never forget the moment I realized you were still alive. Never."

"Thank you, Mary. I cannot begin to tell you how grateful I am." Tobias reached out and covered her gloved hand, squeezing so tightly, her knuckles ground against each other. His Adam's apple bobbed again. For several moments, they shared a profound, deep silence, a commiseration between two souls who had suffered through the same calamity and survived. Was it as difficult for him to gain control over his emotions as it was for her? She'd nearly lost him, and even thinking about the possibility so overwhelmed her, she could scarcely breathe.

When he released her, the spell broke, and she grieved the loss of his touch. If it weren't for holding the reins, she might have disgraced herself by snatching his hand back and keeping it in hers for the rest of the day. "You were going to tell me how you came by that carbine."

"Right." He shifted himself on the bench, and once again the brackets appeared on either side of his mouth. "I stopped to take a drink from the stream I'd been following, and I saw the barrel poking out of the sand. I dug this very carbine out and cleaned it as best I could. Even without ammunition, having a rifle in my hands provided me with a sense of safety. You see, I was the only one who knew it was utterly useless. By then I'd also found two left boots that happened to be the same color—which made it look as if I owned a pair, rather than two mismatched orphans. I'd also found a leather pouch with flint and steel inside. My fortunes had improved considerably. At one time the pouch might have carried ammunition, and with the addition of a handful of pebbles, who could tell it didn't still?"

He barked out a mirthless laugh. "Being outfitted thus gave the appearance I was far better equipped than I was to protect myself.

War brings out the worst in some and the best in others. For too many, the fighting will never end. Some men go mad and believe everyone is out to kill them. I came across one such fellow, or I should say, he came across me. He had a knife, and he intended to slit my throat. In his crazed state, he saw me as an enemy, or perhaps he coveted my two left boots." Tobias sighed heavily and swiped his forearm across his brow.

"Had I not cocked this rifle and aimed it at his heart, I might not be here today." He looked askance at her. "It was quite a standoff and entirely a bluff on my part. In the end, I convinced him I had no wish to shoot him but that I would if need be. He backed down and ran off."

Tobias patted the rifle on his lap. "Having this gun restored to perfect condition was one of the first things I did after I reached Atlanta. I know it's ridiculous, but this carbine saved my life, and I'll never part with it." He peered at her, as if assessing her reaction.

"One day this old gun will hold a place of honor above my hearth, and I will insist it be passed down through the generations of Lovejoys to come. Once I'm settled, I intend to write the story that goes along with it, and that too shall be passed down."

"You must have so many stories to tell, and I hope you write them all down for posterity's sake. What was it like at Fort Sumter? Will you share your experiences with me?"

"Only if you'll also share. The war couldn't have been easy for you either. I'm certain you have stories of your own to tell."

"Talking about my experiences is . . . difficult." He'd eaten worms and pretended to be armed. He'd shared things he believed were a cause for shame, and she owed him no less. Mary bit her lip, considering the story that haunted her dreams the most.

"Other than with you, I haven't spoken to another soul about my father. I haven't known how to speak of that horrible day." Anxiety gripped her, tightening her chest. "I still have nightmares, and . . ." The sight of her father's lifeless body hanging from the rafters came back to her in a rush. Once again Mary was awash in misery—robbed of rational thought, robbed of the present and thrust back into hell.

Laboring to draw air into her lungs, she fought to force all the hurt and betrayal back to the far reaches of her mind. She gripped the leather in her hands as if the reins might lead her back to safety. Once again Tobias rested his hand over hers. Had he sensed her distress?

"Papa *left* me," she blurted. "How could he do that? To this day I still cannot fathom how a father could abandon his only remaining child in such a cowardly, sinful manner." Her voice quavered, and she bit the inside of her cheek in a bid for control over her roiling emotions. Had she been so worthless to him that her father hadn't even spared her a thought? And what of her fiancé? Hadn't he abandoned her as well?

Tobias slid closer, put his arm around her shoulders, and tucked her against his side. Bolstered by his support, she continued. "I know it's foolish to feel I've been abandoned over and over again, but I cannot help myself. First by my mother, next by my brothers, and finally by my father." *And Eldon.* Though she refrained from saying that aloud. "My mother died of a lung fever, and my brothers were killed in the war. Ridiculous—isn't it?—to feel they had any choice in the matter. But Papa did have a choice."

In the throes of rage and bewilderment, she sagged against Tobias, absorbing the comfort he offered. His closeness, the way he smelled of bayberry-scented soap mixed with his own unique essence, calmed her enough that she could draw a deep breath at last.

"You must be so angry," he murmured. "I know I was. Even though my father had no control, I was still furious with him for abandoning me."

"You were?" Her eyes widened.

"Oh yes. Not only did he leave me fatherless, but he saddled me with a man's responsibilities when I was still only a boy. I blamed him for robbing me of the carefree years of adolescence I might have enjoyed. At least, that's how I saw it at the time, and then the war started. My father did not choose to leave us, and perhaps your father couldn't see past his pain. I am certain he could see no alternative either."

She nodded and stared over the backs of his oxen. "Thank you."

"For what?" He brushed his lips across her temple.

She was startled by such intimate contact, and pleasurable shivers skittered down her spine at the brief brush of his lips against her skin. She should have pulled away, but she couldn't bring herself to do so. She risked a peek his way. "For your understanding and for attempting to make me feel less alone. I suffer horrific bouts of shame for feeling as I do, and that is far worse than the anger."

"You have nothing at all to feel ashamed about. You didn't cause your father to do what he did, nor could you have prevented it once his mind was made up. You own no part of his decision."

"I should have realized how despondent he'd become, but I'd just lost both my brothers. I was consumed by my own grief, and I didn't see the signs. I wasn't looking. If only I—"

"Stop, Mary." He ran his hand up and down her arm. "If onlies serve no purpose other than to torture yourself with needless guilt."

"I have not forgiven him, and that is what bedevils me the most," she gritted out. "How could he leave me all alone in the midst of a war?"

"Perhaps he knew how very capable you are. Perhaps he saw in you what I see."

She blinked. "What *do* you see besides a managing, interfering female who insists upon wearing trousers"—she cast him a sideways look—"because they're practical and much more comfortable than yards and yards of skirts and petticoats?"

He grinned. "I see within you a core of tempered strength. You are a woman of indomitable spirit."

"That doesn't sound at all attractive," she grunted . . . unattractively. She should be mortified by what she'd revealed, shouldn't she? Instead, a satisfying kind of lassitude took hold. Emotionally purged, she wanted nothing more than to curl up for a good long nap, preferably snuggled next to Tobias's side like she had last night.

Instead, she flashed him a wry look. "What I hear when you say 'core of tempered strength and indomitable spirit' is interfering and adamant that things be done *my* way."

A reluctant smile broke free at his answering chuckle. "I do know my faults, sir."

"What you perceive as faults, I've come to view as assets." He chuckled again and let her go. "I should have mentioned I also find you quite lovely."

A delicious warmth spread through her from head to toe. "I

do admire a man with good sense," she teased. Sighing, she looked toward the horizon ahead and frowned. An ominous bank of dark grayish-green clouds was heading their way from the northwest. She'd been so wrapped up in their conversation, she hadn't noticed. "I don't like the looks of the weather ahead."

"Nor do I." Tobias twisted around to check the wagons behind them. "It may come to nothing, blowing itself out before it reaches us." He settled back to face forward. "Just to be safe, we should find a good spot where we can wait it out."

"All right. There?" Mary lifted the reins and pointed. The road ran alongside the river they'd camped by the day before. The land sloped downward, and she pointed to a copse of willows.

"That will do nicely," Tobias said. "Once we're behind the rise, turn the oxen so the back of the wagon faces northwest. That will afford the cattle a bit of a buffer from the wind."

Nodding, she turned off the road. Tobias grimaced as the wagon jarred and bounced. "I'm sorry this is causing you pain."

"It's temporary." He gripped the edge of the bench. "I'm glad to be alive and refuse to complain."

By the time Mary got the wagon situated, the wind had picked up considerably, carrying with it the scent of impending rain. The wagons behind them all followed her lead, and Mary sought her cousins. She caught Jonathan's eye and waved. He waved back and nudged his mother. Beatrice nodded at her as she steered the oxen to face away from the coming storm. "Should we head for the shelter of the trees?" Mary pushed the lever for the brake and tied the reins tightly around the handle.

"Hmm." He studied the sky, which was already darkening overhead. "That might be best." He climbed down from the wagon and moved to the back to untie Horace. He led his horse to the front, secured the lead, and then he came to her side and took her hand.

"Let's hurry," he said, tugging her toward the willows.

Many of the other families did the same or took shelter beneath their wagons. Just as they were nearly there, a sizzling bolt of lightning rent the air, followed immediately by thunder so loud the ground shook beneath her feet. The largest of the willows split down the center and burst into flame.

An instant later, the sky opened up, and hail the size of quail's eggs fell in a torrent. Mary covered her head with her arms, crying out against the stinging bites. She didn't know where to turn for safety. Tobias grabbed her around the waist, and they ran back to his wagon. He pushed her beneath and dove in after her, grunting as he hit the ground. Pulling her close, he cradled her head against his chest and shielded her with his body.

The oxen bellowed and lowered their heads. Horace neighed. Stomping restlessly, the cattle tugged against their restraints, and the wind howled. The hail turned to a downpour, and Mary tipped her head back to look at Tobias. Her breath caught. A delicious curl of heat unfurled from her center outward at the tenderness and concern she glimpsed in his expression. The way he held her, as if nothing were more important to him than her safety, made her feel cherished in a way she'd never felt before. Eldon had never held her this way, nor had he ever made her feel as if her safety was more important to him than his own.

"All you all right?" His gaze roamed over her face, coming to rest on her lips.

The sensations coursing through her robbed her of the ability to think, much less speak. She nodded and placed a hand against his chest, only to find his heart pounding riotously against her palm. Her own heart raced to match his. She inhaled deeply, bringing Tobias's scent deep into her lungs. "And you? Your arm is no longer in the sling. You must be in pain."

"I'm fine." He gathered her closer and nuzzled her temple. "Mary, I . . ." His voice came out a hoarse rasp.

"What is it, Tobias?" Breathless, she drew back and studied his face again, a face so dear to her she couldn't imagine her life without him. She smoothed the wet hair from his forehead, then cradled his cheek. His warmth reassured her. She was safe in his arms, the kind of safety she hadn't known in years.

He leaned in and kissed her. Stunned, Mary tensed for an instant, but he was so hesitant, his touch so achingly gentle, she couldn't help but melt into him. She kissed him back. He made a rumbling noise low in his throat and deepened the kiss, plunging his tongue into her mouth.

Rivulets of rainwater running down the slope drenched her side, but she paid no heed. Wrapping her arms around Tobias, Mary lost herself in him, in his scorching kiss. She tilted her head as he nibbled his way to the sensitive spot just behind her ear. Waves of desire consumed her. Instinctively, she tangled a leg with his and pulled him closer, reveling in his weight pressing into her. The effect she had on him, the hardened ridge of flesh against her belly, brought on an answering throb to her core.

"Mary," Beatrice called.

Tobias rolled away, his face flushed and his breathing ragged. "I don't know what came over me. You must think me—"

"I think what I have always thought. You are a good man, Tobias, and as glad to be alive as I am. We could have been beneath that willow when it was struck by lightning. We weren't. A near miss can cause people to . . . to reach for each other the way we did." She was soaked through, and Tobias's sudden withdrawal left her chilled.

"Are you two all right?" Bea leaned over and peered at them through the rain.

"I'm wet and bruised but otherwise unharmed. How about you and Jonathan?" Mary rolled out from beneath the wagon and stood. "Oh . . . *no.*" The canvas bonnet of Tobias's wagon had been shredded by the hail and then wrecked even more by the wind, as had the coverings on all the wagons.

"We're fine," Beatrice assured her. "We need to get the hail out of the wagons while we still can, and those of us who have spare canvases should put them up before everything is drenched."

Tobias crawled out after her, took one look at his wagon, and stomped around in a circle, uttering curses under his breath. "Horace is gone," he bit out.

"He must be terrified." Mary swiped the wet hair from her face. "Go look for him, Tobias. I'll take care of your wagon. You go as well, Bea, and have Jonathan help you put the spare canvas over ours."

"As soon as we're situated, I'll send Jon or one of Cyrus's boys to help you," Bea told her.

Mary nodded before climbing into the wagon. Hail covered every surface, and rain poured in through the rips above. She moved to peer out the front. "Tobias, where do you keep your spare canvas?" she shouted to his retreating, shadowy form. The wind whipped her words away, and the rain lashed them to the ground.

Showing no sign he'd heard her, he strode into the storm with his hands fisted by his sides as if challenging the elements. Should she help him look for Horace? If she did, more damage would be done to his belongings.

Turning back inside, she rummaged through his things until she found the folded canvas. Mary held the heavy tarp to her chest and climbed out of the wagon. She began fastening the covering to the side. The poor oxen huddled as close together as possible, seeking shelter.

Once she had one side fastened, she stood atop the tongue and attempted to drag the spare bonnet over the ruined covering still in place. Just as she got the corner where she needed it, the wind caught the material. It filled like a sail, and the canvas was wrenched from her hand to flap and wave as it fell.

Frustrated and soaked through, she scrambled back down to start over. Once again she gripped a corner of the bonnet and clambered back to her perch. Her teeth chattered from the wet and the sudden drop in temperature as Mary tried again. This time, she held tight to the corner with both hands as she dragged it down over the side.

The wind tugged, and the covering billowed again. Getting the metal eye to the place where she could fasten it to the wagon proved beyond her strength. Overwhelmed with despair, she tightened her grip and sagged against the side of the wagon. If all she could do was hold the covering in place with her weight, then fine. She'd stand in the rain until Bea sent help.

Suddenly the other end of the canvas came over the top, and Tobias appeared at the end, already tying his corner in place. Mary nearly wept with relief. Once his corner was fastened, the canvas settled. She tied her corner and moved to the next tie, with Tobias working toward her.

They met in the middle. "We need to get the hail out of the interior before it melts," she shouted above the howling wind and pounding rain.

"In a minute." Tobias drew her into his arms, pressed her back against the wagon, and kissed her. No hesitation this time, no tenderness. This kiss was frantic, possessive, almost desperate.

Mary went up on her toes, wrapped her arms around his neck, and kissed him back just as fiercely, drawing in his warmth. As much as she wished to remain in his arms, the pressing need to see to salvaging Tobias's belongings took precedence. Mary ended the kiss and stepped out of his arms. A dark stain on his shirt caught her attention. "You're bleeding!" she cried. "Damnation, Tobias, you've opened your wound."

He drew her close again and sheltered her from the storm. "What would you have had me do, Mary? Stand idly by while you struggled alone to protect *my* belongings?" He gave her another brief kiss. "Scold me later. Let's get the hail out of my wagon before everything I own is ruined."

How and why had they gone from butting heads to passionate kissing? Had it been his brush with death that caused Tobias to see her faults as assets all of a sudden? Guilt surged as Mary followed him into the tight confines of his wagon. She had no business kissing him back, but she hadn't been able to resist. "Wait, Tobias. Take off your boots and leave them in the back, or we'll add mud to everything else." She unlaced hers as she spoke. "My feet are sopping anyway."

"Right." He toed his boots off. "Mine are too."

"You didn't find Horace?"

"No, but I'm certain he hasn't gone far. When it's time for his oats, I'm sure he'll return."

"I hope so." She took one end of his sleeping pallet, and he took the other. Together they flung the hail covering his bedding out the rear. They worked in tandem to set things right as much as they could, and all the while, her blood hummed and her nerves tingled. She wanted Tobias Lovejoy, and her desire set off an entire host of conflicting emotions, and she no longer knew what she wanted or needed in terms of her future.

Clinging to the notion she was still engaged had become her security against an uncertain future. Without that security, she was left vulnerable to devastation far worse than the storm wreaking havoc all around her.

LORD, HE HATED BEING AT the mercy of others when it came to tending to his own needs. Tobias sucked in a breath as Mary cleaned, dried, and bandaged the injury on his back. He'd managed to take care of the front himself, but he'd been forced to ask for her help with drying and redressing the wound he couldn't reach or see.

"At least this one didn't reopen," she muttered. "There." She patted his good shoulder. "All set for now."

"Thank you," he gritted out between clenched teeth.

"You're welcome. Perhaps now you'll heed my advice and rest when—"

"Upon sopping wet bedding? I think not." He tugged his only dry shirt over his shoulder and buttoned the front.

"Hello in the wagon," Cyrus called.

"Mr. Oglethorpe," Mary said, scurrying to lift the two layers of canvas at the end. "I hope you and your boys survived the storm with minimal damage."

"Aya, we're fine, and so are your cousins." His gaze slid past Mary to meet Tobias's eyes. "We have your gelding. He's hobbled with the MacGregors' herd of mules at present."

Tobias rubbed his face with both hands. "That is good news indeed. I've been worried."

Cyrus nodded. "Let's see if we can't get a fire started, then we should gather the families together. Half want to move on; half want to stay put until we can dry out some and make repairs. All are chilled and wet. We could use your input."

"All right. I'll be with you in a moment. Just have to find my boots." Frowning, he searched for them. "Mary, what have you done with my—"

"I placed your boots under the bench in front along with mine," Mary said, crawling to the front of his wagon. "I'll get them and meet you at the back."

"I'll have the boys gather firewood." Cyrus flashed him a wry grin. "We are a pitiful sight to see, with our tattered bonnets and every last one of us soaked to the bone."

For the next half hour, Tobias's time was taken up with coaxing a fire to life and waiting as his band of travelers gathered to voice their opinions. He listened and watched the river out of the corner of his eye. The water was rising. Finally, he pointed to the tributary spilling over its banks.

"At the very least, we need to move to higher ground." Tobias moved closer to the fire he and Cyrus finally managed to start despite the damp wood. He surveyed the weary, disheartened faces of the families in his care. Their outfit was nothing if not bedraggled, not to mention sodden.

"But staying here will only delay our arrival in Newburgh even longer. I for one long to be near a town sooner rather than later," Mary asserted. "Some of our families don't have spare canvases, and they'll need to procure coverings for their wagons, replace their spoiled food, and dry out before we continue on to the Santa Fe Trail."

"Yes, but we need to deal with more pressing damage before we continue on," Caroline Cummings said. "Now that it has stopped raining, I'd rather stay here."

"Yes, but it looks like there's more rain on the way." Daniel Morris jutted his chin toward the northwest. "Besides, what can we do in this damp? I say we head out as soon as possible. Staying serves no purpose." He shrugged. "If we leave, we're not going to get any wetter than we already are, and nothing is going to dry if we stay. At least we can make a half day's progress toward the ferry crossing."

Daniel looked around the group. "Besides, the sooner we rid ourselves of them two outlaws, the better I'll sleep at night." His wife nodded her agreement and looped her arm through her husband's. "The better we'll all sleep at night, I reckon."

Tobias's wounds stung, and his head throbbed. "I propose a compromise. I'm starving and chilled to the bone." A chorus of assent met his words. "Do we have pork left over from yesterday?" he asked Cyrus.

Cyrus nodded. "Enough to feed us all if we cook it with beans."

"Coffee would help warm us," Mary offered. "If we start a few pots brewing, we'll have enough to share with anyone who wants a cup." Her eyes lit at the prospect of coffee.

Tobias smiled despite his pounding head. His Mary surely loved her coffee, and he'd see that she always had it on hand. "I have sugar, and I believe today's disaster calls for a bit of sweetness." He met the eyes of each adult in the circle. "I propose we split into groups to accomplish the most immediate and concerning tasks. We'll share a midday meal and set out shortly after. All in favor say aye." All agreed.

"Bea . . . er . . . Mrs. Williams and I will see to the pork and beans," Cyrus said, his face flaming. Mary's cousin folded her hands in front of her and stared at the toes of her boots, where they peeked out from beneath the muddied hem of her skirt. A moment of silence ensued as the adults nudged each other, grinned, and glanced from Cyrus to Bea.

"Mary, shall we provide the coffee and sugar?" Tobias asked.

Mary's brow creased, and she shot him a pointed look. "Certainly, Mr. Lovejoy. I'd be more than happy to see to the coffee with you."

Stifling a grin, Tobias sent everyone off to their chores. Cyrus's younger son and Jonathan had been charged with keeping the fire going, while old Mr. MacGregor and his two strapping sons went to saw wood from the willow that had split. The clouds broke, and a bit of late-morning sunshine burst through. Mary came to stand beside Tobias, her blue eyes flashing reproach. He arched an eyebrow. "Am I about to be scolded again, ma'am?"

"You called me by my given name in front of everyone," she admonished.

"My dear, we've been traveling with the same families for two weeks. Considering everything we've all been through together, don't you think we can dispense with formalities and go by our given names?"

"Perhaps, but—"

"Everyone knows you and I have shared a bed," he teased. "You spent an entire night nursing and nagging me back to life before cuddling up against my side to sleep." He brushed a wet curl from her cheek. "It would seem strange indeed if we did not address each other by our given names after the kisses we've shared. Don't you agree?"

"Why, I . . . you . . . I cannot believe . . ." She huffed and bristled, and her cheeks turned a deep scarlet. "I'll go get coffee and our largest pot. Go get yours as well." With that she lifted her skirt—revealing the trousers she wore beneath—and strode off, her chin raised a dignified notch.

He could get used to teasing Mary and watching the way her long braid swayed in tandem with her slender hips as she strode away. A feeling of rightness came over him, and he couldn't tear his eyes from her. She deserved to have a man by her side who would never let her down. She needed someone like him, a man who would never cause her to suffer the kind of abandonment she'd already endured in her short life.

Gratitude and love weakened his knees, and his chest filled with the weightiness of these new insights and emotions. Even if he did occasionally succumb to the terrors of the past, without a doubt, Mary would recognize what he was suffering. Not only would she understand, but she'd help him return to reality, as he had done with her just a few hours ago.

Life would be anything but boring with Mary, and he wanted that life more than he wanted anything else, including a ranch in Texas.

"You all right, Tobias?" Cyrus came to stand beside him. He carried two pails of water.

Tobias looked askance at his friend. "Well enough. I'd best get my supplies, or I'll soon face Mary's wrath."

Cyrus guffawed. "Aya, and I'd best help Bea gather enough beans to feed twelve families. We were fortunate no one was hurt in the storm and that neither of our prisoners have caused any mischief."

Honestly, he'd forgotten all about the outlaws in their midst until Daniel brought them up earlier. He trusted his men to keep them bound and under watch. However, he had noticed Bea and Cyrus spending more time together, and seeing them enjoying each other's company made him happy. "Your boys seem to get along well with Bea and her son."

"They do, and that's a fact. Beatrice is exactly the gentling influence my boys need."

"And you? Do you need her gentling influence as well?" he asked, scrutinizing his friend.

"I do, and I'm not ashamed to say so. She's . . . well, she's a lovely woman, smart, strong, everything a man could want in a wife, but she's far better than the likes of me deserves."

"She reciprocates your interest?"

"I'm workin' on that. How about you and *your* Mary?" He smirked.

"Heard about that, did you?"

"Aya, everyone's heard."

Tobias rubbed the back of his neck. "It's complicated." How could he explain the nightmares and visions he suffered since the war?

"It ain't at all *complicated*." Cyrus chuckled and set his buckets by the fire. "Think less and persuade more, Tobias." Still chuckling, Cyrus sauntered off toward Mary's wagon, where Bea awaited his help.

"I've had . . . difficulties since the war."

"Who hasn't?" Cyrus averted his gaze, and his Adam's apple bobbed. "It's going to take some time before I can shake loose of the nightmares, and I'm one of the lucky few who came through it with only a musket ball grazing my thigh." He grunted. "I heard you spent the last year of the war in Fort Sumter. I also heard tell that place put hell to shame, it was that bad."

Tobias nodded. "Mary keeps me grounded. I think . . ." He drew in a long breath. "I believe I have fewer nightmares because of her."

"A good woman will do that for a man, and only a fool would throw that away."

"So you believe I should *persuade* more and think less?"

"I do."

"Humph." He hadn't tried persuasion at all, had he? More than anyone, Tobias understood Mary. What she needed most was his assurance that he would never abandon her. No matter what came their way or how melancholy he might become, he would remain steadfastly by her side.

He could not, however, promise never to grow old or to take sick. There were no guarantees against accidents. Death would take him, as it took all mortal souls. How could he promise he'd outlive her? How could he get past her defenses and her fears? Only then would they have a chance at building a future together.

Shaking his head, he set out for his wagon, glad he'd had the foresight to keep his dry goods in a waterproof chest. At the very least, he could promise Mary a fresh, strong cup of coffee, and that would bring a smile to her face.

Chapter Ten

"I REFUSE TO STEP FOOT ON either of those floating piles of rotten wood." Mary studied the two rickety ferries, the swiftness of the current, and the wide expanse of the churning, muddy Ohio River. Her insides twisted into a knot of fear. "There are no sides, only strung rope." She peered at Tobias and then at Cyrus. "Hardly enough to prevent a body from tumbling into the river."

Tobias sighed. "Now, Mary—"

"And what about the livestock?" she continued. "One misstep, and all a family's belongings could be lost. Or worse if children happen to be inside the wagon at the time." A shudder racked through her at the thought.

"True, but many . . ." Cyrus studied her face. "Er . . . *most* make it to the other side with nary a mishap."

"Why can't we take a bridge across?" She clasped her hands together to hide their shaking. "Surely there are bridges nearby."

"Too many bridges were destroyed in the war. We might set out for one on the map only to find it no longer exists." Tobias unclasped her hands and rubbed them between his, bringing back some of the warmth that had fled at the frightening prospect that lay before her.

He arched a brow. "We could continue on and cross at Evansville, but then we'd have to backtrack to reach Newburgh. The only other bridge I know for certain is still standing is in Louisville, and it would likely take a week to reach it. We will be fine, Mary. I promise."

"We will? How can you even say such a thing?" She scowled at him and then at the gray clouds overhead. "We've had so much rain recently. Perhaps we should wait a few days for the water level to recede."

A floating tree branch sped by at a terrifying rate, bobbing beneath the muddy surface, popping back up again an instant later, only to disappear around the bend, gone from sight once and for all. Mary's mouth went sawdust dry. She could end up like that branch, caught in a current so strong she'd be helpless against its force. Unlike the branch, she wasn't certain she'd float. "I cannot and will not cross this river on either of those . . ."—she flapped a hand toward the ferries—"those poorly constructed *rafts*."

"What's the holdup?" George Cummings joined them. "Shouldn't we begin loading? It's going to take several crossings to get all of us to the other side, and it's already midday."

Mary glared. "It's not safe."

George took off his hat and scratched his head. He shrugged. "How do you propose we get to the other side then, ma'am?"

"I don't know." She tugged her hands free from Tobias. "I only know that *I* will *not* cross this river on either of those poor excuses for conveyance." Her heart pounding, she strode off toward her wagon. She was being entirely unreasonable, but she couldn't help herself. Fear had tangled itself into the threads of her thinking, and she couldn't find the loose end to pull it free.

"Mary," Tobias called.

She quickened her stride. "I don't want to talk about this anymore," she called over her shoulder. "Do what you need to do, sir. I'm staying on this side of the Ohio . . . until August if need be. By then, the river will surely be much more shallow." More important, the current would be less daunting.

"We're not crossing without you." He caught her by the arm. "Hear me out, and then we'll make a decision together."

"Fine." She stepped away from him and wrapped her arms around her middle. She refused to look Tobias in the eye. He chuckled, damn him.

"Consider all you've survived during the past four years. Think of every danger you've faced during the war and every hardship you've endured at home and on this journey. Now—"

"I hate to be the bearer of discouraging news, but that's not helping." She huffed out a breath. "Do you have a point, sir?"

"I do." He stepped closer.

His body heat and scent enveloped her. *Distracting. Enticing.* Her scowl deepened. "Well, spit it out. I'm sure *you* wish to cross the river today." A boulder lodged itself in her chest. "If anything happens to you, I will *never, ever* forgive you."

"For abandoning you?"

"No." Her gaze flew to his. Oh God, he was right. If he drowned, she'd be abandoned yet again, and she could not bear even thinking about losing him. "For doing something so foolhardy as to put your life at risk." His probing gaze brought a rush of heat to her face. Unable to bear his scrutiny, she turned away. He must think her behavior childish in the extreme.

"My point is this. You have survived and overcome every single obstacle ever placed in your path. And now you're going to allow one ferry crossing to stop you in your tracks? That's not the Mary Stewart I know." He placed his hands on her shoulders and squeezed, compelling her to once again look at him. "Where's your indomitable spirit, your sense of adventure?"

Damn him again. "When have I ever purposefully sought adventure?" Mary blinked furiously. "Never, I tell you."

"Mary . . ." His wonderful brown eyes filled with concern.

"I'm frightened," she whispered. "More frightened than I ever thought possible. The thought of drowning in that . . . that murky, churning river is more than I can face." She stared down the road. "The town of Owensboro is only a few miles away. Perhaps I can start a school for young ladies there."

"Mary, don't you know how to swim?"

"No, I do not know how to swim. Swimming was never part of the curriculum in finishing school, and I could hardly learn in the midst of cotton fields, could I? Unlike you, I was never free to tear around the countryside or visit the local watering holes."

Tobias's gaze intensified. "We'll go together, and I shall hold you the entire way."

Two of their wagons were already crossing, and she watched in horror-stricken fascination, expecting the entire undertaking to fall apart halfway to the opposite side. Her friends would surely disappear forever, snatched away from her by the rain-swollen river. "Perhaps if we go last and I see everyone else has made it safely that might help." She sent him what she hoped was a brief, imploring look, though she suspected it was more pitiful than imploring.

"I'm willing to wait until you're ready, however long that might take. Only . . ."

"Only what?"

He shrugged. "Wouldn't you rather cross in full daylight? If anything *should* happen, it's more difficult to see when the sun begins to set. Wouldn't you agree?"

"Thank you so very much for adding yet another worry to my list," she snapped and took off for her wagon again. What she planned to do once she got there, she had no idea. Perhaps she'd turn the team and set out alone for Owensboro.

He caught up and stopped her. "What about Beatrice and Jonathan?"

"What about them?" Guilt nipped at her tattered nerves. Hadn't she just that minute considered leaving without them?

"Do you mean to trap them on this side with you because you're unwilling to cross the river? After all, you and your cousins share your wagon and oxen. Not only your belongings fill the back, but theirs as well." He arched a brow. "You are the only one of our party who is unwilling to cross, I might add."

"I would prefer it if Bea and Jonathan remain on this side with me, but if my cousins are determined to cross, I am sure Mr. Oglethorpe will be glad to take them with him. If not, I am certain Bea and I can start an enterprise in Owensboro as easily as in Houston."

"That's true, but are you prepared to let go of your reasons for traveling to Texas? Have you given up hope of finding—"

"I do not appreciate being manipulated, sir." She stomped a foot and fisted her hands like she had as a three-year-old in the midst of a tantrum.

"Forgive me." He rubbed the back of his neck and peered over her head toward the landing. "What can I do to convince you to cross with me? None of us want to leave you behind."

She blinked. "Others have said they don't want to leave me behind?"

"Yes. We discussed the matter and took a vote. I'm to throw you over my shoulder and carry you onto the ferry if need be. And that will cause me considerable discomfort, seeing I'm wounded and all." One side of his mouth quirked up for an instant, and he reached for her hands again. "Please trust me to keep you safe."

"You think me a ninny."

"Not at all." He shook his head, and once again his expression filled with tender concern.

Her heart melting, she sighed and studied the Ohio. "I am a ninny."

"I won't let you fall into the river, and if any man calls you a ninny, I shall knock him to the ground."

"What if it's a woman who says it?"

"I shall glare her into taking it back."

She couldn't help but smile at his outrageous claim. "I refuse to wear a skirt. If you should lose hold of me and I do fall into the Ohio, I am certain the weight of a skirt would drag me under more quickly."

"All right. Trousers it is."

"I'm not even a little bit fond of you right now, Tobias, and I meant what I said. If you fall into the river and drown, I shall never forgive you, and if I fall into the river and drown, I shall haunt you for the rest of your days." The thought of losing him to the murky depths of the Ohio scared her even more than falling in herself.

"I agree to your terms, ma'am. George and Cyrus are taking care of my wagon and cattle. I will see to yours, and we'll cross together with your cousins. Let's get going before you change your mind."

Her insides roiling with trepidation, Mary followed Tobias to her wagon. "Stay here. I'll be out in a moment." She climbed in and divested herself of the skirt and petticoat she wore over her trousers. Bea and Jon were already at the ferry landing, leaving her to drive the wagon and team toward certain death. Her cousins could have at least walked along beside the wagon in a show of support.

Climbing to the front, she took her place on the driver's bench and motioned for Tobias to join her. "Are you sure you want to hold on to me as we cross? If I fall, you're likely to topple in with me."

Tobias climbed up to join her. "Unlike you, I know how to

swim."

Reluctantly, she started the oxen down the hill. "Yes, but you're wounded." Already horrifying scenarios flitted through her imagination. She'd fall in. Tobias wouldn't be able to help her, but he'd try anyway, and they'd both perish.

He tugged at her braid. "We have rope, and we have friends who will help. Quit your worrying, Mary, or I might just throw you over my shoulder after all."

"If I could *quit* worrying, don't you think I would have done so already?" She scowled at him again, eliciting another of his annoying deep-chested rumbles. By the time they reached the landing, her throat had closed, and breathing had become a chore.

"Climb down," Tobias commanded. "I'll lead the oxen aboard."

"Miss Stewart," the elder MacGregor called. He approached, carrying a small barrel.

"Yes?" Mary's feet hit the ground, her trembling legs barely supporting her.

"This is for ye," he said, thrusting the barrel into her hands.

"Thank you, Robert." Her brow rose in question. "What am I to do with it?" The barrel had a rope attached at either end.

"Barrels float, and this'n is just right for ye to wrap your arms 'round." The elder MacGregor took hold of the rope and dropped it over her head. He drew her arm through the cord so the strap crossed her chest, and the barrel rested against her hip. "If ye fall in, this'll keep ye afloat until we can fish ye out. See?"

"Oh." Warmth and gratitude flooded through her. "How very clever." She smiled into the older man's eyes. "Thank you."

He tugged at the brim of his hat. "Think nothin' of it. Don't ye worry none. Ye and Mr. Lovejoy go on aboard now. Me and one of my sons will be right behind ye, with ropes at the ready in case anythin' goes awry. That should put yer mind at ease, aye?"

"It does ease my mind considerably." She ran her hand along the stout rope.

"We're all glad Mr. Lovejoy didn't need ta toss ye over his shoulder and force ye to cross after all."

MacGregor winked and walked away just as Bea and Jonathan joined her. "Ready?" Bea asked.

"As ready as I'll . . . never be," she muttered. Her grip on the rope tightened. Jonathan's eyes sparkled with excitement, and he darted ahead to help Tobias lead the oxen aboard. The weight caused the ferry to dip low enough so that water skimmed over the edge. Mary squeaked in alarm.

Bea took her by the arm. "It'll right itself. You'll see."

"If you say so." Her heart in her throat, Mary boarded the weathered wooden planks and hugged the barrel to her chest. She took up a position as near to the center of the platform as possible and held her breath, as if that might help steady the ferry.

Tobias came to stand beside her. Circling her waist with his good arm, he drew her close. "I've got you."

Robert MacGregor and his eldest son's family boarded next, and their wagon balanced the load. The ferrymen poled them away from the bank and worked the cable and pulley rig to get them across. The smell of pickles rose from the barrel she gripped, and the ferry rocked and surged with the current. Nauseated, she closed her eyes, which only made things worse. "I'm going to be sick."

"Fix your gaze on the boathouse or the pier on the other side," Tobias ordered. "Doing so will help settle your stomach."

She cast him a doubtful look but did as he suggested anyway.

"Better?" he whispered in her ear.

"A little."

"Breathe deeply." He tightened his arm around her. "That will also help."

She took in the smells of woodsmoke, cattle, the fishy scent of the river, and even a bit of fresh air, all mixing with the vinegar-and-dill scent from her barrel.

Mary's nerves steadied some as she watched the second ferry returning to the opposite bank to pick up more of their families. Finally, she could take note of her surroundings. The clouds were breaking, and everything was budding and blooming. The two handling their ferry were grizzled, wiry old men who paid their passengers little heed. "I wonder how many times these men have crossed this river?"

"I imagine thousands of times in all kinds of conditions. They know what they're about."

Mary twisted around to peer at him. "You're trying to reassure me."

"Is it working?"

She smiled. "It is. Along with the fact the ferrymen have made it to old age doing what they do."

"Shall I let you go now?"

"At your peril." She gripped his forearm where it circled her midriff. Rewarded by the amusement in his smile, she relaxed against him. "After this, everything will go smoothly for us. We've endured spring storms and endless mud. We've thwarted and captured wanted criminals and dealt with shredded bonnets and broken wheels and axles."

"Don't forget bugs in our food." He squeezed her for an instant.

"And the bugs. In a few weeks, things will be drier, and the going will be easier."

"Is that what you think?"

"Not really." She turned a wry look his way. "It's what I hope. At least we'll be free of the outlaws in a day or two."

"There is that, and don't forget the reward."

"I do hope there's a café and a hotel in town," Bea said as she joined them, her son's hand held firmly in hers. "I think we should splurge and have a meal or two cooked by someone else. Crisp fried chicken or perhaps roasted beef with thick gravy and all the fixings. I'm sorely tired of beans."

Mary's mouth watered. "A meal that doesn't include ashes from the fire and weevils in the flour sounds lovely. Perhaps we can have pie or cake for dessert. I sorely miss sweets."

"We can use some of the reward money," Tobias suggested. "And invite all the families to join us. After all, everyone has done their share and pitched in."

"Excellent idea." She patted his forearm.

Distracted by thoughts of something to eat other than beans and bacon, Mary hadn't even noticed they'd already reached the other side. The ferry thumped against the riverbank, and the ferrymen threw ropes to boys on the pier who secured the vessel so the passengers could disembark.

"Things will go better now," she repeated. "You'll see. We'll restock our wagons in town, and then we can make repairs and dry our belongings." Her legs no longer shook, and Mary walked down the ramp to solid—more slippery mud than solid—ground. She might even book a room if Newburgh had a hotel. She'd order baths prepared for her, Bea, and Jonathan, and they'd sleep on soft mattresses rather than on the hard ground or in the cramped interior of their wagon. Would Tobias spare them a few days to rest and recover? "Don't forget, Tobias. You promised we'd hold a social once we reached Newburgh."

"I haven't forgotten." He moved her barrel out of his way and took her by the elbow. "Will you dance with me, ma'am?"

"I will indeed, sir."

"I don't suppose you'll wear a dress for the occasion," he muttered under his breath.

"I might." Awash with relief, Mary laughed. She wouldn't have to haunt Tobias for the rest of his life after all. He'd been there for her, a source of support and reassurance, and she'd been there for him when he'd been shot. Her heart wrenched at the thought of how their paths would diverge once they reached Texas.

But he had his dreams, and she had hers. A rancher's life in the wilderness of Texas was not for her, not that he'd asked her to join him. She needed to live near people. After the fear and isolation of living at Marilee Hills during the war, settling near a town appealed to her. This journey had also taught her how much she valued companionship. No doubt she'd wither in the wilderness with only one soul and a few hired hands for company. Her heart skipped a beat. Was she setting up more barriers, rationalizing with herself to protect her heart?

Why were her thoughts taking this direction to begin with? Tobias had never mentioned a future together, despite his passionate kisses and frequent touches. His kisses, she was certain, grew out of his near-death experience. They were close, after all, and they had shared the harrowing experience. It was only natural to reach for each other. Still, she needed to quash any further advances on his part. Didn't she? She bit her lip, recalling how utterly safe and cherished she'd felt in his arms.

He left her side to lead the oxen down the ramp, and she was struck once again by the broadness of his shoulders. Tobias possessed a lean strength and an air of confidence that appealed to her. As attractive as she found him, she had no right to burden him with her unsolicited feelings for him. She hadn't wanted to grow so attached to him in the first place.

Best to remain focused upon her own goals: find out what became of Eldon, and if he'd departed this world, she'd start a school for young ladies in the growing city of Houston. And if Eldon hadn't died, and she found him? Then what?

What could or should she say to the man who had asked her to marry him and then left her without a word for nearly two years? Whatever she'd felt for him had perished from neglect long ago, and she wasn't certain she wished to revive those feelings should their paths cross again. Her attention strayed to Tobias, and her heart pitter-pattered away as if it had a mind of its own.

HUDDLING INTO HIS DUSTER AGAINST the drizzle, Tobias leaned against the back of the wagon bench as Mary drove his team. He stared at the plodding gait and bobbing heads of his oxen. He'd seen far too much of the backsides of cattle and sorely needed a change of scenery or a distraction. "At least it's not a downpour," he muttered.

His companion gave no response. In fact, Mary had been far too quiet since they'd left the ferry landing yesterday, and he had no idea why. "You're awfully quiet. Is it the rain, or is something bothering you?"

"Why would you think something is bothering me?" She shifted to face him, a look of puzzlement crossing her features. "Can't I be quiet without there being something amiss?"

"Not that I'm aware of." That bought him a disgruntled look, along with an unladylike snort. Trousers, grunts, and snorts—any day now she'd take up the habit of chewing tobacco, and then she'd add spitting to her repertoire. He could hardly wait. "Fine. Nothing is bothering you."

So much for her company to distract him from the itch and throb of his overtaxed wounds. Sullen weather and a mood to match, this was not shaping up to be one of their best days traveling together.

"How far are we from Newburgh right now, do you suppose?" she asked.

"We've barely been on the trail for five miles this morning. From the ferry landing, Newburgh is about twenty-two miles. Feel free to do the math."

"No need to be rude, sir."

"I'm being rude?" He turned to face her. "You have not said a word to me since we set out this morning. If I've done something to offend you, at least have the courtesy to inform me what that might have been."

"You've done nothing to offend, Tobias. I beg your pardon if I've given you the impression that you have. I am simply not in the mood to talk."

"In that case, I shall leave you be. Pardon me for intruding upon your privacy." He had a mother and two sisters. If he'd learned anything from living in a household dominated by females, it was how to tread lightly and give them space when they needed or requested to be left alone. Only he hoped that's all it was, and she wasn't brooding over her future plans.

Yesterday she'd threatened to settle in Owensboro, as if parting ways with him meant nothing at all to her. Lord help him, she'd leave him once they reached Texas, if not before. He swallowed the panic rising to engulf him.

They continued on in silence, and Tobias wished he'd brought along at least one of the books on animal husbandry he'd been studying. At least then he might be able to bore himself into a stupor, or better yet, into a nap.

Lowering the brim of his hat, he watched the Ohio River flow by and surveyed the landscape. The sight of the broad river running through gently rolling hills and fertile land soothed him. Despite the gray and the drizzle, his mood lightened, and he took in the sweet smell of alfalfa, clover, and flowering bushes and trees. This was a good place, a peaceful place, and the tranquility gradually seeped into his soul, offering him a respite from the carnage always lurking in the recesses of his mind.

They rounded a bend, and his gut clenched at the sight of a cabin that had burned to the ground. The stone hearth was all that remained standing amid the blackened ruins of what had once been a home. The cabin had surely sheltered a family at one time. Memories of that first glimpse he'd gotten of his family's burned-out mercantile engulfed him, and all the fear and worry he'd carried during the war for his family came back to him in a rush. And of course, that path led him to the misery of Fort Sumter, with all its smells and horrors.

"Do you think that happened during the war?" Mary asked.

Struggling to shake loose of a past that had him in its grip, he concentrated upon breathing—in, then out—over and over until he was able to answer. "Could be, or it could've been an accident. Perhaps the cabin was struck by lightning during a storm."

An outhouse stood nearby. The charred remains of its roof had caved in, but the walls were intact, along with a ramshackle barn and a paddock showing signs of neglect but no scars from burning. The cabin had been built at the crest of a gently sloping hill overlooking the Ohio. A cluster of weeping willows grew along the riverbank.

Patchy corn and wheat had begun to sprout in the surrounding fields, though the ground had not been plowed. The place gave the appearance of having been abandoned. Sadness pressed in upon him as he imagined the losses the poor family must have suffered before walking away. A shiver slid down his spine, and he hoped they'd walked away.

Think about something else. He drew in a long breath and let it out slowly as he studied the homestead. With the river right there, transporting and receiving goods would be easy. Folks would travel west, then south, by this route. The farmstead lay roughly ten miles from Newburgh, and from there, probably another eleven to Evansville, a major city. Ah, but he was thinking like a merchant, not a rancher.

Once again his gaze drifted to the Ohio, flowing steadily toward the Wabash River, there to merge and turn south for a time before heading west again toward the Mississippi. Rivers were unaffected by war, ambition, or the foibles of man. "Humph."

Mary shot him a questioning look. "What?"

He jutted his chin toward the Ohio. "I was just thinking. Rivers are entirely indifferent to the plight of mankind. This is a peaceful place. Don't you agree?"

"Yes, I—"

A single gunshot rent the air, destroying the slice of peace he'd been savoring. Flinching, Tobias swore under his breath as Mary brought the wagon to a halt.

She engaged the brake and coiled the lines around the lever. "What now?"

"More trouble, that's what," he groused. Tobias peered behind them. "I'm afraid it's your wagon this time. Looks like the front axle broke, and you've lost a wheel."

"Wonderful. We gave our spare axle to George Cummings after theirs broke."

By the time the two of them reached her wagon, Cyrus and Douglas, the older of MacGregor's sons, were assessing the damage. Bea had organized volunteers to empty the cargo. Her son stood off to the side, pale and trembling. He clutched his left arm to his chest.

Mary crouched down in front of him. "What happened, Jon?"

"I-I fell from the wagon when the wheel came off." He sniffed. "Mr. Oglethorpe says my wrist isn't broken, but it sure feels like it is." His chin quivered, and his eyes were wide and luminous with unshed tears.

"We'll fix a sling for you nonetheless. You and Mr. Lovejoy will be a matched pair." She smoothed Jon's hair from his forehead before cradling his cheek in her palm. Jon leaned into her, and she embraced him and ran her hand up and down his back in a soothing motion.

Jon shot him a shy glance from the comfort of Mary's arms, and Tobias winked. He lifted his own sling in commiseration. "Between the two of us, we'll have one compete set of arms. We'll manage together, won't we?"

Jonathan brightened and nodded, and Tobias was struck once again by Mary's talent for spreading calm and optimism when faced with one crisis after another. So long as the crisis didn't involve crossing a river atop a *poor excuse for a conveyance*, anyway. His heart filled with love for her, and he couldn't keep from staring. His gaze met and held hers, and her cheeks flamed.

Right then and there he wanted to pour out everything he held in his heart for her, but that would not do. This was neither the time nor the place. Tearing himself away, he joined the two men assessing the damage. "How bad is it?" he asked Douglas.

"The iron skeins are in good shape, but the axle's shot." Douglas widened his stance and crossed his arms in front of him while scanning the area. He nodded toward an island of trees in the closest field. "There's oak and maple here. Me and Pa can build a new axle, but it'll take some time, and the wood'll be green."

Tobias shook his head and huffed out a breath. "It's one thing after another, isn't it?"

"Aya," Cyrus added. "The wheel that came off will have to be replaced or repaired. The rim is bent and the wood splintered. I'll lend them my spare, and they can replace it once we're in town. I could fix the wheel if I had a forge, but truth be told, it would be faster to see if a spare can be had in Newburgh."

Mary joined them. "Will we be staying put?"

Tobias surveyed the rest of their families. Everyone seemed to be in the process of setting up camp already. The two Morris brothers guarded the prisoners, while their wives provided the outlaws with water and some of their jerky and biscuits left over from breakfast. Lord, he wanted to be rid of the two thieving murderers. It didn't sit right with him that the two were using up the supplies of the good folk they had intended to rob and possibly murder. Anger surged, followed by a wave of frustration that had been building with every setback they'd endured since leaving Atlanta.

"I need to think." Mostly he wanted to remove himself before he did irreparable damage by snapping and snarling at anyone who dared come close. He'd begun the day in a foul mood, and it hadn't improved. He rubbed the back of his neck and glanced at the river. "I'll be back in a bit. In the meantime, get started on the new axle."

Without another word, he strode off toward the river, continuing his pace until he stood beneath the lush, green canopy of the largest of the willows. Slowly his fists uncurled, and he relaxed in small increments, measured by the movement of the willow branches in the breeze and the steady flow of the river.

A few of their families still had nothing but the shredded bonnets covering their wagons. Everyone's belongings were damp, and the stench of mildew permeated everything. Soon enough, heat and humidity would descend upon them, and the sun's intensity would add further misery. More axles would break, and tempers would flare. He snorted. Hadn't Mary asserted things would go easier from here on in?

He picked up a small stone and cast it into the Ohio. Did a letter from Bradford await him at the Schmitt farm? If so, he feared what he might learn, for it would fall to him to pass the news along to Mary. He couldn't bear to be the one to break her heart, and one way or another, the news would break her heart.

Mesmerized, he watched the Ohio's hypnotic flow, and the

longer he watched, the calmer he became. Finally, his mind quieted. Everything was so green. Birds trilled in harmony with the constant background chorus of tree frogs. Even the hum of bees in the overgrown raspberry blossoms nearby soothed him. If the raspberry bushes were pruned back, they'd surely provide an abundance of sweet berries come summer. His mouth watered just thinking about the tart sweetness of the fruit bursting in his mouth. Were they black or red?

Tobias turned back to face the river, and a half smile broke free. He could see himself growing old in a place like this. Here the river would remind him the troubles of man were temporary and small, passing out of sight like the debris caught up in the current and swept downriver.

He glanced at the canopy of the willow he stood beneath. How much would this tree grow in five years, ten? If this were his land, he'd plant a row of walnut trees from the crest of the hill all the way down to the bank where he now stood. Then he and his family would always have shade from the trees, and the walnuts would also be a good addition to their larder. This would be a lovely spot to build a bench where he and Mary could sit, holding hands as they grew old together, surrounded by their children and grandchildren.

"Humph." He pinched the bridge of his nose and shook off his fanciful thoughts.

He had two priorities: rid his party of the two outlaws, and visit the Schmitt farm to see if they'd received a letter for him. Still, he couldn't deny the longing this place evoked, and he couldn't prevent the seed of an idea from taking root. And the more consideration he pored over the notion, the more the idea grew in his mind.

"Tobias, is everything all right?" Mary came to stand by his side.

He struggled against the desire to haul her into his arms and holding her so tightly she'd never be able to leave him. He heaved a sigh. "I'm frustrated with all the delays and the damage done by the storm." He studied their camp and the ruined cabin behind him. "I wonder who lived here and if they've abandoned their home forever."

"Perhaps there is no one left to inherit this homestead. I hope there were no children inside when—"

"As do I." Mary's tender, open heart humbled him. He reached for her hand and twined his fingers with hers. "I've been thinking."

"Yes. You mentioned needing to do just that. And where have your thoughts led you, Tobias?"

She smiled, and his heart leaped. His thoughts led to her, always to her. "I want to take the Morris brothers and head into town to turn our captives over to the local sheriff. I also think it would be a good idea to visit the Schmitt farm to inform Andrew Offermeyer we're close. While we're gone, the MacGregors will build your new axle, and folks will have time to regroup a little more from the storm."

"How long will you be away?"

Did her voice quaver slightly, or had he imagined it in the hopes she'd miss him? "Three days at the most."

"Three whole days?"

His focus sharpened, and he caught a flicker of fear—or was it panic?—flitting across her features. All the words he longed to say crowded into his chest, and the pressure to give voice to them was so great he feared he might burst. Unable to stop himself, he drew her into his arms and cradled her close to his heart, exactly where she belonged. He rested his chin atop her head, and a deep sense of homecoming descended over him. They were hidden from view beneath the hanging branches of the willow, their very own sanctuary.

"I'll be back before you know it, and I'll even bring you something sweet from town. What would you prefer, my dear? Lemon drops or peppermints?"

"Why don't I come with you?" she asked, tipping her face up to beseech and beguile him with her larkspur-blue eyes. "You might need my help."

"No, Mary." When had she wrapped her arms around his waist? He couldn't contain his grin, and it grew even wider at her disgruntled expression at his refusal. "I need you here to keep everyone organized and productive."

"No, you don't." She backed out of his arms. "You're only saying that to appease me, and I am not at all appeased." She blinked rapidly before turning away and stomping off.

"Does this mean you don't want me to bring you anything from town?" he called after her.

"Lemon drops would be much appreciated," she called without turning around. "Thank you, *sir*."

He stifled the urge to laugh. Filled with nervous energy, he raked his fingers through his hair and paced. Her reaction, the look of panic at the thought of parting with him for only three days, gave him such hope he could hardly contain the optimism thrumming through him.

In his present state, he could move mountains and change the course of the Ohio River, with vigor to spare. Mary cared for him. She'd fret and worry about him while he was gone. Hell, she'd miss him as much as he'd miss her. Now, how to go about convincing her to admit it to herself? That was the challenge before him, and he was determined to do whatever it took to triumph over her fears and defenses. Turning back to camp, he considered his options and formed strategies for the siege to come. He would not accept defeat.

Part Three
A New Beginning

Chapter Eleven

Growing smaller and smaller the longer Mary watched, Tobias and the Morris brothers rode off without her, the outlaws bound and tethered, trailing behind them. She saw nothing out of the ordinary, but still a sense of impending doom overtook her. Why she should feel that way at all was beyond her, but she couldn't shake free from the anxiety churning deep in her gut. Maybe not doom exactly, but foreboding, definitely foreboding.

Something had shifted between her and Tobias again. She couldn't put her finger on what exactly that might be, but she'd seen it in his expression when he looked at her. She'd felt it in his incessant restlessness. He'd been tromping all over the abandoned farmstead as if he couldn't be still. The change showed clearly in the set of his jaw and the glint of resolve she'd caught in his eyes. *What is on his mind, and why hasn't he shared his thoughts with me?*

"Mary, watching Tobias leave will not bring him back any faster," Bea murmured beside her.

A blush rose to her cheeks. "I was not *watching* him; I was just thinking while I happened to be facing his general direction is all." She waved a hand in his *general direction*.

"If you say so." Bea looped her arm through hers. "The clouds are breaking, and now would be a good time to lay things out to dry."

"Except the ground is wet." She frowned at the horizon, where the five men disappeared altogether from sight. What if the two outlaws managed to free themselves? Would they finish the job their brother had started? Her lungs seized at the thought of harm coming to Tobias or the Morris brothers.

"We can drape things over bushes and low-hanging tree branches."

"I suppose you're right." She bit her lip. "I'm out of sorts, Bea. I'm tired of damp, tired of mud, and sick to death of the stench of cattle and mildew."

"You're not the only one. I'm tired of sleeping on the ground and eating the same food day in and day out," Bea commiserated. "My joints ache from walking or being jostled all day long, and we've only been traveling for two weeks. How are we going to fare after a month or two?"

"Why are we doing this again?" Mary slid her cousin a wry look. "Whose foolhardy idea was it to travel by prairie schooner from Georgia all the way to Texas by way of Indiana anyway?"

"It's pointless to lay blame, dear cousin-whose-idea-this-was-in-the-first-place, so I will refrain."

Mary grinned. "Well, come on then. Since our wagon has been unloaded, we may as well see what we can do to make improvements." She glanced at the island of trees where two of the MacGregors were cutting down a maple for her axle. "We are fortunate to have the MacGregors with us, are we not?"

"Indeed, and it's also a good thing the pump on this farm's well still works, because the Ohio is frightfully muddy," Bea said.

"There's clean water to be had?"

Bea nodded and pointed toward the group of women gathered around the pump. She and Bea reached their pile of belongings, and there they found Jonathan showing off his swollen and bruised wrist to his friends.

Bea made a clucking sound. "I'd best wrap his injury again and badger him into keeping his arm in the sling."

"While you badger your son, I'll fetch water." She scanned their camp. "If it clears, we should have a picnic supper by the river."

"My dear cousin, *all* our meals are picnics." Bea sighed heavily.

"True, but we don't generally gather together as a group. We can read to the children around a fire this evening. I am sure they would enjoy a bit of storytelling."

Bea's brow furrowed. "I do hope the few books we packed haven't been ruined by the damp."

"They're wrapped in oiled canvas and tucked into a trunk," Mary said. "I'm sure they're fine. *The Swiss Family Robinson* will do nicely."

"Or fairy tales."

"Hmm." Mary considered the books they'd brought. "Fairy tales can be frightening, and we don't want to cause any of our young ones bad dreams."

"Speaking of bad dreams, does camping so near the river make you nervous?" Bea asked.

Mary shrugged a shoulder. "Not so long as I don't have to cross to the other side."

"There will be other rivers we must cross along the way, you know."

"I know, and I'll clutch my pickle barrel during every single one." Dear old Mr. MacGregor. She'd have to think of something special to do for him to show her gratitude for his thoughtfulness. His sons and their wives were wonderful as well, always willing to offer a kind word or a helping hand. Tobias really had done an amazing job of vetting the right people for this journey.

"Speaking of your barrel"—Bea rummaged through their fabric remnants and rags—"I prefer the smell of pickles to the stink of mildew permeating everything."

"One stench cutting through the other, I suppose it does help." Mary averted her gaze. "Did you notice Tobias's odd behavior yesterday afternoon and again this morning before the men left?"

"Odd behavior?" Bea frowned. "Do you mean the way he tramped off alone down by the river and all through the surrounding fields?"

"Exactly." Again foreboding cramped her stomach. "Something is bothering him."

"That surprises you, Mary? You know how his experiences during the war have affected him. I'm certain there are times when he feels the need for solitude. It could not have been easy for him to come face-to-face with the sight of that burned-out cabin," Bea said. "It's not even a full year since he found his own home and mercantile destroyed by fire. Perhaps he needed the time alone to cope with his memories."

Mary smacked her palm to her forehead. "I'm certain you're right. I'd forgotten his home had burned, and Tobias has shared with me some of the difficulties he faced on his journey home. It's a wonder he survived." Mary picked up their buckets. "I'm certain the shock of seeing the cabin is the reason for his solitary walks. Thank you, Bea. You've put my mind at ease."

The coil of anxiety unwound, and she could finally breathe deeply. "I'll be back in a moment with water, and then I'll start a fire for the wash."

Her heart lighter, she set off to join the ladies and children already in line beside the pump. "Good morning," she greeted. "Looks like it will be a lovely day, doesn't it?" Engaging in small talk with her neighbors lifted her mood.

She'd been fretting over nothing. Perhaps if they'd encountered a stable instead of the cabin, sight of the rafters might have set her off, and she would've been the one seeking solitude. All the families she traveled with had tragedies they were leaving behind, but they also had much to look forward to, thanks to Tobias. Even thinking about him brought a thrill to her heart.

Her attention strayed to the river and the willows growing along the shore. This homestead certainly was a lovely spot. Now that she'd let go of her anxiety, the utter peace of her surroundings seeped into her bones. The sun had come out, and everything around her was fresh and green. She was among friends, and they had the day to recover from the storm. Tobias would return in three days. Three days was nothing in the grand scheme of things. For the moment, everything in her world settled, and she was content.

THE METALLIC CLANK OF THE cell door closing reverberated through the office as the sheriff locked up the two outlaws. Tobias set the worn wanted poster he'd carried with him on the scarred wooden desk in the main room. His attention drifted to the Morris brothers, who spoke quietly to each other while studying a great number of similar posters nailed to the wall. Too great a number.

"You two thinking of becoming bounty hunters?" Tobias teased.

"Nah, just curious." David grinned at him over his shoulder. "Our wives would put bounties on *our* hides if we even considered such a scheme."

Sheriff Ramsay returned and dropped the ring of keys into a desk drawer. "After a bit of... persuasion, those two corroborated your story about how their older brother died. You were a lucky man that night, Mr. Lovejoy."

"Don't I know it," he said, lifting his sling slightly.

"The reward is for dead or alive." He sauntered over to the wall holding the pictures and descriptions of wanted criminals and tore down the poster identical to the one Tobias had placed on the desk. "Do you plan on sticking around for a while? It's going to take a few days and some paperwork before the bank can free up the reward money."

The Morris brothers looked to him, and Tobias nodded. "Yes, sir. We're camped down the road a piece. We have repairs to make, and I know our families will agree to remain for a spell." He shifted his stance. "Can you tell me how to get to the Schmitt farm from here? I have business with their son-in-law, Andrew Offermeyer."

"Sure can. The turnoff to their spread is less than a mile west of town. Can't miss it. Just look for three large elms, and you'll see the tracks from their wagons right there."

"Thank you." Tobias turned to his companions. "Why don't you two go on down to the café and order lunch? I'll be there in a minute. I have a few questions for the sheriff."

The brothers exchanged a pained look. "That's not necessary," Daniel said, not meeting Tobias's eyes. "We have jerky and biscuits."

He'd been thoughtless. Clearly the two didn't have the extra coin to spend at a café. Every last penny they had would go into starting their farms. "Lunch is on me today, gentlemen. After all, we do have that reward money coming to us."

"In that case, we're on our way." David grinned and grabbed his brother by the shirtsleeve. "Do you want us to order for you, Tobias?"

"Sure. Whatever the special is would be fine." The brothers nodded and tore out of the sheriff's office, and Tobias was struck by how very young the two were. Hopefully homesteading would work out well for them. At least they had each other to rely upon for support and help.

Sheriff Ramsay sat down, propped his bootheels on the top of his desk, and regarded Tobias curiously. "You have questions?"

"Yes." Tobias's heart raced at the thought of what he hoped to accomplish, what had occupied his mind since Mary's axle had broken. "Can you tell me anything about the burned-out farmstead about ten miles east of Newburgh?"

"Why're you asking?"

"I want to know if it's available, for sale or . . ." He rubbed the back of his neck. "Just wondering, I guess."

"Hmm." The sheriff canted his head. "A young couple, the Andersons, homesteaded the farm going on four years ago now. The husband went off to war. Rumor had it his wife had been faring poorly, and they were going through tough times. He joined the army for the steady pay. Problem was, he never returned. His widow moved back to Vincennes to live with her folks. They didn't make it the required five years to make the homestead theirs. Unless someone has already filed for the plots, I'd guess the land is once again available."

"Any idea how the cabin burned?"

"We were at war." The sheriff shrugged. "Your guess is as good as mine. Might've been arson; might've been hit by lightning." He scrutinized Tobias. "Might've been the widow burned it to the ground herself out of grief. Didn't you say you're leading a wagon train to Texas?"

"I did."

"Changed your mind, have you?"

"I reckon that property might be better than anything I can find in Texas. I'm considering a change in plans."

"If you stay here, where will that leave the families you're leading?"

"I'm hoping to persuade them to stay with me, and if they choose to continue on to Texas, I believe every man among them is more than capable of taking my place."

If he could persuade Mary to become his wife and to stay here with him, they'd have a far easier life than if he became a rancher in Texas. He'd heard how tough and isolating a rancher's life could be. At the time he'd made the decision to transition from shopkeeper to rancher, isolation appealed to him, but things had changed since that dark time in his life. Mary had brought the light back to him.

The idea to stay put had taken root and spread like creeping vines. As he'd explored the abandoned farmstead, he'd decided the location was as close to perfect as he was likely to get. If others agreed to stay with him, perhaps he and his group of pioneers could start their own town. The farmstead wasn't too distant from Newburgh or the growing city of Evansville. The families he traveled with possessed skills and abilities that would surely help them prosper.

"Is there a land office here in Newburgh?" Once again excitement thrummed through his veins, and his hopes took wing. The land here was fertile, and the place he wanted couldn't be any better situated for commerce.

More important, something about the land beside the river called to him. Though he couldn't put a name to whatever quality the land possessed, he soaked up the offered comfort like dry dirt took in the rain. The picture he'd formed in his mind, the one where he and Mary sat by the river holding hands while surrounded by their family, had intensified to the point where he almost believed it was a foretelling, not just a dream.

"Nope. We haven't had a land office here since before the war."

"Do you know where I might find the closest one?"

"I do." The sheriff opened a desk drawer and pulled out a piece of paper. "To file for homestead, you'll have to head into Evansville. I can give you the location." Ramsay picked up a pencil and began writing the address. He even drew a map. "Stop in at our courthouse here to get the identifying information you'll need for the land you're interested in owning. Just tell the clerk it's the Andersons' abandoned homestead."

"I'm much obliged."

"Best of luck to you, Mr. Lovejoy." The sheriff handed him the paper. "Perhaps everything will work out in your favor, and we'll meet again."

"I hope so." Tobias folded the directions and tucked the paper into his back pocket. "I'll stop by on my way back from Evansville and let you know." He held out his hand, and they shook.

Tobias's mind spun with possibilities, and he couldn't keep the grin off his face. If he could homestead the initial one hundred sixty acres and buy even more, he'd have something tangible with which to bargain and entice others to stay. He'd offer to sell smaller plots to those who agreed to settle and build businesses, asking only what he'd paid for the land himself. Of course, his offer would be granted only to the original twelve families he'd been traveling with and Andrew Offermeyer. No reason why he shouldn't earn a tidy profit should outsiders wish to settle in their town.

In the meantime, a hot meal beckoned. Tobias stepped out of the sheriff's office and headed for the café. The moment he walked into the building, delicious smells wafted over him, causing his mouth to water. The Morris brothers sat at a table next to the window. They waved him over, and he wended his way through the tables to join them.

Should he share his thoughts, or should he keep them close until he knew something for certain? The brothers planned to farm together. If the parcels he wanted were available, surely more land thereabouts would also be available. Between the brothers and their wives, the Morris families could secure over six hundred acres of prime farmland. Plus, they had a portion of the reward money coming to them, which would help get their farms off to a good start.

He slid into his place at the table, and a matron wearing a ruffled apron appeared almost immediately. She set a plate down at each of their spots. Each plate was heaped with thick slices of roast beef and mashed potatoes, both smothered in thick gravy. A basket filled with freshly baked bread and a dish of butter had been set in the middle of the table, along with a small bowl of raspberry preserves.

"I'll be right back with stewed tomatoes. Would you like something to drink?" she asked him. "Coffee comes with the meal, or tea if you prefer."

"Coffee would be fine," Tobias said. "Thank you."

Daniel cut a chunk of beef and dredged it through his mashed potatoes and gravy. "So what did you talk to the sheriff about?" he asked before stuffing the forkful into his mouth.

David pushed his brother's shoulder. "Ain't none of our business."

His mouth full, Daniel shrugged unrepentantly.

"Actually, I'm glad you asked," Tobias said. The woman

returned with his coffee and a large bowl of stewed tomatoes, with a large serving spoon resting on the inside rim. As the three of them ate the first decent meal they'd had in days, he shared his plan.

"I want the land where we're currently camped. After we're done here, I have a few errands to complete, and then I'm riding to Evansville."

He intended to buy a pair of gold wedding bands and, of course, a sack of lemon drops. He'd also stop in at the courthouse for the identifying information for the plots he coveted.

"We can stop at the Schmitt farm on our way back. No sense talking to the folks who are joining us until I know what I'm going to do. Would either of you be interested in coming along to the land office with me to see what else might be available?"

Daniel swallowed a mouthful and leaned back in his chair. "I didn't know there was still land to homestead in Indiana. We thought only the far west still had parcels to offer."

"Nope. There's good land right here."

The two brothers shared a long silent look before turning back to Tobias. "Hell yes, we'll go with you." David thumped the table with his palm. "My wife recently informed me I'm going to be a papa come fall, and I don't much like the idea of putting her through another month or more of misery traveling by wagon all the way to Texas. It's too dangerous for a woman in her condition. She needs rest, good food, and a roof over her head."

"Count me in." Daniel grinned. "David and I took a look at the soil where we're camped. It's good, real good, and if we're going to get crops in the ground yet this year, now's the time to start breaking sod. We plan to raise hogs too, and of course we'll have chickens and a small herd of dairy cows." He looked at his brother. "Our wives will want to plant a large vegetable garden."

"It's settled then." Tobias could wait until they returned from Evansville to buy rings and the candy he'd promised, but he didn't want to. Something about having tangible evidence of his hopes and dreams in his pocket filled him with optimism. Perhaps he'd succumbed to an outlandish superstitious belief having the rings would make everything come out the way he wished.

"It's settled then. After lunch and my errands, we'll ride out." With every fiber of his being, this was what he was meant to do.

He'd convince Mary to relegate her long-lost fiancé to her prewar life, part of the past. Tobias was her present and her future. If Smythe had meant to send for her, he would've done so long ago.

He suspected she'd clung to the notion of still being engaged as a means to cope. Smythe was a memory, nothing more. Tobias, on the other hand, was solid and real, and he loved her beyond reason. Once he swore he'd never let her down, surely she'd agree to marry him, and the sooner the better. Perhaps one day she'd even return his love.

"It's another eleven miles to Evansville. We'll have to spend a night there, and we can visit the land office first thing tomorrow morning." Tobias glanced at one brother and then the other. "I'll get a room, and you two can bunk with me."

"Dessert first." Daniel waved his fork over his plate. "I haven't had dessert for I don't know how long, and today's dessert is chocolate cake with chocolate buttercream frosting. I ain't passing that up, Tobias. You're just gonna have to hold your horses."

"All right." Tobias laughed. "After dessert."

He'd made a good start, already securing two farming families to populate and help feed the new community. Two of the MacGregors were carpenters, and the third was a mason. Everyone who agreed to stay would need housing, and surely several would want to build businesses—incentive enough for the MacGregors to stay. Oglethorpe was a blacksmith, farrier, and cooper as well, all important skills for a growing town. If he could convince Andrew Offermeyer to join them, they'd have a butcher shop and green grocer as well. They'd need a school, a church, and a flour mill. He'd build a mercantile of course.

Once again restlessness assailed him, and he wanted to charge forth right that minute. He was ready, more than ready, to build a new life here in southern Indiana with Mary by his side. He meant to provide her with a good life and a comfortable, secure home in which to raise their children.

Children. He wanted a passel of sons and daughters to fill a noisy, happy home. As he finished his meal, he imagined how Mary would look, her belly rounded with his babe growing beneath her heart. His own heart swelled at the thought, and a powerful longing gripped him for the life he imagined. Determination stilled his restlessness. He *would* make it happen.

"THERE ARE THE ELM TREES the sheriff told me about." Tobias pointed. "The Schmitt farm is down the lane from them." Tobias eyed the landmark ahead. Would his news be met with anger, or would Andrew embrace what was now more reality than dream? After all, he'd agreed to lead the Offermeyers and two other families to Texas.

Along with the rings and candy, Tobias had the homesteading documents in his saddlebag. He'd filed for the homestead, and he'd also put money down to buy a good chunk of land on either side. He'd also secured the forms for Mary to file for the one hundred sixty acres adjacent to his. Since they weren't yet wed, she'd have to file for it on her own. She'd like knowing those one hundred sixty acres belonged to her anyway. If he knew anything at all about his love, it was that she'd need to be an equal partner in this venture from the onset, or nothing would work out between them.

More than anything, he was tempted to skip stopping at the Schmitt farm for now, dig his heels into Horace's sides, and gallop all the way back to camp, back to Mary and his land. Pride welled, and he sat a little straighter in the saddle.

"Let's not tarry, Tobias," David said. "I'm mighty eager to tell my wife we're staying put. She'll be worrying about now, 'cause we're a day behind schedule."

"I don't intend to make this a long visit, David. More like, here's how it is, and you can join us, or you can travel on to Texas with whoever chooses to go from our group." He'd also taken the time to draw up a map of sorts, showing the plots that were available adjoining the parcels he owned. "We'll give them a few days to think about it and to discuss things with the other two families, and then they can send word."

David and Daniel had filled out the forms to homestead four parcels bordering Tobias's spread to the north, and he couldn't be happier. Their property had a small river running through it toward the Ohio. They also owned several acres of valuable timber as well, which they could sell. It was fertile land and the perfect place to raise a family.

Tobias grinned at the two. "I sure hope we can convince the

MacGregors to stay. Robert and Douglas are carpenters, but Allen is a mason. Did you know that?"

"That's good. Real good." Daniel nodded. "You think Oglethorpe will stay?"

David snorted. "If Mrs. Williams stays, there's no doubt Cyrus will settle here too. Haven't you seen the way the two of them look at each other?"

"Well, of course I have. Everybody has. But if Miss Stewart moves on, her cousin is sure to follow."

"Miss Stewart will *not* be moving on." The words were out of his mouth before he thought better, and the heat of mortification rose up his neck to heat his face.

"That so?" Daniel quipped, sharing a smug grin with his brother. "Says who?"

"Mark my words; she'll stay." Tobias looked from one brother to the next. "You *did* see how crossing the Ohio affected her, did you not? When confronted with the prospect of settling here versus crossing several more rivers, I'm sure she'll choose to stay."

"What about her long-lost—"

"It's been nearly two years since her fiancé left her behind." One side of his mouth turned up. "A bird in the hand is worth two in the bush, so to speak."

"Oh?" David laughed. "I'm guessing you're the bird in the hand?"

"More like a strutting rooster," Daniel chortled. "Don't think we can't all tell you're smitten. *My Mary,*" he teased, and then he made kissing sounds. "We saw you, you know. The day of the storm, you grabbed her, and—"

"Didn't look like she was puttin' up much of a fight, neither." David laughed.

Tobias scowled. "How old are you two again? Ten and twelve?" With that feeble retort, he spurred Horace into a canter, leaving the two brothers and their grating laughter behind. He turned onto the lane, and the Schmitts' farm came into view around the first bend. Tobias's pulse kicked up at the sight of the whitewashed frame house. Three men were working in the field to the north of the house, and he waved. Andrew, Ambrose's older son, and the reason they'd traveled out of their way to Newburgh, was one of them.

How would Tobias respond if Andrew and his wife were unhappy with him for breaking his word? At least worrying about the Offermeyers' reaction replaced the mortification of being ribbed by the Morris brothers. Tobias had thought for sure his stolen kiss with Mary had been hidden by the rain, if not by his wagon. Lord, she'd be wroth with him if she knew they'd been seen. Except, didn't their kiss being witnessed give him an expedient argument for the two of them marrying?

The Morris brothers came up behind him as Tobias reined in Horace next to a hitching rail. The other two men from the field approached, and the Morris brothers dismounted and tied their mounts. Was he doing the right thing, or was he letting a whole lot of folks down for his own selfish reasons? He dismounted just as Andrew reached his side.

"Tobias Lovejoy, you're a sight for sore eyes," Andrew said, striding toward him. His childhood friend slapped Tobias on the back as they shook hands.

"You look good, Andy. You've recovered from your illness, I take it." He and Andrew were close in age and had been close as boys. His friend's color was good, and though he was thin, he appeared to be healthy. "Farming agrees with you," he remarked before making introductions. "Daniel, David, this is Andrew Offermeyer. He grew up across the street from me in Atlanta."

"Nice to meet you." Andrew shook their hands. "The young man still working the field is my brother-in-law, Benjamin, and here is my father-in-law, Abelard Schmitt."

"Call me Abe," the older man said, offering his hand. "Come on in. If my wife ain't already done so, we'll put on a pot of coffee and scare up something in the way of sustenance." He steered them all toward the steps leading to the side porch.

Andrew hung back to walk beside Tobias. "I have recovered, thanks to Bonnie and her family's excellent care, but it's just recently that I've been able to help with the farming and chores around here. I'm growing stronger every day, and I can't tell you how good it is to finally feel well." He glanced toward the main road. "Where's the rest of your pioneers?"

"We're camped down the road a piece." They entered a large kitchen, and the delicious scent of fresh coffee and something sweet and laced with cinnamon baking in the oven filled the air.

"Bonnie, Minerva, we got company," Abe called. "Come on through to the parlor." He gestured toward a door to their right.

Two women met them there. One he recognized as the young schoolteacher who had stolen Andrew's heart while teaching in Atlanta, and the other had to be Bonnie's mother-in-law, a middle-aged woman with silver-streaked brown hair.

The corners of Minerva's eyes creased with her smile. "Welcome, welcome. Here I was expectin' that other feller." She waved toward a settee and several chairs. "Sit. Bonnie and I will be right back with coffee and cinnamon rolls."

Bonnie greeted him, and Tobias noticed the slight swell around her middle. She and Andrew were expecting, and the joy of seeing his childhood friend hale and happy brought a smile to Tobias's face. Andrew put his arm around his wife's shoulders and made introductions, pride shining in his eyes. As they all settled, Mrs. Schmitt's words finally registered. "Other fellow?" Tobias's brow rose in question.

"Yep, this feller's been comin' 'round every day, asking about you and the folks traveling with you," Abe told him.

"Hmm." Had Bradford come all this way to tell him what he wanted to know? "One of the reasons I stopped by is to see if you might have received a letter for me from Texas."

"Nope." Abe shook his head and reached for a pipe and a pouch from the mantel above the hearth. "Not a one." He leaned over and tapped out the remnants from the pipe into the ashes. Then he packed the bowl with tobacco and lit it with a match. A cloud of fragrant smoke floated through the parlor.

The ladies returned with trays laden with coffee and cinnamon rolls. Tobias was about to ask for the *feller's* name when there came a knock on the front door. Had to be Bradford. No one else knew to look for Tobias here at this time. Andrew headed for the door, and Tobias couldn't fathom why Bradford would come all this way just to talk to him. As happy as he would be to see his old friend, he'd rather be on his way back to camp. He had things to do, like declare his undying love and propose marriage.

He'd been rehearsing how he'd ask her to marry him ever since he'd filled out the forms to homestead. Nervous energy brought him up from his chair. A conversation ensued in the foyer, and he didn't recognize the second voice. If not Charles Bradford's, then whose? He frowned as Andrew led a tall, blond man with friendly blue eyes into the parlor. The stranger dressed like he had money.

"Andrew tells me you're Tobias Lovejoy." His commanding voice drew everyone's attention. The man approached Tobias with his hand outstretched.

Tobias nodded, and wariness crept up his spine. "I am." They shook.

"You're here at last." The stranger released Tobias's hand and gazed around the room, as if making certain all eyes were on him. "If you don't mind my asking, where are the rest of the good people traveling west with you? In particular, I'm looking for Miss Mary Stewart."

"Miss Stewart?" Tobias's vague uneasiness grew.

"Yes. She *is* traveling with you, is she not? I spoke at length with Charles Bradford, a Texas Ranger who came to me in Houston. He said you requested that he look into my whereabouts on Miss Stewart's behalf." He placed his palm over his heart and smiled, revealing a straight row of very white teeth. "I'm Eldon Smythe, Miss Stewart's fiancé."

"Well, I'll be damned," Daniel muttered. "Weren't we just—"

"Watch your language, Dan," David hissed. "There are ladies present."

Tobias's dreams shattered like the clay jars Mary used for target practice. All the air left his lungs, and a sheen of sweat broke out across his brow. His heart had never pounded this hard in his entire life, not even in the midst of battle, and he wasn't sure he'd survive the hammering.

"Best sit down, Tobias." Andrew took him by the elbow. "You've gone pale. Are you ill?"

"Pale as bread dough," Daniel supplied helpfully.

"I'm fine," he murmured. "Since the war, I have these . . . spells."

"You can't possibly think you and Miss Stewart are still engaged, do you?" David glared. "Not after all this time without a single word." He glanced at Tobias. "How long's it been?"

"Almost two years." Tobias did a bit of glaring himself, all along visualizing his fist connecting with the man's even, white teeth. "Mary has not heard a single word from you or your family in nearly two years."

"*Mary*, is it?" Smythe turned his hat over and over in his hand, his eyes not quite so friendly now.

Mr. Smythe," Minerva interjected, "have a seat and take refreshment with us."

"Thank you, ma'am." Once again Smythe showed off his dazzling smile.

The light-headedness passed, leaving Tobias seething. Why had this man appeared now, at a time when all Tobias's dreams were about to come to fruition? Even more salient, why would Smythe still refer to himself as Mary's fiancé?

Tobias rubbed his temples and closed his eyes as coffee and cinnamon rolls were passed around, and the hum of empty pleasantries being exchanged filled the room. Coffee was the last thing he wanted. His stomach already churned with frustration and uncertainty. Who and what would Mary choose? Him and a life in Indiana, or Texas and life with her long-absent fiancé?

Tobias lowered his chin and speared Smythe with a look. "What excuse could you possibly offer Mary for abandoning her in the middle of a war? She was left entirely alone to fend for herself. Did you *know* and simply not care?"

Smythe returned Tobias's sharp look with one of his own. "What possible reason do *you* have to suppose any of this is your concern?"

"Oh, it's his concern, all right," Daniel snapped. "Just like it's my concern, my brother's, our wives', and every single one of the good folks traveling with Miss Stewart. Anyone who knows her can't help but care about her. She helps everybody. She's smart as a whip, and she never lets any of us wallow in a dark mood for long before she comes by to lift our spirits." He looked to his older brother for agreement.

David nodded and gestured toward Tobias. "Why, she even saved Lovejoy's life. Killed a thievin' outlaw about to shoot him in the back." He grunted. "Whenever there's trouble, Miss Stewart is always first in line to help out. She's a good-hearted, generous woman. She even gave her spare axle to the Cummingses when theirs broke, which left Miss Stewart without when hers busted."

"That's right," Daniel said with a nod. "We don't take kindly to anyone who might mean her harm."

Daniel's and David's willingness to jump to his defense and heap praise on the woman he loved touched a place deep in Tobias's heart. "She means a great deal to all of us, and we won't see her hurt."

"I'm not here to *hurt* my intended. I am here to reunite with her. My *excuses* and what I have to say to her are none of your business." He leveled his gaze toward Daniel and David for a second before settling it on Tobias. "Though I appreciate the sentiments you've expressed, I feel no compunction to share our personal business with any of *you*. After Miss Stewart and I have spoken, if she chooses to share what was said, that is her prerogative."

"Spoken like a lawyer or a politician," Tobias snapped. "Which are you, Mr. Eldon Smythe?"

"Both."

For several loaded seconds, Tobias took the man's measure, and Smythe took his. He couldn't picture his trousers-wearing, stubborn-as-granite woman paired with this fancified, slick-tongued abandoner of damsels in distress. He just couldn't, and more than anything, that buoyed his resolve. "I must insist that I speak to her first once we return to camp. Then you are free to say whatever it is you came to say before heading back to Houston." *Without her.* God help him, he hoped that's how it turned out.

"Fine," Smythe said. His expression smug, he sipped his coffee and turned his disingenuous charm on their hosts.

Hadn't Mary told him more than once she took her promise to her fiancé seriously? What if her word of honor meant more to her than her own happiness . . . and his? Tobias nearly choked on his rising insecurities, and trepidation threatened to fell him where he sat.

Chapter Twelve

MARY BROUGHT THE BLADE OF the axe down in a wide arc, hitting the upended log squarely in the center. A satisfying crack resounded, and the wood split into two even pieces. *Perfect.* Chopping wood was another skill she'd been forced to learn during the war. Oddly enough, she enjoyed the labor. If given the choice between doing the wash or chopping wood, she'd choose the axe every time. She placed one of the halves on the stump, raised the axe, and brought it down again. The maple split right down the middle. Smiling, she mentally patted herself on the back for a job well done.

Bea came to stand beside her. "The men have returned. They're within sight of camp."

"About time." She glanced at the afternoon sky. "Tobias said three days, and this is the afternoon of the fourth day they've been gone."

Her cousin shielded her eyes from the sun and peered westward down the road. "There's another man with them."

"Andrew Offermeyer or someone else from one of the families joining us, no doubt." She set another log on the stump and fixed her attention on her task.

"Perhaps, but . . ." Bea gasped. "Oh, Mary."

"What?" Mary split the hardwood with swift precision. Tobias should not have told her three days at the most, and she had no desire to appear overly eager at his return—even though she'd been worried sick each and every hour of his absence.

"Dearest, you may want to brace yourself."

"*Brace* myself? What for?" She leaned the axe against the stump and gathered the quartered pieces of wood from the ground, stacking them neatly out of the way. The MacGregors had cut logs for everyone after taking down the tree that would become her new axle, another favor she owed the family.

"I do believe Mr. Lovejoy was able to discover Mr. Eldon Smythe's whereabouts after all."

"Whatever do you mean, Bea?"

"He's here. Mr. Smythe is the fourth man riding with Tobias and the Morris brothers."

"Don't be ridiculous." Mary's breath hitched. "Perhaps Tobias's ranger friend has—"

"Mary." Bea nodded toward the road. "See for yourself."

Her heart pounding, Mary huffed and cast her cousin an incredulous look. "You must be mistaken."

"Look." Bea's brow rose, and she nodded in the direction of the road again, this time more forcibly.

Crossing her arms in front of her, Mary turned. Her heart tripped and tumbled down to the pit of her stomach. There before her, riding toward their camp as if he hadn't a care in the world, was her long-lost fiancé.

All the hurt, all the terror and loneliness amassed over the past two years coursed through her in a current far stronger than any river's, no matter how wide. "I can't . . ." She staggered back a step as all the blood rushed from her head. Stars danced before her eyes, and a tremor started in her ice-cold hands. "This can't be."

The worst, the very worst part? She hadn't the strength to run away, and the need to run far from the pain of betrayal overwhelmed her. He was alive. After all this time, Eldon was alive and well, and he hadn't bothered to reach out to her. Not one word.

The months and months of waiting for him to send for her unfurled between them. He hadn't been there for her when she'd received word of her brothers' deaths. She'd had no one to wipe the tears from her cheeks or to hold her when her father had taken his own life. During the darkest time of her entire life, she'd been alone, and now here he was, hale and whole.

Anguish surged, and only pride kept her upright. "Bea," she pleaded, unable even to form a coherent sentence.

Her cousin wrapped her arms around her. "Where to?"

"Anywhere away from . . ." A stunning grief for all she'd lost swallowed the rest of her words. She couldn't say the man's name aloud. How could Tobias bring him here without sending her a word of warning? She could have prepared herself, shored up the battered walls around her heart enough that she could at least talk to Eldon. Oh, but what was there to say? She'd clung to Eldon's memory in much the same way she'd clung to her pickle barrel. Hadn't she wondered and speculated over and over about what kept him away? Now she wasn't certain she wanted to know, because whatever his reasons might have been, they were sure to pierce her heart and cause her even more pain.

Bea turned Mary's quaking body around and moved her forward. She hadn't a care where her cousin took her, so long as she didn't have to look at or talk to anyone—so long as her cousin led her to a place where she'd be shielded from prying eyes. God, she hated for others to witness her humiliating breakdown.

"Cyrus," Bea called in a firm tone, approaching his wagon. "I must ask a favor."

"Anything for you, love," he said, coming around the corner of her wagon. "Oh. Didn't know we had company." His eyes widened. "What is it? Are you ailing, ma'am?" He dropped the hammer he'd been holding and hurried to Mary's side. "You've gone white as a sheet."

"If you wouldn't mind, may Mary lie down in your wagon for a bit?" Bea asked. "She's suffered quite a shock, and—"

"Aya. No need to even ask. We'll help any way we can." Cyrus supported Mary on one side, while Bea held her up by the other. "Winston, Junior," he called to his sons. "Clear a spot in the wagon for Miss Stewart."

Cyrus Junior peeked around the end of the wagon, took one look at her, and scrambled into the interior. "Right away, Pa." Winston scurried after his brother an instant later.

Focusing on the scraping sound of objects being moved, Mary waited. Had the men reached camp yet? Had Eldon seen her? If he had, he couldn't possibly have recognized her. He'd only ever seen her wearing wide hoops and elaborate gowns, with her hair fashionably coifed. She'd carried parasols to protect her complexion from the sun back then, and now her skin was tanned and freckled. Today she wore hand-me-down breeches and worn leather gloves, and her hair hung down her back in a simple braid. Not to mention she'd lost weight since the war, almost to the point of gauntness.

The grunts and scrapes from within the wagon continued. Lord, the few moments it took to rearrange the wagon lasted an excruciating eternity. Shouts rang out as folks greeted the Morris brothers and Tobias. She could imagine their curious stares as they looked upon the stranger their men had brought into their midst.

Mary shrank into herself, separating from those around her. Hadn't she done the same when her father had shamed her by taking his own life? Eldon's abandonment felt no different to her than her papa's. She hadn't mattered to Papa or to Eldon. That she'd loved and needed them both hadn't made a damn bit of difference. In the end, they'd left her anyway.

"We made a nice bed for you, ma'am," Cyrus Junior told her. He came to stand before her, took off his cap, and waved it toward the wagon. "I hope you feel better soon."

"Is she sick, Pa?" Winston whispered to his father.

"No, Win. She's just . . ." Cyrus scratched his head and looked to Bea for guidance.

"She needs a bit of privacy to rest and settle her nerves." Bea led her to the back of the wagon.

"Thank you, boys, Cyrus," Mary murmured. Cyrus and Bea helped her into the wagon, and then they dropped the canvas curtain and left her in peace. The cozy nest of blankets the boys had arranged for her warmed her frozen heart. Sighing, she dropped to her side, rested her cheek on her folded hands, and curled into a ball of misery.

Privacy at last. Other than greeting the men who returned, the familiar sounds of living in a camp resumed, while her life had been turned upside down. Children played, chores and repairs were being made, and the constant low hum of familiar voices lulled her.

Mary rolled to her back and closed her eyes. Thoughts skittered through her mind like wood ash caught in a breeze. All the promises she and Eldon had made to each other, his plans for their life in Houston, memories of their courtship so many years ago assailed her and squeezed at her heart. Why was Eldon here? Surely he didn't mean to take up where they'd left off. Did he still believe they were to marry? She had given him her word and she still wore his ring, but so much had changed. She had changed.

Tobias's steady, supportive presence, his passionate kisses, weighted the other side of her mental scale. When had she begun weighing sides? Did it matter? No. What mattered was Tobias had never let her down. Not once.

If only he'd left well enough alone and not offered to help her find Eldon, she would have come to terms, let go of the past, and embraced the future. Perhaps she and Tobias would eventually have grown closer.

"Mary?" Tobias knocked on the side of the wagon.

Her heart leaped to her throat, and she hadn't the breath in her lungs to respond.

"I know you're in there. I need to talk to you," he said. His words came out hoarse. *"Please."*

"All right," she managed to utter. She could listen at least, even if responding was beyond her. And if she were honest with herself, from the moment he'd ridden off with the Morris brothers, she'd yearned for his return. More than anything, she needed to lay eyes upon him to assure for herself he was well. Somehow Tobias had become as essential to her as the air she breathed, and she needed his presence to anchor herself amid the turbulent storm of her thoughts and conflicting feelings.

He climbed into the tight confines of the wagon, and she wanted to throw herself into his arms and rail at him for being away for so long. Mary pushed herself up to sitting and scooted over to make room for him.

He lowered himself to sit and handed her a small paper packet bound with string. She took it and looked at him in question.

"Lemon drops." He untied the string for her and folded the paper back. "I promised I'd bring you lemon drops. Remember?"

Another promise kept—a promise so small as to be insignificant, yet to her, the candy she held in her gloved palm meant the world. "Thank you," she whispered.

Tobias's Adam's apple bobbed, and he breathed in shallow sips of air. Even in the dim light, she detected the pounding of his pulse at the side of his neck. "What is it you wish to talk to me about, Tobias?"

"I know you are already aware Mr. Smythe journeyed with us back to camp. He met us at the Schmitt farm." His words came out in a rush. "Bradford told him where to find us . . . find you, and he's here to . . . He wants to talk to you, Mary, but I needed to speak with you first." He drew in a long breath. "There are things that need to be said, and I'm here to say them."

She nodded and stared at the sweets in her hands.

"The thing is," he began, pausing to clear his throat. "Before we went on to Evansville to file for homestead, I—"

"You did what?" She blinked. "You filed for—"

"This is *our* land now. Yours and mine. This farm was abandoned, and I filed for one half of the original claim and brought you back the forms to file for the other."

"*Our* land?" His words muddled her thinking even more than it already was. "I'm not following you."

"I know. I know. Damnation, I'm not going about this right at all." Tobias took the lemon drops from her and set them aside. He tugged off her gloves and clasped her hands between his. "Mary, Eldon says he's here to reunite with you, but there's something you need to know before you make up your mind." His gaze drilled into her, searching to the very depths of her soul.

"And what is that?"

"You see, before I knew Eldon was coming for you, I bought these." He let her go and took something out of his back pocket, a small box made of leather. "I'm in love with you, Mary, and—"

"You are?" She gaped at him as his words sank in.

"Yes, and I had planned to return, tell you of my decision to remain where we are, and then I meant to beg you to marry me." He placed the box in her hand. "Nothing would make me happier than to have you by my side for the rest of my life."

If her thoughts had been muddled before, his revelations rendered her unable to think at all now. Fixed in his hawklike perusal, Mary opened the case. Inside, she found two shiny gold wedding bands. Her insides melted, and the bands blurred before her misting eyes. "Oh, Tobias, I—"

"Don't say anything now." He closed the box holding the rings and folded her hands around the leather. "Just know that you have a choice. With everything that I am, I love you. I cherish everything about you, Mary, from your larkspur-blue eyes to your trousers-wearing stubborn and brilliant self, and my greatest wish is to see you happy. Whatever you decide, I want you to be happy."

"I'm *not* stubborn." She frowned. "I'm persistent. There's a difference." She gripped the container holding his promise of a future together and blinked away at the moisture filling her eyes. He made that deep chuckle sound she so adored, and her insides melted all over again.

"Hear what Mr. Smythe has to say, and then we'll talk." He placed his hands on her shoulders, leaned in, and kissed her forehead. "While you listen to what *he* has to say, don't forget that I love you with all my heart and always will, no matter what. Should you accept my proposal, for as long as I live, I promise you will never be alone again. I will not leave you, and though we might become miffed with each other from time to time, I shall remain steadfast. I'll leave you to think now, but I'll be nearby should you need me."

With those words, he climbed out of the wagon. He'd homesteaded this very place, this wonderful, peaceful place with its rich soil and the Ohio River flowing by. No wonder he'd spent all that time tromping through the fields and along the riverbank. He'd been making plans for their future, and now she knew what had altered between them. He wanted her, and he'd taken careful, methodical steps to ensure his plans bore fruit. And then he'd been confronted with the sudden appearance of her fiancé. How awful that must have been for him.

Her fiancé. Did the promises they made so long ago mean anything today? If Eldon had jilted her or if he'd meant to abandon her, why come all this way? Why not send word through Bradford, releasing her from her vow? Only one way to find out: she needed to talk to him, and dammit, she had no intention of donning petticoats and a dress to do so.

The woman she was now no longer resembled the woman she'd been when Eldon asked for her hand, and he needed to know that before a word was spoken between them. She was no longer the privileged daughter of a wealthy plantation owner. She was her own woman. She'd made her own way in life, and she had choices.

Tobias loves me. Her heart turned over. Hadn't he said he cherished everything about her? "From my larkspur-blue eyes to my trousers-wearing stubborn and brilliant self." *Larkspur-blue eyes?* My, who knew Tobias hid such a poetic, romantic nature. Tucking the ring box into her pocket, she prepared to confront Eldon, her word of honor at war with her heart.

TOBIAS PACED BY HIS WAGON. How could he not when his entire future hung in the balance? If Mary chose Eldon, losing her would gut him. He needed something to do, something to force his attention away from his dandified rival. He glanced toward Eldon, who appeared entirely too calm as he awaited Mary's summons.

"Tobias," Cyrus said as he strode toward him. "What's this I hear about yon stranger?" He tilted his head in their guest's direction. Eldon sat on a tree stump, his horse tethered beside him. "Is he really—"

"Yes. Mary's prodigal fiancé has come at last to fetch her." The very words turned his stomach.

Cyrus scratched at his beard. "Humph."

"Indeed." Tobias caught movement from the corner of his eye. No matter how hard he tried, he couldn't prevent himself from watching as Mary's cousin approached Mr. Smythe. She said something to him and gestured toward Cyrus's wagon. Eldon nodded and followed as she led him to Mary. Tobias's mouth went dry. His gut twisted, and the urge to do anything in his power to keep his rival from getting anywhere near Mary almost defeated his good sense.

"The Morris brothers are spreading tales," Cyrus said, drawing Tobias's attention back to him. "Is it true what they're saying?" Cyrus scrutinized him. "Did you homestead this farm? Do you mean to stay here?"

"It's true." Tobias sighed. Since he couldn't keep the smooth-talking lawyer away from Mary, his only recourse was to distance himself. "Walk with me through camp, and I'll tell you what I have in mind." Gazing toward the Ohio, he was reminded how very small his troubles were in the grand scheme of things.

"Aya, I'd very much like to know what you're thinking."

Did he detect the hint of anger in his friend's tone? Cyrus beside him, he headed down the worn tracks of the many travelers who must have passed this way. He'd told Mary he wanted her happiness, and he'd meant it. He should have told her *he* could make her happy in ways Eldon never could.

"Had it not been for the unexpected appearance of one Mr. Eldon Smythe, I would have gathered everyone together to share my news right away."

"I'm certain our *guest's* appearance is an unwelcome surprise."

"You've no idea." A growl of frustration escaped him. "I had planned to propose to Mary once we'd returned, and I meant to ask you, the MacGregors, the Cummings family, the Morris families, and anyone else who might be interested to stay here with us. I want to build a town."

"I see." Cyrus nodded, his expression grave.

"I put money down on a few adjacent plots, and I'm willing to sell smaller parcels for no more than what they cost me. That way, folks will have a place to set up their businesses and build their homes. You could open a forge, Cy. The MacGregors could put their carpentry skills to good use, and perhaps start a wood mill or a brick foundry. I'd open a mercantile. I spoke with Andrew Offermeyer and his wife. They're expecting a child, and they've decided they want to stay in Indiana, rather than risk Bonnie's health traveling to Texas. They'll open a butcher shop and a green grocer here.

"We'll need to put in a pier, and that will open up a flow of supplies and a venue to sell whatever products we produce." Tobias waved a hand toward the river. "We'd need a school and a church." He'd thought about running a bank along with his mercantile. But that would be down the road some. "There will be enough work and commerce right here for all of us to prosper."

"Hmm." Cyrus nodded.

"But now, I don't know." Tobias shoved his hands into his pockets. Without Mary, none of his grand plans mattered. Without the woman he loved in his life, he might as well return to Atlanta or continue on to Texas. Where he lived wouldn't make a bit of difference. He studied his boots, his insides a painful tangle.

"She can't want him still." Cyrus laid a hand on Tobias's

shoulder. "Not after the way he's neglected her. Not after leaving her without a word all this time." He squeezed Tobias's shoulder and let go. "Did you tell Miss Stewart what is in your heart?"

"I did." Tobias grunted. "But she's been telling me all along she's not free. Her word means a lot to her, and she made a promise to Eldon. Her words, not mine."

"Don't seem like his promise meant all that much to him."

"I should have knocked him senseless and put him on the nearest train or stagecoach back to Texas."

"I would've helped."

"Good to know. I'd do the same for you, by the way." Tobias slanted his friend a look of gratitude. "Speaking of hearts, have you shared with Bea what's in yours?"

"I have."

"And?"

"She likes to remind me we've only been acquainted a very short time, and it's too soon for her to know what she feels for me yet." The big man shrugged. "It's gonna take a bit more convincing, but I'm not giving up, and neither should you."

"I told Mary I want her to be my wife and that I adore everything about her." His chest tightened with uncertainty. "But the choice is hers. If there's anything you think I could do to persuade her, I'm happy to hear what that might be."

"Well, it's still not too late to knock the man senseless and put him on the nearest train." Cyrus snorted. "I'm certain Daniel and David would help too. We trussed up them outlaws and brought them to justice. We can surely handle one citified lawyer type. Hell, I'll bet he don't even own a callus on either hand."

Touched by his friend's willingness to tip the scale on his behalf, Tobias smiled, the first smile he'd been able to muster since Eldon Smythe sauntered into the Schmitts' parlor. Would Mary forgive him if he sent Smythe off? Eventually. After several years of proving to her how much he loved her. Perhaps after a decade or so, she might even be amused by the tale. "That plan is not out of the question, Cy."

Chapter Thirteen

MARY REFUSED TO SMOOTH HER hair or check her clothing for stains or tears. Straightening her spine, she kept a level eye on the man she once thought she would marry. Eldon approached Cyrus's wagon, his all-too-familiar smile lighting his handsome features. Smiling or not, he couldn't hide the way his gaze traveled over her from head to toe. Did his smile falter just then? *Good.* "Eldon." She held tight to her one-word greeting, lest she let loose a diatribe over all the months' worth of frustration she'd suffered.

"Mary, I cannot begin to tell you . . ."

Were those tears causing his eyes to shine so? Mary glanced at her cousin for her aid or to beseech her for privacy; she couldn't say which impulse was the stronger.

"Well," Bea said, looking from her to Eldon and back to her, "I imagine you two have much to discuss, so I'll leave you now. Mr. Smythe, I'm glad to see you're alive and well. You see, after all this time without a single word, we *feared* you had perished."

Eldon flinched at her words, and Mary's frozen heart thawed the tiniest bit. Bea left, and once again she was at a loss. Studying the old gloves she held in her hands, she racked her poor brain for a way to begin this most awkward conversation.

"You look . . . different," Eldon said. He stepped closer and leaned down to catch her eye.

"War and poverty change a body." Mary met his stare, hers maybe a little accusing.

"You must think me the worst sort of—"

"I haven't *thought* about you at all for quite some time." She gripped her gloves all the tighter, and the lie tasted bitter upon her tongue. The alternative was to rant, to rave, and to pound his chest with both her fists. But doing so would expose how very vulnerable his abandonment had left her and all the bewildering hurt she'd suffered on his account. She did have her pride, after all. Still, she longed to throw her broken dreams at his feet and to point to them as an indictment for all the wrongs he'd committed against her. But to what end? The past could not be changed.

"Can we walk a bit, Mary? Perhaps distance ourselves from your overly protective neighbors?"

She surveyed their camp, catching the stares turned unabashedly their way. "They're curious is all, and why wouldn't they be? Everyone knows I lost a fiancé somewhere between Savannah and Houston. How long has it been, sir?" Lifting her chin, she dared him to explain. "Almost two years if I'm not mistaken."

"They are more than curious, my dear." He sent her a sheepish look. "I've been warned by several, including your cousin, not to cause you any further hurt, or else. You are well loved by everyone in this community. But then, you've always had that effect on those around you. You must know that is one of the qualities I cherish most about you."

"Really." She swallowed the lump constricting her throat.

"You doubt me, and I cannot blame you. There is something I'd like you to read." Eldon glanced around the camp again. "Not here, though."

Sighing, she acquiesced. "All right. Let us walk to the river. There are willow trees growing along the bank. We can at least take advantage of the shade." *Something to read?* After all this time, she deserved to know why he'd left her the way he had, and her curiosity had been piqued.

"Thank you." He offered her his arm.

She almost snorted; it seemed such a ridiculous gesture. Placing her hand at the crook of his elbow, she wondered at the picture they made—he in his finely tailored suit, she in her brother's hand-me-down trousers and her old, scuffed boots, a favorite misshapen old straw hat upon her head. She looked like a poor farmer, while he appeared to be a gentleman of means, which he was.

They walked in silence, and when they reached the riverbank, she was surprised to find a crude bench of sorts, part of the maple trunk split in half and placed in front of the willows. The flat side made a decent place to sit. The work of the MacGregor brothers, no doubt.

"This is a lovely spot," Eldon said, supporting her as she took a seat. Another ridiculous gesture.

"It is." And part of it was hers if she chose to claim half of this farmstead. Tobias had brought her the forms, and all she had to do was fill in the blanks and file. How like him to understand her need to own a part of his dream for their future. He'd let her know without words he saw her as his equal. Bolstered by that thought, she patted the spot beside her. "Please sit, Eldon, or I'll get a crick in my neck from looking up at you."

He chuckled as he sat. "Another characteristic that drew me to you, the charming way you always speak your mind. You are entirely without artifice, and it's a quality I've always admired. It's a refreshing trait and one I've sorely missed."

Then why hadn't he sent for her? Her mind reeled with his declarations, setting her off-balance. "I am confused, sir. If there was so much to love, why did you abandon me? Did you meet someone else and come to regret—"

"Never," he rasped out.

She slanted him a look filled with skepticism. "You said you had something for me to read." Biting her lip, she peeked at him as he reached into his coat and brought forth what appeared to be a letter. He hadn't changed at all. He'd matured, but he was the same handsome, polished man he'd always been. She frowned as he handed her the yellowing paper. "What is this?"

"I sent a packet along with a business associate on his way to Savannah to see my father. The packet contained my letter to you, instructing you and your father to take a stage to Savannah, there to join my parents as they traveled by coach and train to Houston for our wedding. I had asked my mother to find a reliable way to get my letter to you." Eldon shook his head, and his mouth tightened into a straight, unhappy line.

"Why did you not send my part directly to Marilee Hills?"

"With Atlanta burned to the ground and no reliable mail service going out or in?" He shook his head. "I couldn't chance word not reaching you in a timely manner. Besides, I had already arranged and paid for your journey, and the tickets were enclosed. I didn't want to risk having them stolen."

His gaze met hers. "Everything had been arranged: the church where we were to be wed, the home I'd rented until we could build our own. I could not wait to make you mine, and what you hold in your hand is the response I received from my mother."

She blinked, her confusion so complete it took several seconds before she could open the letter and begin to read. And as she did, anger and disbelief ignited into a red-hot flame.

My Dearest Eldon,
It is with a heavy heart that I must inform you that Miss Stewart and her father both recently passed. From what I have learned, it seems Mr. Stewart took ill, and in nursing him, your dear Mary also contracted the fever that took them both . . .

Gasping, Mary placed a hand over her heart. "How could she? How could she tell you such an outrageous lie? I am the one who wrote to your parents. *I'm* the one who informed *her* of my father's death. I hadn't heard from you for two months by then, and I'd asked your mother to send my letter on to you in the hopes they knew where you were."

Mystified, she gaped at him. "Why on earth would she tell you I'd died of a fever? I always thought she liked me. I was under the impression she approved of our union. Our fathers were close friends, business associates. Why would she do such a thing?"

"I have no idea, but rest assured, once I learned you were alive, I wrote her a letter demanding an explanation and expressing how angry I am at her betrayal. I didn't wait in Houston for her answer but left immediately. A Mr. Bradford, a Texas Ranger who came to me, told me of your plans and the route your group would take. The desire to arrive in Newburgh around the same time you did far outweighed my need to hear any excuse my mother might make."

"My father didn't die of a fever." Tears pooled, and she stared in disbelief at the letter she held in her shaking hands. In several spots the words had blurred, as if drops of water had landed on the ink. *Oh God. Not water—tears. Eldon's tears.* "I think I know why she did this to us, Eldon."

"Please enlighten me. I cannot begin to tell you the grief my mother's deceitfulness has caused. I may never speak to her again."

Mary placed a hand on his forearm. "Your mother has always been extremely sensitive regarding the opinion of society. Has she not?"

"Yes, but I fail to see—"

"And deeply involved in her church. Her beliefs are singularly strong, wouldn't you agree?"

"Overly zealous and judgmental, you mean." Eldon grunted and placed his hand over hers. "What has that to do with us? You and I have always been in accord on matters of faith, how we would raise our children and conduct our lives."

She slipped her hand back to her own lap and stared at the river's steady current, recalling Tobias's words. The river didn't concern itself with the petty problems of humanity. The Ohio would continue on its course long after she, Eldon, and Tobias turned to dust in the ground. "Yes. We were, weren't we? We were in accord on most everything."

She drew in a fortifying breath. "As I said, Papa didn't die of a fever. Once he learned he'd lost both his sons to the war, and he realized our way of life would never be the same, he hung himself from the rafters of our stable. My mistake was in telling your mother how he died. Perhaps I should have kept the details to myself, but I was not in my right mind at the time. I'd lost my entire family, you see, and I hadn't heard from you in so long."

She handed him the letter, and he tucked it back into his pocket. Mary sighed. "I suppose I'd hoped your family might take pity on me and invite me to live with them until we married."

"As they should have. I *did* write to you, Mary, every single week, but with the war . . . I am not surprised you didn't get my letters." He shook his head. "I received only one from you during those two months as well. I blamed it on the upheaval, which is why I sent my packet along with a friend who was traveling to Savannah on business."

"I am sure you are right, and our letters never made it through." A tear trickled down her cheek. It was all so unfair and so very tragic.

"Mother could hardly blame you for your father's death," Eldon bit out. He took her hand, brought it to his lips, and kissed her knuckles. "My God, you must have been devastated."

"I was, but as you can see, I survived and adapted." She ran her hands over her trousers. "Your mother could not blame me, but she would not have tolerated the stigma of my father's mortal sin staining your family's good name either. I'm certain she feared it might hinder your family's social status and perhaps even your career aspirations." She paused to steady her nerves.

"Besides, when you and I became engaged, I was the wealthy daughter of a plantation owner. By the time I'd written that letter to your parents, my family's fortunes had declined." She glanced at him as heat flooded her face. "They'd dwindled to nothing, in fact. Then my cousin learned she'd been widowed. She and her son came to live with me, and we supported ourselves by selling eggs and vegetables to the green grocer in Atlanta."

Once again her attention drifted to the steady, calming flow of the river. "Finally I sold Marilee Hills to finance this journey. I had intended to put the remaining funds into some sort of business for myself and Beatrice so that we might support ourselves and her son."

"My God, Mary, what you must have gone through, and on top of that, you believed that I had . . . that I . . ."

"Exactly. I feared you had jilted me or worse. I didn't know if you'd fallen gravely ill or if you had died. I wrote letter after letter to your parents, and I never received a single reply."

"My mind is made up. I shall never speak to that woman again." His grip on her hand tightened.

They sat in silence for several moments. She needed the time to reconcile herself to this altered version of the past. All this time, so much needless suffering caused by . . . "Eldon, do you suppose your father could have been complicit in your mother's deception?"

"I don't know," he rasped out. "I would like to think not. I shall have to write him as well. *That* letter I shall post to his place of business." He squeezed her hand again.

Mary nodded. Emotional fatigue stole over her, as if the weight of the past she'd carried for so long had finally been lifted and she could finally rest. "I am so sorry."

"Neither you nor I have anything to be sorry about. As far as I'm concerned, nothing has changed." He touched the sapphire ring he'd placed upon her finger so long ago. "Seeing you still wearing my ring gives me hope. My practice is thriving, and

Houston is growing. You will love it there, Mary. There are theaters, fine restaurants, society events, and all the modern comforts you could imagine. I've taken on two partners, and I'm considering running for state office or perhaps for a judgeship. Think of the life we could have together, my dear."

Everything had changed. She wasn't the same person she'd been when they'd whispered tender promises to each other. She'd continued to wear his ring only as a shield against more heartache. She'd used Eldon to protect herself, and doing so no longer made any sense. "Eldon, I—"

"Don't."

"Don't what?" Her pulse pounded so hard she could hear the hammering inside her head.

"*Don't* make a decision in haste. Don't think I am not aware that I have a rival for your affections, and don't dismiss the promises we made to each other. They mean as much to me now as they did the day I asked for your hand in marriage and you accepted."

He swallowed hard a few times. "Most important, *don't* break my heart all over again. I thought I'd lost you, and it nearly broke me. Not a day has gone by since that I have not thought of you and missed you desperately. There hasn't been anyone else for me, and I doubt there ever will be. You are still the woman I want by my side, and you always will be."

Oh God. What was she to do? She'd given Eldon her word and agreed to marry him. Their separation was no fault of his, and yet . . . Tobias's image came to her mind. His soulful brown eyes, passionate kisses, and all the secrets they'd shared. Even the way they were free to expose their worst selves, with no lasting ill effects. She more than loved Tobias; she needed him. No single, all-encompassing word for what he meant to her existed. He was her touchstone, her confidant, and her very best friend in the world.

"I need time to think." She removed her hand from his and rubbed her temples. "This has all been such a shock, and—"

"Of course. Take as much time as you need." He rose from his place beside her and reached out to help her up. She took his hand and found herself drawn into his arms.

"I have a room in Newburgh's hotel. If you wish, I could secure a suite for you and your cousins. It can't be comfortable for you living here as you are. Come to town with me, Mary. Let us dine together this evening, and we can spend the next few days becoming reacquainted."

"I appreciate the offer, but—"

His lips covered hers in a tender kiss, and he drew her closer. In the past, she'd reveled in his embrace and welcomed his kisses. Could those feelings be rekindled? Right now, everything about being in his arms felt . . . wrong. Placing her palms on his chest, she broke the kiss and stepped back. "I'd prefer to stay here for now."

The sting of her rejection flitted across his features, and her heart wrenched. Neither of them carried one whit of blame for the dilemma closing in around them, and once again anger toward his mother burst into flame.

Eldon's jaw tightened, and his struggle to contain his emotions showed plainly. "As you wish." His gaze roamed over her face as if he meant to memorize every freckle. "Shall I escort you back to camp?"

Mary looked toward camp as her conscience warred with her heart. "If you don't mind, I believe I'd like to sit here a while longer. I have a lot to sort out just now, and I wish to be alone to think things through." That and to have a good cry in private while cursing his mother to perdition.

"Indeed." A strangled, mirthless laugh escaped him, and he cleared his throat. "I shall leave you for now, but I will return tomorrow and every single day thereafter until you tell me what you have decided. I have never stopped loving you, my dear. As you consider your options, do not forget that you still hold my heart in your hands."

With that he strode off, and she was left alone to think. Or at least to try and think, for her mind was in such a state she could not make sense of anything. What should she choose: honoring the vow she'd made to Eldon or honoring her heart's desire? How could she live with either decision, knowing she'd cause another such pain?

She believed she'd been in love with Eldon once, but that seemed a lifetime ago. Could she start over with Eldon and live a life of luxury amid the high society in Houston, or did she want to build a new life from the ground up with Tobias here in

Indiana? She huffed out a breath. Did what *she* want even matter? "What is the *right* thing to do? That is what matters." Wasn't it?

More than one terrible injustice had been perpetrated against her: first by her father, and next by the woman who was to have been her mother-in-law. Ripples from that woman's single act of cruelty had the potential to break all three hearts involved. Tears flooded her eyes and trickled down her cheeks. She'd given her promise to Eldon, but she'd given her heart to Tobias. Perhaps it would be best for all involved to refuse them both.

CURSING UNDER HIS BREATH, TOBIAS broke out in a cold sweat. From the moment he'd watched Smythe walk with Mary to the willows, his insides had frothed with helplessness. And anger. Dammit, Mary was his, and *he'd* claimed the willows as their special place. What right did this interloping, slick-tongued lawyer have to wreck everything? Groaning, he raked furrows through his hair. Dammit all to hell, didn't he deserve happiness?

He couldn't keep from watching as the reunited couple made their way to the privacy of the willows. When Smythe returned alone to camp, triumph surged, and Tobias's knees weakened with relief. Mary's long-absent beau strode to his horse, tightened the girth strap, and mounted. Tobias's opponent looked none too happy, a good sign.

"Leaving so soon?" Tobias approached on shaky legs.

Eldon aimed a disdainful look his way. "For now. My fiancée has suffered more than one shock today, and she has requested time to adjust."

Did he speak the truth? Had Mary told him she wanted to *adjust*? His flare of triumph sputtered out.

"I'll be back tomorrow." The man rested his hands on the pommel of his saddle and scrutinized Tobias. "What do you have to offer her, Lovejoy? A crude cabin far from town?" He stared pointedly at the burned-out husk marring Tobias's property. "Poverty and a life of hard labor, eking out a living from the soil? Mary deserves better. She was born to better."

"I'm no farmer, and your assumptions regarding my solvency don't much signify." Tobias's hands fisted by his sides. "I can promise never to betray her trust. I can promise to stand by her side for as long as I live—something *you* failed to do at a time when she needed you most."

His words hit their mark, and Tobias caught a glimpse of strong emotion flickering through Smythe's eyes. "I can provide Mary with a comfortable life," Tobias continued. "She's not the same person she was before the war. You don't know her at all. I do."

"Then I look forward to getting to know who she has become. I'm certain doing so will only deepen what she and I have together." He tipped his hat. "Good day to you, sir, and good luck. You'll need it." He kicked his horse and rode off.

Tobias groaned. More than anything he wanted to go to Mary and beg her to stay with him.

"Don't much like that man," David said, appearing by Tobias's side.

Daniel joined his brother. "Me neither," he added.

Cyrus came to stand at his other side. "Ain't too late to . . . er . . . put him on a train, if you catch my drift."

Tobias's sigh bore with it the weight of his anxiety. "As much as I'd love to do just that, Mary would never forgive me."

"That's a fact. You should go to her," David said, his expression solemn. "A shoulder to lean on and a willin' ear go a long way where womenfolk are concerned."

Daniel nodded. "Might just tip the scale in your favor."

Tobias's attention drifted to the willows. He could see her where she stood, hurling stones into the river. He frowned. She was using quite a bit of force to throw those stones. "I will."

"Before you go," Cyrus said, placing a beefy hand on Tobias's shoulder, "we come to tell you we've shared your plans with everyone. All but two families have agreed to stay and help build a town. The other two said they would, except they have kinfolk waitin' for 'em in Texas."

"Oh?" He peered at the three men standing beside him. They'd become close friends, and he was grateful for their presence. Could he muster the enthusiasm to build a town if he lost the love of his life? He couldn't say for certain. "Andrew should be here the day after tomorrow with word from the other two families who had planned to travel with us." He shared a look with each of his companions. "I'd say we've made a damned good start, wouldn't you?"

"Aya, now go talk to your woman."

"I don't know what to say to her," he admitted, his chest tightening into a painful twist of hope and despair.

"Just let *her* do the talking—or the cryin' if need be." David gestured toward the river. "Whatever she needs, you make sure *you're* the one to provide for her."

"Sounds easy enough." He jammed his hands into his pockets. "But what if—"

"Go on, now." Daniel glowered. "The longer you stand here like a fool with them hangdog eyes, the more time she has to think about Smythe and his pearly white teeth."

"Good point." Placing one foot in front of the other, he started down the hill. *Don't try and force her to see things my way; just be there for her.* Lord, he hoped they were right. Mary must have been so absorbed in her own thoughts, she didn't even notice his approach. He stood behind her, his heart pounding and his palms sweaty. The unevenness of her breathing, the hiccupping sounds she made cut straight through him. "Mary, how can I help?"

Gasping, she dropped the stones she'd been holding and whirled around to face him. Her eyes were red and puffy, and her beautiful face presented a picture of abject misery. "Oh, *Tobias*," she whispered. A tear trickled down her cheek.

He couldn't get to her fast enough, the need to wipe away the hurt so overwhelmed him. Drawing her close, Tobias cradled her head against his shoulder and rocked her gently to and fro. "Tell me, dearest."

Her tears dampened his shirt. The sounds of distress she made pierced him to his very soul. Her scent, having her slight form against him, this was as close to heaven as he'd ever come to in this world, and dammit, he wanted to spend the rest of his life with her in his arms and by his side.

"How can I help?" he murmured, nuzzling her forehead with his cheek. "Tell me what I can do to make it all better."

"H-he's not a b-bad man. This w-would all b-be so much easier if he w-were," she cried against his neck.

Did that mean she'd decided to refuse Smythe? As much as he wanted to ask that very question, instinct and the advice of his friends kept him quiet. *Give her what she needs, and make no demands.* "Do you wish to talk about what kept him away for so long, or would you prefer nothing more than a shoulder to cry on? Whatever you need, I'm here for you."

Mary sniffed. "I haven't a handkerchief."

"Take mine." He reached into his back pocket, thanking his lucky stars his happened to be clean. She stepped away and took the square of cloth he offered. He needed her in his arms again, now and forever. She wiped her eyes and blew her nose. He waited.

"Eldon did send for me. Shortly after I'd informed his parents of my father's suicide, in fact. His mother wrote back to him, and she told him that my father and I had both perished from a fever. All this time Eldon believed I had died."

"You know this for a fact?"

Mary nodded. "I read the letter his mother wrote him myself." She peered up at him through her wet lashes. "It wasn't until your friend came to him in Houston that Eldon learned the truth."

He never should have enlisted Bradford's help. "I'm so very sorry."

"As am I." Her voice broke, and she sniffed again.

"And now he wants you back."

"He does." She bit her lip. "What am I to do?"

Her pleading tone tugged at his heart. "Are you asking *me* to advise you, knowing as you do that I want you for my very own? I must tell you, I'm not at all certain I can give you an unbiased answer."

That brought the merest hint of a smile to her face. "Try. I've always been able to depend upon you for honest counsel, and I need to hear what you have to say."

"Mary, in good conscience, I cannot tell you what to do, but I can share an observation. For as long as I've known you, I've noticed you always put everyone else's needs before your own. Every single person here will tell you the same.

"Today I asked myself whether or not I deserve happiness," he said. "I believe I do, and my happiness is very much bound to you, by the way." He stood before her, lost in the clear blue of her eyes and the sprinkle of freckles across her cheeks. "Perhaps it's time you asked yourself the same question."

"How can I be content when no matter what I decide, someone will be hurt?"

"How can you sacrifice your own happiness for the sake of someone else's? For once in your life, put yourself first. That is all I can say on the matter."

Cradling her beloved face between his palms, Tobias wiped away her tears with his thumbs. "I don't want to be the man whose hopes you dash, but I promise you this: *You* deserve the very best life has to offer. No matter what you decide, I will never stand in the way of your happiness. It would destroy me to see you unhappy, Mary."

He stared deeply into her eyes, praying she'd see inside him to the truth of his words. "If it's Eldon you want, you have my blessing." *And my forgiveness, for I shall be desolate without you.* "No matter what, I am your devoted friend for life."

She blinked up at him, her lovely blue eyes awash in anguish. Her hands came up to cover his. "I do love you, Tobias. I hope you know that."

His heart dropped. "Do I hear a 'but' in there?"

She shook her head. "I've never been so torn before in my entire life. I feel as if we've just gotten through one war, and now another has started inside me." Stepping back, she pressed both of her hands against her midriff. "I gave my promise to Eldon years ago, and through no fault of his, we were torn apart. I don't know what to do. I don't know what will make me happy, but you deserve to know how I feel about you."

"Fair enough." He knew better than to plead, argue, or cajole her into choosing him. "Come back to camp. You must be starving. Thanks to Oglethorpe's boys, there's rabbit stew to be had." He placed his hands on her shoulders and kissed her forehead.

"One would think all this emotional turmoil would make it impossible for me to eat, but you're right: I am famished." Mary let loose a shaky breath and touched the spot on her forehead where he'd kissed her. "Thank you, Tobias."

"For what?" For his willingness to let her go should she choose her past over their future? He placed his hand at the small of her back and started her up the hill.

"For being my very best friend."

"Always." As they walked side by side back to camp, he told her of his plans to start a town and of their friends who had already committed to staying in Indiana to help. She listened, made sounds of approval and—dare he hope?—excitement.

For his part, he could hardly breathe, the need to hold her so consumed him. That and the desire to beg. *Choose me. Choose me, and I shall spend the rest of my days making sure you never have cause for regret.*

Chapter Fourteen

Mary inspected the almost completed axle in the gathering twilight. "It looks good, Mr. MacGregor," she said as if she knew what qualified as *good* where axles were concerned. She'd only come to check on their progress in an effort to distract herself. She still had not recovered from all the shocks she'd suffered earlier today. Tobias's proposal, Eldon's reappearance in her life after all this time, and finally, the awful letter written by Mrs. Smythe. Mary ran her hand over the smooth wood and swallowed against the tightness in her throat.

"It'll be finished first thing tomorrow morning." Robert straightened. "Me and my boys will put yer wagon back together afore noon."

"Thank you."

"So that feller what come to see ye today." Robert took a handkerchief from his pocket and mopped the sweat from his brow. "Heard tell you *used* to be engaged to him. It'd be a shame if we lost ye now." He raised a single bushy eyebrow. "What with all us pullin' together to build a town right here, aye?"

Her heart tripped, and the familiar heat of mortification rose to her face. "I suppose everyone is talking about—"

"Oh, I suspect they are, but it's out o' caring, ma'am." He fixed her in his sights, his expression one of concern. "If'n ye don't mind my sayin' so, Tobias is a good man. We all think so, ye ken."

"No one knows better than I what a fine man Mr. Lovejoy is, sir." So much for distracting herself. "Well, I'd best be . . ." She searched her mind for something she needed to do, but all the chores had been done. She had nothing but her tumultuous thoughts to fill the evening. Was it too dark to split more wood? "Good evening to you, Robert."

"And to ye, Miss Mary." He continued to scrutinize her from beneath his bushy white eyebrows. "We all hope ye'll choose to stay."

In other words, they all wanted her to choose Tobias. If only it were that simple. She nodded and took her leave. Tobias and a group of men had begun clearing the debris and taking down what remained of the burned-out cabin. He'd told her about his plans to build another cabin in a nearby spot, because he intended to eventually put a grand house where the ruined cabin now stood.

A bonfire burned atop the hill, consuming the charred wood that could not be salvaged and casting orange and golden sparks against the deepening twilight. She stared at the flames for a while, trying to decide what she wanted to do right now. She needed to talk to Bea and hadn't had the chance yet.

She, her cousins, and Tobias had joined Cyrus and his sons for lunch. Tobias had left them the moment he'd finished. Cyrus had hovered around Mary's cousin like a bee after nectar, going on and on about his plans for a forge and his desire to expand his business into designing fancy fences and banisters for the folks who would surely want such things.

Needing to get away, Mary had left them to go for a walk, a long walk, until it became clear placing one foot in front of the other would not lead her to a solution to her problems.

She searched for her cousin, finding her by their wagon, reorganizing or repacking things in one of her trunks. Mary strode to her side. "Bea, I need to talk."

Her cousin straightened and smiled. "I can imagine you do. I'm sorry Cyrus wouldn't let me leave his side after lunch, but he's so very excited about his plans." She laughed softly. "Ever since Tobias asked him to stay, Cyrus has been wound tighter than a clock spring."

Bea closed the trunk and sat on the top, gesturing for Mary to sit on another nearby trunk. "I've been dying to hear what Eldon had to say."

Rather than sit, Mary paced. All the day's revelations filling her head and her heart poured forth in an unstoppable torrent of words. She began with Tobias's proposal and ended with the awful letter. "Eldon still wants to marry me, Bea. I don't know what to do. I gave him my promise, but . . ." Her voice broke.

Bea stood up, put her arm around Mary's shoulders, and guided her to a trunk. There she gently urged her to sit. "Oh, my dear, I cannot imagine being in such a position. Why on earth would Eldon's mother do such a thing?"

Mary shook her head. "I believe she did what she did because my father took his own life. She would have been ashamed to associate her good name with ours."

"Mmm. You may be right." Bea studied her. "What's in your heart, Mary?"

"Too much." She groaned and covered her face with both hands. "I once loved Eldon, at least as much as a girl of eighteen *can* love a man." She lifted her tormented gaze to her cousin. "You see, I agreed to marry Eldon, and it's not his fault we were separated the way we were."

"And?" Bea nodded encouragement.

"I've changed so much between then and now. I'm not sure I can go back to hoops, gowns, and idleness."

"Yes, I can see that about you, but I asked what is in your heart."

Mary bit her lip, her throat and chest tightening. "Tobias fills my heart. I love him with a depth I did not imagine possible."

"There you have it," Bea said, patting Mary's arm.

"But I gave my promise to Eldon first, and he still loves me. He said I'm the only woman he will ever want to marry, and he begged me not to break his heart a second time. I am fond of him. He has many fine qualities." She shrugged. "Perhaps in time what I feel for Eldon will deepen."

"Perhaps; perhaps not," Bea murmured.

Mary swallowed a few times. "What about you and Jonathan, Bea? Do you want to stay here, or would you rather continue on to Texas?"

"Oh no, you don't." Bea shook her head. "I refuse to answer, because I know you too well."

"Whatever do you mean?" Mary blinked and swiped at her cheeks.

"You want to know what I want to do, so that you can accommodate *my* wishes rather than face your own difficult choice. I won't let you avoid making a decision regarding Eldon and Tobias based upon what I want or need."

Mary opened her mouth to reply, but nothing came to her.

"Don't forget I've known you your entire life." Bea's brow creased. "After your mother died, you set out to gain your father's affection and approval by doing everything in your power to comfort him. You were just a child. It was he who should have done everything in his power to soothe your grief, not the other way around, my dear. And once you returned from finishing school, you took over managing every aspect of your father's household, seeing to his needs before your own."

"Did I?" Mary thought back. True, she had wanted to make her father happy, because doing so just might gain his attention. But no matter what she did or how hard she tried, she never quite breached his indifference toward her. Nothing she did prevented him from sending her away to one boarding school after another, as if he couldn't wait to be rid of her. The pain of his ultimate abandonment swept through her, and a boulder lodged itself in her throat.

"I believe your earlier attempts to take care of your father have led you to become far too concerned about the welfare of those around you, and I fear it's often at the expense of your own well-being."

"That's a bad thing?"

"No, but perhaps just this once, you might want to consider your own happiness first. After all, this is the rest of your life we're talking about. It's not your responsibility to protect anyone's heart but yours. Eldon will be hurt, but his hurt will pass. If he decides to continue on as a bachelor for the rest of his life, that's his choice, and you are blameless."

Her mind reeling, Mary peered at Bea. "When did you become so wise?"

Bea laughed. "I've always been wise, but you've always been so determined to . . . er . . ."

"Do things my way?" Mary choked out a breath. "Be in charge?"

"No. I was going to say you were always so determined to be

the one who took care of me, Jonathan, Ezra, and Mabel that you would not let us take care of you. We allowed you to do so, because we felt you needed to fill that role in order to get through the war."

Mary's eyes widened. "You're right. I needed the responsibility in order to keep moving forward." Doing so gave her direction and purpose. Also, protecting them meant she could keep them with her. "I could not have borne being alone—especially after my father's death."

"You'll never know how grateful I am to you, Mary, for I could not have borne being alone either." Bea let loose a long sigh and studied Mary. "For once in your life, let someone take care of you. Let *me* take care of you. Will you?"

Mary squirmed where she sat, and her heart thumped. "All right, but it's not going to be easy."

"I know, but you must give it your very best effort." Bea chuckled. "Listen carefully, my dear."

Sighing, Mary nodded. "All right."

"First, your father was a thoughtless, selfish man who did not deserve the devotion you showed him. You are not to blame for his death any more than you are to blame for his neglect. He failed you, not the other way around."

Mary's eyes filled again, and the truth of Bea's words pierced her heart. If she ever had children, she would make sure they knew without a doubt they were loved and wanted.

"Second, you love Tobias, and he loves you. Never have I known a couple better suited to each other than the two of you. You deserve to be happy, Mary. You deserve to be taken care of by a man who will appreciate being taken care of by you in return. Tobias Lovejoy is the right choice for you."

She deserved to be happy? What a novel idea, a revelation. "I do deserve happiness," she whispered, trying on the notion for size. Did it fit? She hoped so with all her heart.

"Yes, you do." Bea squeezed Mary's hands. "What happened between you and Eldon is tragic, but you deserve more than to become his prized accessory."

She frowned at Bea. "I don't understand."

"Oh, Mary, don't you see?" Bea sighed. "Eldon has always been ambitious. In his mind, you would be the consummate, beautiful hostess to adorn the grand life he has planned for himself. You would become his adoring devotee, accompanying him to all the important social functions meant to advance his career and his standing in society. You would give *him* adorable children to fill his grand house, which again will enhance his standing."

Bea shook her head. "Your ambitions, your dreams of having any kind of meaningful work for yourself will never figure in to his schemes, unless what you wish to do benefits him personally. I'm not saying such a life wouldn't be fulfilling for someone. At one time, you might have been content in that role, but . . ." Bea paused again, as if weighing her words and choosing exactly the ones needed. "My dear, you have been independent and self-reliant for far too long to be anything but frustrated and resentful in such a scenario."

"Oh."

"Exactly."

"Thank you, Bea, for being honest and for caring about me."

"You're entirely welcome. Thank you for taking care of me and Jonathan the way you have. As I've said before, I'll never be able to repay you, but if you'll let me, I'd love to return the favor and take care of you as well." Bea straightened. "I'll leave you now. Supper will be ready soon. Until then, stay right here and think things over. I will make sure no one bothers you."

"I will." Once again her attention gravitated toward the bonfire. Bea was right. Mary had no desire to return to the life of being nothing more than a hostess or a society lady trussed in corsets and hoops. Here she'd be an integral part of starting a new town. She and Tobias would work together as partners to build a new life from the ground up. She knew in her heart Tobias would welcome her suggestions and input. Eldon would find her desire to contribute amusing, and eventually he'd find her advice annoying. The challenge of creating a new town held great appeal and the potential for deep satisfaction.

Besides the challenge staying here offered, she wanted Tobias to the point of distraction, to the point where she ached with needing to have him close. He would take care of her, and she would take care of him. Her heart took flight at the thought of going to sleep in his arms and of waking every morning beside him. The past was the past, and it was time to let it go.

TOBIAS WATCHED AS MARY AND Eldon walked together, their heads bent in earnest conversation. Every fiber of his being tensed, and it was all he could do to keep from running after them. He and Mary hadn't really spoken since yesterday when he went to her after Eldon left her crying her eyes out by the river.

Anxiety roiled through him, and his breakfast turned to a lump of clay in his gut. What was she saying to Eldon? Did she favor a life of luxury in Houston over a life with him?

"Tobias, are you going to join us, or are you planning to stare at Miss Stewart all morning?" Douglas MacGregor asked, his gaze following Tobias's. "We're ready to pace off the dimensions of your cabin, and I imagine you'll want a say, right?"

"Right."

Douglas jutted his chin toward Mary and Eldon. "Can't do nothing about that right now, anyway. May as well turn your mind to something else."

Tobias grunted. "I don't think it's possible to turn my mind to something else, but I'll join you nonetheless."

Douglas scratched at his beard and shrugged. "Miss Stewart is a woman of good sense, else a man like you wouldn't want her the way you do. True?" He cast Tobias a slanted look, his brow raised.

"True. Miss Stewart does possess an overabundance of good sense." Which meant absolutely nothing if she desired a life of luxury with a gentleman who could give her all the finer things in life. Tobias wanted to give her those things as well, only fate had given Eldon Smythe a head start. He cursed under his breath. "Yes, let's pace off the dimensions for the cabin. I want mine to be larger than the cabin that stood here before. Two bedrooms, a great room, and a loft."

He took one more long, anguished look toward the love of his life, and then he turned toward the MacGregors. All three now stood waiting for him in the spot he'd chosen for his temporary home. Three pitying looks were aimed his way. "I'm coming," he grumbled.

One day he'd build a grand house where the original cabin had stood. He'd already imagined how elegant it would be, overlooking the river and the willows growing along the bank. His and Mary's home.

For the rest of the morning, he forced himself to immerse himself in work. He and those who offered their help managed to put together a good-size corral by the old barn. They used what rails they could from the original corral, adding newly split timbers where needed. The MacGregors had set themselves to repairing the existing barn and putting a new roof on the privy. By lunchtime, Tobias was sweaty and starving.

He walked to the water pump, splashed water over his face and at the back of his neck, and then he took a long cold drink. Drawing his handkerchief from his pocket, he straightened to dry off. His heart stuttered and skipped as he caught sight of Mary striding purposefully toward him. All the air left his lungs, while at the same time his stomach lurched. He tried like hell to read her expression, trying to get a sense of what was to come. He hadn't a clue. Everything around him stilled, as if the entire world held its breath and waited to hear his fate. He couldn't utter a word if his life depended upon it.

Mary came to stand before him. She tilted her face up, and tears immediately filled her lovely blue eyes. *God, no.* He got the shakes, and his knees nearly buckled. "Mary," he managed to rasp out.

"Tobias," she whispered. She swallowed a few times, their gazes still locked. "I want very much to marry you."

"But?" There had to be a "but" in there. He was certain he'd heard one, and dread turned his blood to ice and his bones to jelly.

One side of her mouth quirked up. "No buts. I love you more than you could possibly imagine, and there's nothing I want more than to share the rest of my life with you." She blinked several times, but her eyes never wavered from his. "If this journey has taught me anything, it's that you and I are partners in every sense of the word. No one understands me the way you do, Tobias. No one could possibly take care of me the way you do." She swallowed. "Just as no one could possibly love and care for you as well as I can."

He didn't say a thing because her words refused to sink in or make sense. He'd been expecting something entirely different.

All morning long he'd been bracing himself for the worst. He searched her face, her beloved, beautiful face, looking for guidance. Such love reflected back to him that his eyes filled, blurring his vision. He cleared his throat a few times. "Come again?"

She let loose a shaky sigh. "I *said* I want to marry you. More than anything, I want to spend the rest of my life loving you and being loved by you." She lifted her chin in that way she did when she was determined to have her way.

His hands went from cold to warm. Air filled his starved lungs, and his heart filled with such happiness he feared it might burst. He reached for her, encircled her waist, and lifted her off her feet. He swung her around in a circle and shouted at the top of his lungs, "*Yes!*"

Whoops, whistles, and clapping filled the air as he set his bride-to-be on the ground. Her face had turned pink, and her expression could only be described as joyfully radiant. Tears streaked both their cheeks, but he didn't care.

"You've made me the happiest man on earth, and I promise never to give you cause to regret your decision. I love you, Mary, more than you can imagine."

He drew her tight in his embrace and kissed her thoroughly, heedless of who might be watching. She wrapped her arms around his waist and kissed him back. If he didn't stop soon, he'd embarrass them both by laying her on the ground right there and showing her just how much he wanted her.

Breathless and aching, he broke the kiss and tucked her head beneath his chin. She fit perfectly against him of course. "Tomorrow, let's ride to Evansville so you can file for your homestead, and on the way back, we'll stop in Newburgh and talk to the preacher about arranging our wedding. I don't want to wait."

She chuckled and leaned back to smile up at him. Her eyes glowed with happiness. "I don't want to wait either."

"Where would you like to be married? There's a lovely little church in Newburgh." He smoothed an errant curl from her cheek, tucking it behind her ear. Unable to resist, he trailed kisses across her forehead and down the side of her soft-as-a-rose-petal cheek. He inhaled her unique essence, imagining she smelled of sunshine, wildflowers, and happiness.

Mary snuggled closer. "I want to be married next to the river among our willow trees."

"Next to the Ohio, you say? I suppose you'll want to wear trousers and your pickle barrel," he teased.

Mary made a clucking sound and poked him in the chest. "No. I'll wear a dress. I can't promise I won't have my pickle barrel nearby, though," she teased back. "We'll have all our friends around us. Perhaps some of the men might agree to hunt, and we can have a feast and a dance after the wedding."

"Outside by our willow trees is the perfect place to hold our wedding, and this land is the perfect place to begin our life together."

"I agree." Swiping at her cheeks, Mary stepped out of his arms. "Well, I'm glad that's settled.

He laughed, his smile so wide his cheeks ached. "As am I." He took her hand in his. "Come, let's talk to the others. Some of our neighbors will want to join us on our journey to Evansville, so they can file for land grants."

They turned to join their friends, and Mary pointed down the road. "Someone is coming."

Tobias shielded his eyes and spotted the loaded wagon heading their way. "Andrew and Bonnie Offermeyer." He waved, and a deep sense of rightness settled over him. He surveyed the land, his and Mary's land, his mind already planning for their future. He harbored no doubts where Mary was concerned. They were meant to be together. "Once our house is built, I want to plant a few fruit trees."

Mary made a noise he took as agreement as they made their way into the midst of their town's fellow founders, and he was content to the very center of his soul. Mary had chosen him, and that was all that mattered. The scars from their pasts could not defeat them or bring them low, because their love and understanding would always be strong enough to lift them above their sorrows. "I just thought of something," he said, squeezing her hand.

"That is one of the things I love most about you, sir. You are always thinking of something." She smiled and squeezed back. "What, pray tell, were you thinking about this time?"

"You can be my pickle barrel through life's dangerous waters, and I'll be yours."

She laughed, and the sound rained over him in a deluge of jubilation. "Come, let me introduce you to Andrew and his wife. Do you remember them at all from Atlanta?"

"Vaguely."

Together, they set out to welcome another family into the fold. The future stretched before them, and the possibilities were endless now that he had Mary by his side.

Epilogue

1869, Along the banks of the Ohio River

TOBIAS HELD BOTH HIS SON'S hands while the rambunctious toddler attempted to pull his father toward the Ohio River. He steered his dark-haired scamp back on a course toward his mother. Mary sat upon one of the sturdy benches they'd had the MacGregors make for them for their special spot by the river. Here he and Mary often discussed important topics or news of their days. "So? What do you think, my dear?" he asked, gazing lovingly at his very pregnant wife.

"I think the plans for our new house are wonderful, but can we afford this much house, Tobias?" She glanced up from the blueprints, her larkspur-blue eyes questioning.

"We can. Our store and the bank are both doing extremely well, and as our town continues to grow, so will business." Their town now boasted a pier, where steamships filled with goods could dock, unload, and then reload with the goods produced by the local residents. Many more people seeking a fresh start had settled nearby, and Tobias had made a tidy profit selling off the land he'd purchased at the same time he'd filed for his land grant.

He swung his son into his arms and brought him to the bench. His active little boy squirmed and fussed to be put down, but he held firm. Tobias sat beside his wife, placing Michael between them.

"By the way, the town council has finally come to a consensus on a permanent name for our town, and we're finally ready to incorporate." He snorted and shook his head. "The council has asked me to run for mayor, as if I don't already have enough to do."

"Oh, you must." Mary leaned over their son and kissed Tobias's cheek. "Do you know, back when I was pestering you to allow me and my cousin to join your wagon train, even then I recognized you are a natural-born leader."

"Did you? And here I'd been hoping you were noticing my natural good looks."

"That too."

His wife's gentle laughter sent a thrill down his spine, and he grinned wolfishly her way. When she'd been pregnant with Michael, he'd been surprised to discover how very enticing he found her while she carried their child. Not that he didn't find her enticing when she wasn't carrying—hence, their second child—but something about her rounded figure, rounded because she sheltered and nurtured their precious child, melted his insides and made him want to fall to his knees before her in adoration.

"Did I ever tell you how infatuated with you I was as a girl?"

"Do tell." He made a grab for his son, who tried to make his escape by sliding off the bench. "No, you don't, little man," he admonished, only to have Michael fuss at his attempt to keep his little boy safe.

"That reminds me, dearest. Can we add a fenced-in yard between the back of our house and the carriage bays? Chasing two children at once is going to be a challenge, and with an enclosed space, we can give them a safe place to play while keeping them well away from the river."

He'd offered to hire someone to help her with their growing family, but she'd refused, insisting they raise their children themselves. They'd compromised, and he'd hired help with the housework and cooking.

"Consider it done, and I'll have Cyrus design some kind of latch their little fingers won't be able to open." He hoisted his son to his lap, slid closer to the woman who made up the center of his world, and wrapped his arm around her. "Every single morning I awake to find my love for you, Michael, and the little one you carry has grown by leaps and bounds. I never knew this kind of happiness was possible."

His son finally gave up the struggle and settled himself on

his father's lap, and Tobias relaxed. He drew in a long breath, savoring the late-summer smells, even the slight stench of hogs that sometimes drifted their way from the Morris brothers' farms.

"I feel the same, my love." Mary leaned against him, resting her head upon his shoulder.

Michael patted her belly. "Baby," he said.

"That's right, son. You're going to be a big brother." Tobias tousled his son's thick chestnut mop of hair. "It's a big responsibility, young man, and I trust you will take it seriously." His son responded by sticking his thumb into his mouth.

"So what did you and the council decide to name our town?" Mary rolled the blueprints for their house into a tight cylinder and tucked them into their leather tube.

"Well, since you would not allow me to suggest Maryville, I went with another. I'm sorry to say they would not agree to Heaven, Indiana," Tobias grunted. "I did my best to convince them, but out of the nine council members, Heaven only got two votes, mine and George Cummings's." He peered at his wife, whose hair caught the sun just then. Her curls turned to polished strands of copper and gold, and he brought his hand up to wrap one of those silky ringlets around a finger.

The day she'd come to his mercantile demanding to join his wagon train flashed into his mind. He'd probably fallen in love with her then and there, only it took a while for his brain to catch up with his heart.

"We compromised in the end." He chuckled. "Don't tell the rest of the council, but I got my way after all."

Mary's knowing smile sent heat curling through him, that and a deep, abiding satisfaction with his life. The day he'd been released from Fort Sumter, he hadn't believed such contentment would ever be possible for him. He no longer had nightmares or visions of the dead. Those visions had been replaced by the image of him and his wife, surrounded by their family, sitting in this very spot and enjoying the view of the Ohio River.

"Tobias?"

"Mmm?"

"The name. Let me guess." Mary nudged him. "Perfect?"

He nodded. "Perfect, Indiana. How did you guess?"

"This is the *perfect* place to hold our wedding, the *perfect* place to raise our children," she mimicked him. "This is the *perfect* spot to build our new house. This is the *perfect* place for the new school, the church, a bank, the butcher shop. I swear, Tobias, you dub one enterprise after another as *perfect* at least ten times a day to all and sundry."

"Planting the seed, my dear. I was planting the seed, because this *is* the perfect place for all the above, and I can't imagine living anywhere else." He slid her an appreciative look. "Or sharing my life with any other woman but my sweet, stubborn Mary Lovejoy."

"I agree with everything, including my sweetness, and now it's the perfect time to put Michael down for his nap, and then you and I can share a few moments of peace before you head back into town."

"What kind of *peace* did you have in mind?" He waggled his eyebrows and offered her what he hoped was his most seductive look.

"Actually, I was hoping for a nap myself." She yawned and tucked the blueprints under her arm.

Tobias rose from the bench, and his heart swelled with tenderness. "Your wish is my command."

"Good. Then I command you to help me off this bench." Mary snorted and held out her hand, her eyes sparkling with amusement.

He hefted Michael onto his shoulder. His son yawned and snuggled against Tobias. "A nap it is, and I shall hold you in my arms until you fall asleep."

"That would be—"

"Don't say it," he groaned as he helped her to stand.

"Perfect." Mary laughed again and wrapped her arm around his waist. "By the way, Bea, Cyrus, and their brood are coming for a picnic Saturday. Bea says David is teething, and she hopes having activity going on all around him might take his mind off the discomfort."

"That sounds . . . perfect," he teased, chuckling at the way she rolled her eyes. "Let's invite Andrew and his family to join us as well." His childhood friend now had two daughters, and their butcher shop thrived.

"Let's." She sighed. "I love it here, Tobias, and I love you with a fierceness you cannot imagine."

"Oh, I can imagine, for I love you that much and more." Tobias grinned from ear to ear as he escorted his reasons for drawing breath to their humble cabin . . . for a nap. Unless he could persuade Mary into more. He was certain he could. By her own admission, she could not resist his kisses or his caresses, nor could he resist hers, because they were perfect together.

ACKNOWLEDGMENTS

THEY SAY IT TAKES A village to raise a child, and the same can be said for raising a "child of the mind"—a story. I've worked with the same incredible critique partners for over a decade, and a big thank-you goes to Tamara Hughes and Wyndemere Coffey for your insightfulness and friendship!

I want to also thank the Kindle Press team for giving *Close to Perfect* a home. A huge thank you goes to Kelli Martin, for her editing expertise. Finally, I want to thank my readers, because you make this writing journey a joy.

About the Author

INTERNATIONAL AMAZON BESTSELLER, **BARBARA LONGLEY** is the award-winning author of the Novels of Loch Moigh, and the Love from the Heartland, Perfect, Indiana series, The Haneys and The MacCarthy Sisters.

Ms. Longley moved frequently throughout her childhood and learned how to entertain herself with stories. As an adult, she has lived on an Appalachian commune, taught on an Indian reservation and traveled the country from coast to coast. After having children of her own, Barbara stayed put.

Barbara holds a master's degree in special education and taught for many years. She enjoys exploring all things mythical, paranormal and newsworthy, channeling what she learns into her stories. She's a long-standing member of Romance Writers of American, and is listed on their Honor Roll of Bestsellers.

Barbara loves to connect with readers via Twitter @barbaralongley, on Facebook at www.facebook.com/Barbara-Longley, or through her website, *www.barbaralongley.com*.

Readers can also learn all about her new releases through her Amazon Author Page, *www.amazon.com/Barbara-Longley*

Made in the USA
Lexington, KY
25 April 2018